Kitty Kendall is a bucket list achieving, junk jewelry collecting, hopeless romantic who loves great wine and a good adrenaline rush from time to time. She also collect classy shoes and expensive perfume. But her greatest thrill in life is writing romance and the steamier the better.

Bring It On!

She's travelled extensively, some 37 countries and counting and she's addicted to experiences that make her scream... white water rafting, scuba diving with sharks and hang gliding are just a few. Her stories reflect her sense of adventure and her love affair with her very own hero.

Kitty also writes romantic suspense under the pen name of Kendall Talbot. She's won numerous awards including Romantic Book of the Year, Best Romantic Suspense and Best Continuing Series. Several of her books are Amazon bestsellers. Check out www.kendalltalbot.com to find out more.

Read more at www.kittykendall.com

BOOKS IN THIS SERIES

Rise of Memphis Box Sets:

Rise of Memphis Touch Me (January, February, March)
Rise of Memphis Tempt Me (April, May, June)
Rise of Memphis Tease Me (July, August, September)
Rise of Memphis Tame Me (October, November, December)

Rise of Memphis Monthly Chronicles

Rise of Memphis January Chronicles
Rise of Memphis February Chronicles
Rise of Memphis March Chronicles
Rise of Memphis April Chronicles
Rise of Memphis May Chronicles
Rise of Memphis June Chronicles
Rise of Memphis July Chronicles
Rise of Memphis August Chronicles
Rise of Memphis September Chronicles
Rise of Memphis October Chronicles
Rise of Memphis November Chronicles
Rise of Memphis December Chronicles

Rise of Memphis
Tempt Me

This three book box set contains:

Rise of Memphis April Chronicles
Rise of Memphis May Chronicles
Rise of Memphis June Chronicles

KITTY KENDALL

DEDICATION

This book is dedicated to all the women out there who need an adventure.

1ˢᵀ APRIL
MY KINKY IRISHMAN
Room 34 - Hot Horizon Hotel

I knew Savannah's seventh birthday party would be noisy with twelve squealing seven-year-old girls in one room assaulting my ears. Include all those girls, *and* my best friend Lolita's blasting Singstar music, and the noise became downright torture. None of the other women at the party seemed to notice. They all carried on conversation as if they were the only humans in the place. Maybe once a woman had a child she somehow became oblivious to noise.

I wouldn't know.

I couldn't stand it anymore. With Lolita distracted as she set up another song, I snuck out of the party onto the back patio and slid the glass door closed behind me. The change in volume was instant relief, and the ringing in my ears nearly drowned out the blasting music I still heard through the door. *Nearly*.

With my wine glass in hand, I made my way out to one of the wicker deck chairs by the pool and eased onto it. I closed my eyes and tugged my skirt higher so I could enjoy the sun on my legs. It was lovely, not too hot that I'd need to cover up in five minutes and not too cold. Queensland weather was perfect at this time of year.

"May I join you?"

I jumped and swiveled to the man's voice. He was already opening the pool gate. "Sure." I didn't really have a choice in the matter.

"The noise in there is doing my head in."

I smiled at the kindred spirit. "I agree."

"So which one is yours?"

I frowned at him. "Sorry?"

"Which one of the girls is your daughter?"

"Oh." I chuckled. "None. I'm Lolita's friend Jane."

"Oh." The way he said it made me wonder if he was Lolly's husband's single friend that she'd mentioned. I tried to ignore the way he looked at me. It was like he was sizing me up for a ball-gown.

For three years, no man had looked at me. Nada. Zip. Zero. Zilch. Now, though, men seemed to be coming out of the woodwork like a plague of termites. Not that I was complaining; it was a pleasant change.

"And you are?" I made a show of eyeballing him up and down.

"Sorry." He grinned at me and held his hand forward. "That was very rude of me. I'm Clayton." His honesty had me quickly forgiving him as he took my hand in a firm shake. "It's just that when Lolita mentioned you, I imagined someone different."

"Oh." I cringed, as I wondered what exaggerations she'd conveyed. "What did she say?"

He shifted in his seat. "Well, she said you were single and hadn't had a date in three years."

Great. Just great. *I'm going to kill her.* "Okay. And what exactly should a single woman who hasn't had a date in three years look like?"

He cleared his throat and squirmed some more. "I umm . . . I don't know exactly. But I didn't picture a woman as gorgeous as you."

As I blinked at him, I wondered if the ringing in my ears had messed up my hearing.

"Oh my God. That sounded totally like a line. Sorry. I'm not used to this kind of stuff."

My head spun. Clayton was handsome. The epitome of tall, dark and handsome, actually. He had thick, ebony hair that had a slight wave to it. His dark eyes, nearing the color of a perfect hot chocolate, were framed with long black lashes.

"What stuff are you referring to? We're just two people trying to escape that bedlam inside."

He chuckled. It was a nervous chuckle, and I wondered what else Lolly had told him. If she'd even so much as hinted at my dirty little secret, I was definitely going to kill her.

Clayton gulped back the beer. "Yes, you're right. Just two people chatting."

Now I really was convinced Lolita had told him more. "Okay, go on. Tell me what else you know about me."

"Alright, let me see." He rolled his eyes to the clouds. "She said you were twenty-eight?" He said it as a question, and I answered with a nod. "She said you'd moved to the Gold Coast after, and I quote, 'your cheating bastard ex-fiancé slept with everyone in your small country town who had a vagina.'"

I burst out laughing. How could I not? Lolita had described my previous love life perfectly.

Clayton grinned at me now, and his shoulders relaxed. "Did I get that right?"

"Yes. Exactly. So it seems you know everything about me. How about you tell me about you?"

"Okay. I'm thirty-one."

He looked at me as if seeking approval of his age. In light of the variety of ages of the men I'd experienced recently, age was no longer important. I refrained from reacting, and he carried on. "I manage a jewelry store. Paradise Jewelers at Broadbeach. Do you know it?"

I shook my head and wriggled my unadorned fingers at him. The most expensive piece of jewelry I'd ever owned was my engagement ring, and I'd thrown that from my balcony weeks ago. Hopefully it was someone else's prized possession by now.

"I play squash twice a week." He grinned at me. "Oh, I love to cook. Italian is my specialty. I make my own pasta—"

"Daddy. Daddy." A little girl came running toward us. "Come on, Dad, it's cake time."

I glanced from the cute little girl in a pink and yellow sundress to Clayton, whose cheeks had flushed maroon in an instant. He glanced at me then turned his attention to his daughter. "I'll be there in a second, sweetheart."

The little girl dashed off.

"I'm also a single dad," he said.

That caught me by surprise. I blinked at Clayton, expecting him to elaborate, but instead he silently stood up and followed his daughter into the house. I waited until he'd disappeared through the glass sliding doors before I re-joined the party.

Homemade birthday cakes are just one of Lolly's abundant skills. If I'd never met Lolita Bell in person, I'd never have believed a woman like her existed in real life. She was beautiful, athletic, smart, funny, a great mother, could hold her own in a room full of politicians, a green belt in karate, and to top that off, she was the best friend a girl from the country could ask for. Savannah's cake was a replica of a fairytale castle, smothered in no doubt delicious pink icing and decorated in sweets and hundreds of colorful sprinkles. It was demolished in a matter of seconds and received the praise it deserved from everyone in the room, including me. The cake hidden beneath the icing was a rich white-chocolate mud cake. I forked aside some of the icing but would've been prepared to lick the plate for mud cake crumbs if it'd gone unnoticed.

With overflowing sweet-bags in all the little the girls' hands and dramatic air-kisses from the immaculately dressed women, the guests vanished in a matter of minutes. Clayton gave me a fleeting glance before he hugged Lolly and left, holding his daughter's hand.

Lolita, Savannah and I were the only remaining people when the dust settled, and my ears were grateful. Savannah ran off to the sunroom where her abundant selection of new birthday gifts were on display.

I collected the plates off the table. "I don't know about you, but I'm exhausted."

"It was fun though, don't you think?" Lolita looked like she could do it all again, ten times over. The woman was a machine.

"It was fun. Loud, but fun."

"Pfft, you think that was loud? Wait until Maddox's party. Boys are way worse."

"Where are Calvin and Maddox anyway?"

"Cal took Maddox to his mate's place. Savannah didn't want her stinky brother at her party."

I could clearly picture Savannah requesting that. For a seven-year-old, she knew how to get her own way. Much like her mother.

"So," Lolly said, as I filled the sink with water, "what'd you think of Clayton?"

"Thanks for that." I ensured there was sufficient sarcasm in my voice.

"What? Oh Jane, what's wrong with him? He's gorgeous."

"He's a single dad."

"So? Open your horizons, babe."

"I *have* opened my horizons. In fact, they're so far open I've fallen into some weird wonderland."

Lolly laughed so hard her boobs threatened to shake out of her sunflower-yellow strapless dress. "You've had a man twice your age."

I rolled my eyes at her. "I didn't 'have him,' as you put it."

"But you would have."

Would I have? *Yes, probably.* "That's different. And you know it."

"What's wrong with a single dad?"

I scrubbed icing off a plate and rinsed it under the running tap. "I'm just not ready for that."

"Well what are you ready for, babe?"

I sighed. "I don't know yet. But I'm enjoying finding out."

"You are, huh? Still on track?"

I nodded, hardly able to believe it myself. "Thirteen men in thirteen weeks."

"Holy shit, babe. And you haven't actually had sex with any one of them. That's gotta be a Guinness record or something." She held her hands up like she was reading a giant banner. "Gold Coast Woman Pleasures Herself With Multiple Men. No Penetration."

"Lolly!" I slapped my wet hand on her shoulder, and she doubled over laughing.

I couldn't hold back my chuckle either. Maybe it was some kind of record. "Actually . . ." I drew the word out.

Her eyes bulged. "Holy fuck! You've had sex and you didn't tell me."

I couldn't hold back my excited grin.

She turned to the fridge, plucked out a bottle of bubbles, then clutched my wrist and dragged me toward the table. "Details, babe. I want all the juicy details."

She plonked me down amongst the demolished birthday cake and hundreds of colorful sprinkles, and then she dashed across the open-plan room to the kitchen to fetch fresh glasses.

"Tell me all about it. Was it hot? Was he hot? Did you get your fucking rocks off?"

I glanced around at all the remnants of the cute seven-year-old girl's birthday party and decided this wasn't the time or place to divulge my naughty little romp. Lolly wasn't going to be happy.

I looked right into her beautiful blue eyes. "I'll tell you all the details, but not now."

"You can't—"

"Today is for Savannah," I interrupted, something I rarely did to Lolita. "Tuesday you'll get it all, and trust me—I won't leave out a single thing." Except for the name I'd invented for my naughty twin, that is. If I told her that, she might think I really had gone crazy.

Her frown deepened, and the way her eyes drilled into me, I was certain she was reading my mind. "You've been holding out on me."

I shook my head, ready to deny it, but she had an uncanny ability to sniff out a lie. I'd hate to be her kids.

"Maybe, but just one thing." I scrunched up my nose. All of a sudden, the name I'd chosen was embarrassing.

"Tell me." Her eyes nearly jumped out of their sockets.

My shoulders slumped as I realized there was no getting out of it now. "Don't laugh."

She cocked her head. "I can't promise that. Come on, spit it out."

"Oh alright. You know how my favorite song is Marc Cohn's 'Walking in Memphis?'"

"Yeah."

"Well, the name I use when I get into my disguise is Memphis."

Lolly covered her mouth, but I saw the laughter in her eyes.

Within seconds, she was chuckling. "Oh that's golden. Memphis! What . . . and none of these men question it?"

"None so far."

"Fools! Hey, it's April Fools' Day today. Maybe you can snag another fool tonight."

I frowned at her. "They're not fools."

"I know, babe. I'm just messing with you. You know that, right?"

I nodded. Lolita was the closest thing I had to a big sister. If I hadn't met her when I'd first arrived on the Gold Coast just over three years ago, I probably would've already gone back home.

I checked the clock on the kitchen wall. Forty-five minutes until my shifts started. "I better get going. Sorry I can't help clean up."

"Do you want me to drive you home?"

"No, don't be silly."

We hugged and said our goodbyes. I walked to the station and caught the tram to Florida Gardens.

The trip took all of fifteen minutes, yet I was certain I spied at least four men looking at me during that journey. I was beginning to wonder if I had pink icing in my hair or something.

All of a sudden, men had taken to checking me out, and it was getting weird.

* * *

It was eleven p.m. and two and a half hours into my shift when my 'fool' showed up. I mentally slapped myself at that thought. He wasn't exactly a fool, but he was a jolly fellow. An Irish jolly fellow, to be exact. He laughed to himself as he entered the lobby. Maybe it was because he saw me grinning at him, but for whatever reason, he approached the counter.

"G'day, I'm Finn Hanson." With his Irish lilt, it sounded ridiculous. Maybe that's why he laughed as if what he'd said was the most hilarious thing in the world.

His laugh was wickedly funny, and I found myself laughing along with him. "How can I help you, Finn?"

He drove his fingers through his strawberry blond curls. "I'm beyond help apparently."

I shifted my gaze, quickly running my eyes over his crumpled blue business shirt and pausing high on his chest at the Penoptic Solutions insignia. I'd never heard of it. "Looks like you've had a fun night."

"Nope," he said. "Bloody boring. Had to drink myself silly to enjoy it."

"That's a shame."

"Not really. My boss is an ass, and he was paying the bill." He roared with laughter.

I could one hundred percent appreciate his plan. My boss was a complete loser, and if he ever shouted drinks, I'd probably do the same, too.

He pointed his finger at me. "Guilty."

I blinked at him. I was definitely guilty, but right now I wasn't sure what guilt he was referring to. "Pardon?"

"You, madam . . . know exactly what I'm talking about."

I swallowed. "No. I'm not sure I do."

He slapped his palm on the table. "Your boss is an ass, too. I'm right. Aren't I?"

Relief washed through me and I nodded. "Yes, you're right."

"I can smell a shithead boss a mile away. Lord knows, I've had enough of 'em. Say, how about you join me for a drink? Don't worry; I won't tell your boss." Finn's smile was a cheeky one.

His idea was very tempting. But I couldn't; I'd already risked too much with my secret trysts with hotel guests. "Sorry, I'm working."

He held his hand across the counter. "Well, it was a delight to meet you—"

I reached over the counter and we shook hands. "Jane."

He gave me a salute and swaggered away. When he reached the entrance to the Triple H bar, he clutched the doorway like it were a stripper's pole. "Jane," he yelled across the lobby, "Have a great night."

I giggled as he slinked off the wall and disappeared.

Mr. Finn Hanson had just volunteered himself as my fourteenth pleasure partner.

He just didn't know it yet.

* * *

The morning sun slithered across the white lobby tiles, announcing both a new day and nearly the end to my shift. I wrapped up the last of my duties, and was more than ready to leave when my boss, Needledick, arrived. After the quick changeover, I left reception and made my way up to my room on the fourth floor.

As I showered and applied my makeup, I thought about the Irishman waiting for me three floors up. Well, not exactly waiting for me—when I'd seen him roll from the Triple H bar to the elevators at about one a.m. this morning, he'd looked close to passing out. The chances of him even being awake when I went to him were miniscule. That didn't bother me. I think half of the men I'd selected this year were asleep when I began my act. None of them complained.

Deciding that my Irishman would get a giggle out of it, I chose the French maid outfit again. I selected hot pink matching lingerie and a pair of Christian Louboutin black shoes with a pink ankle strap and pink heels. The shoes were a gift from me for my birthday last year, yet this was the first time I'd worn them. At least today, they'd have a lovely memory to go with them.

My reflection in the mirror always surprised me. It was like looking at a sexy stranger. The fact that it was me still didn't register, even after three months of dressing in this disguise. I checked my blond bob wig was secured in place and glided on the final touch—Pinky Promise lipstick.

With my trusty black trench coat on and my bag over my arm, I strode from my room, leaving Plain Jane behind. By the time I was in the elevator, I was in Memphis mode and so ready for whatever my morning held with Finn Hanson.

On the sixth floor, I strode to room thirty-four and stopped to listen. Nothing. I knocked and quickly plumped up my boobs as I waited. The door opened in a couple of seconds, and I stepped back in shock. Finn did a double-take when he saw me, and I did the same. I'd expected him to be drowsy after the drunken state he was in late last night, but instead, Finn's bright eyes and quick grin showed the opposite.

"Hello, hello. Have I died and gone to heaven?"

I chuckled and made a show of looking him up and down, admiring the half-naked body that'd been hidden in his work shirt earlier. Finn's chiseled torso was a pleasant surprise. "No, you haven't." I ran my tongue over my lip. "May I come in?"

He glanced over his shoulder, as if looking to someone else for approval, then he stepped aside. "Of course."

As I strode into the room, I undid the belt on my trench coat and glided it off my shoulders. I tossed it over the chair, ran my hands over the skirt of my French maid costume, and turned to Finn.

The door clicked closed behind him as he whistled, then clicked his fingers. "April Fools' joke, right?" His gaze drifted from me to the bathroom door and back again.

Lolly's comment rolled around my head. "No. No joke."

He tucked his thumbs into his blue-check boxer shorts and adjusted the elastic. Once again, he glanced at the bathroom, and I wondered if he needed to go or something.

"I have a little problem." I reached down and unhooked the ankle strap from my high heel.

"Mmmm, doesn't look like you do." He grinned and nodded with ridiculous eagerness.

"I'm horny, and I hate being alone when I feel this way." I was getting good at this.

"Holy shit! Okay." He swallowed loud enough for me to hear him, and once again, glanced at the closed bathroom door.

"So, do you like to watch?"

"Hell yes." There was movement in his shorts.

8

"Yes, I think you do." I made a show of looking at his groin. "We're not going to have sex. Okay?" I felt the need to lay down strict ground rules until I assessed the situation.

"Okay then. So what do I do?"

"Just watch." I turned a fraction and bent over so he could get a good look up my skirt while I undid my second shoe. Once removed, I flicked the heel toward the other one.

Finn still stood halfway between the front door and me. I clutched a handful of my skirt and lifted my dress up over my head, careful not to remove my blond wig with it. But as I watched Finn's hungry eyes travel from my half-clad body to over my shoulder, I sensed a change in the room and turned.

My blood drained in a flash.

A woman, a beautiful young woman, strolled from the bathroom toward the bed. I snapped my arms over my breasts in a feeble attempt to cover myself. She was wearing sky blue French knickers. Just French knickers. She walked with a bold confidence, and her perky breasts moved very little as she sashayed across the carpet.

"I'm sorry, I thought . . ." I grappled with my costume, trying to work out top from bottom.

"No need to be sorry." She flicked her long amber hair over her shoulder. "I hear you'd like us to watch." Her voice was a seductive melody.

My heart exploded in my chest. I held my dress over my torso. "This is a mistake."

"No, it's not. Don't worry. We won't touch you. Will we, lover?" She patted the bed.

Finn's eyes, greedy with lust, travelled between the two women in his room. His cock was now a full-blown pole, ready to burst from his shorts.

My feet were frozen to the floor. My breath was trapped in my throat, and my heart was set to explode as I flitted my gaze from Finn to the beautiful young seductress near the bed.

Finn strode to the other woman, and as their mouths met in a heated kiss, I was unable to pull my eyes away. My face flushed, and the heat between my legs inflamed. His hands were on her breasts, manipulating them with eager fingers.

Their heady breathing matched my own as Finn's shorts were lowered by the woman. His cock bounced out and aimed toward her, seeking attention. She obliged by wrapping her hand around it and gliding her closed fist up and down the solid muscle. As if choreographed, they stopped kissing and glanced at me together.

"Are you okay?" The woman sounded so sweet and genuine.

I nodded, completely lost for words. I knew I could leave. *Should leave.* I'd walk out of here completely naked if I had to.

And yet, for some inexplicable reason, I wanted to stay.

The admission both horrified and titillated me at the same time.

While she was looking at me, the woman carried on caressing Finn's cock as if she were just patting a puppy. I guess my reluctance to leave was the signal she needed, because she sat on the bed, leaned forward and wrapped her lips around his cock. Finn's entire body tensed. His focus remained on me and when our eyes met, he smiled. The way he looked at me, literally devouring me with his gaze, had my knees weakening and a steady beat pulsing from my clit.

I was unable to look away, and yet I couldn't believe what I was about to do. With my heart thundering in my chest, I reached behind my back and flicked off my bra. That one simple move confirmed I was staying. Not only that, it showed me a hell of a lot more about myself than I was willing to admit right there and then.

The woman stopped sucking Finn's cock with a loud smacking noise. When her eyes turned to me, I suddenly felt very naked. I'd never had a woman look at me like this, and I couldn't decide if I liked it.

"Are you going to join us?" she asked.

Words were impossible to form. My mind flipped with abundant possibilities as I shook my head.

"Your loss; he's an incredible fuck."

The way she said it convinced me their relationship was forbidden. One or both of them were having an affair, and this, whatever this was, was a complete secret.

Just like me being here. A complete secret. Nobody, not even Lolly, would learn of this one. *I hope!*

Finn eased the woman backwards onto the already crumpled sheets, but he remained standing beside the bed. He tugged her French knickers from her body and flung them toward me. This time, it was the woman who watched me as Finn fell to his knees and lowered his head between her legs. Her eyes rolled. Her hips raised to meet him. A gasp tumbled from her mouth.

A moan tumbled from mine.

She spread her legs wide, allowing me to watch the show, and I could just see his tongue, gliding up over the pink folds of her sex. At the swollen nub right at the top of her pussy, the flick of his tongue had her writhing on the sheets. When Finn moaned as if he was tasting the most delicious thing in the world, the woman he was enjoying, fisted the bed sheets and tore them from their fittings.

The sight of them, their sounds, the tangy smell of their sex, their unbridled passion—all of it shredded my inhibitions.

I drove my fingers into my panties and found my pulsing pussy. It was wet, hot, and so ready to be fucked. My legs threatened to buckle as I plunged my fingers deep into my hole.

I clutched at the dining table and I bent my knees in time to the rhythm of each thrust of my fingers.

Deeper. Harder. *Faster.*

Finn's groan had me opening eyes that I hadn't realized I'd closed. I froze at what I saw. The woman was on her hands and knees now, and Finn thrust into her from behind. Her fingers clutched at the sheets with each driving force of his enormous cock into her body.

She glanced at me, although her eyes were glazed, lost in a glorious world, and I wasn't certain she could actually see. Her mouth was open, as if she were gasping for her last breath. Her breasts swung in a pendulum below her chest, rocking backward and forward to Finn's timed thrusts.

Finn's cock, slick with the woman's juices, glistened when it slid out of her pussy, and his balls looked rock hard as they slapped against her ass with each powerful drive into her. His eyes were closed and his clenched jaw gave me the impression he was savoring every sensation.

I drove my fingers into myself, and the orgasm I'd been riding hit me.

It was sudden. Uncontrollable. *Glorious.*

I must've screamed or something because in a flash, both of them were at my side. I allowed them to take me to the bed and lie me down. Finn removed my panties and I spread my legs, showing him I wanted him. He fell to his knees, and as his tongue travelled the length of my pussy, I turned my head to see the woman at my side, on her knees, her own fingers inside herself.

I came. Quick and explosive. A rolling orgasm started deep inside my belly and shuddered through my body again and again. The woman screamed and I watched her slick fingers jam inside her vagina over and over. Her juices spilled onto her hand and wet the bedsheets between her knees.

Finn launched himself on her, thrusting his cock into the woman who lay right beside me. I resisted the powerful urge to touch her, to touch him.

To get involved was barely inches away.

Her breasts bobbed back and forward, matching his thrusts. He hooked his elbows under her knees, dragging her closer to him and raising her hips so he drove his cock into her like a jackhammer. She gasped with each thrust and her head rolled toward me. Her unseeing eyes shot open, glazed in their own world.

Finn plunged faster, thrusting, pounding. His groaning grew louder.

Suddenly, he stopped. His entire body tensed. He sucked his breath between his teeth. It was a moment frozen in time—his body glistened with sweat and his chest heaved with each ragged breath. Then he closed his eyes and slammed all he had into the woman. Over and over and over.

She yelped. He groaned. The bed came alive.

It was an eternity before his rhythm slowed. His cock relaxed and he fell onto his hands and lowered his head onto her belly.

She glided her fingers through his hair like a familiar lover would do.

Feeling like I was witnessing a special private moment in their lives, I looked away. It was a weird thought, given what I'd just seen. The bed creaked as I wriggled off it, and I began to gather my things from the floor.

I tugged on my coat and stepped into my shoes as I wrapped the belt around my waist. The couple were still together, regaining their breath, and I was happy to slip out of the room unnoticed.

"Did you have fun?" the woman called to me as I neared the door.

Had I? That was an unmistakable yes. I turned to her and nodded.

"What's your name?" she asked.

I swallowed the dryness from my throat. "Memphis."

She nodded as if she expected that to be my answer. "Don't judge us, Memphis. Finn's the only thing keeping me married to my boring husband."

I resisted letting my jaw drop as I struggled to comprehend what she'd said. It took all my effort not to ogle them. Instead, I reached for the handle and opened the door.

"See you next time, Memphis," Finn said as I left the room.

I floated to my room through an air of confusion and glory. As I showered, I thought about what the woman had said. Could sex with another man really be the solution to an unhealthy marriage? I didn't think so.

Deep in my heart, I looked forward to falling in love. When I did, that man and only that man would give me mind-blowing sex. And I was going to give him the same.

Especially with everything I've learned this year. I'll teach him a few moves he'd have never even thought of.

Later, as I sat on the edge of my bed, I reached for my diary. At the top of the page for 1st of April, I wrote *Finn Hanson - Room 34 - My Kinky Irishman.*

As I detailed what had happened in room thirty-four, I realized that watching a couple have sex had taught me a lot. Previously, when I'd had sex with Alexander, my cheating bastard ex-fiancé, we'd nearly always done it with the lights off. Having the lights on offered a whole lot more to the experience. To see expressions, how bodies moved and open eyes lost to another world was incredibly intoxicating.

It was a glorious thing to have witnessed a couple having wild, unadulterated sex. As I crawled under the bed sheet and rolled onto my side, I tried to convince myself I'd never do it again.

6TH APRIL
THE PERFECT STRANGER
Room 29 - Hot Horizon Hotel

I wiped the sweat from my forehead as I tugged a chair out from our favorite table at the Blue Haven Cafe. High off the horizon, the sun was a blazing white ball, and ridiculously hot given that it was the middle of autumn. Fortunately, the red umbrella above us offered just the right amount of shade, and there was a slight breeze coming off the beach.

Lolita, my best friend, had worked my ass off at the gym today, and my muscles were already feeling it. Apparently, she was punishing herself for missing our last session, and I was the collateral damage.

"I can't believe I missed last week, of all weeks," Lolita said, as soon as we were seated. "Okay, I'm ready. Tell it all, and don't cut out any details."

I couldn't believe she'd missed it either. Lolita and I have been meeting at our gym every Tuesday for three years, and that was the first time Lolly had ever missed a session. Lolita's daughter must've been really sick, because it would've killed her to stay home, especially after I'd hinted at my news more than a week ago.

Matt, the waiter, had his usual dour expression as he strolled toward us. He looked particularly lost today. I never understood how he kept his position. If I owned this cafe, I'd have asked him a long time ago to either snap out of his sad-sack demeanor or find another job.

"What would you like?" he said, in his uninterested drawl.

"Green tea." Lolly ordered the same thing she did every Tuesday. Matt need not have asked.

"I'll have a skinny cappuccino and a lemon cupcake, please."

Lolita shot me her customary disappointed glare at my choice of treat, and I ignored her. Everything so far had been typical of our Tuesday morning routine.

However, that was all about to change.

"So, come on," Lolly said as soon as Matt left our able. She leaned forward on her elbows and her brilliant blue eyes pierced me with their intensity. "You've been acting weird all morning. The suspense is killing me."

"I haven't been acting weird."

"Like hell you haven't. You're grinning like a woman on a drug induced high."

I tried to stop smiling as I debated hiding my last crazy romp from Lolita. After all, what I did took me so far from my comfort zone it was a wonder I wasn't in a strait jacket. But it was pointless. Lolita was a predator when it came to sniffing out the truth. I decided to settle her curiosity with the one I'd already hinted at, and tell her the second tidbit after I'd finished my cupcake. I'd need the sugar rush. "First of all, let me just say that I hadn't planned it."

"Oooh sounds exciting."

"It was. I still can't believe it."

"Come on, babe, stop holding out on me." She drilled her long red nails on the table.

I let out a deep breath. "I did it after my shift."

"Tell me about the sex."

I cocked my head. "Will you let me talk!"

"Sorry. Carry on."

"He was tall, dark and handsome—I know it's cliché, but it's true. And smart; he's a computer technician, so he had really nice hands, and he seemed gentle. That's what appealed to me."

"Yes, yes, but what was his cock like?"

"Lolly!"

"What?"

The waiter's timing was impeccable, and Lolita showed her frustration by tapping her nails as he placed our drinks and my cupcake on the table. I laughed at her as she displayed her impatience and I wouldn't have been surprised if she booted Matt out of the way. She lived for gossip like this, although I trusted her not to tell anyone about my dirty little secret. Except for Calvin, her husband, of course—apparently she told him everything.

The second the waiter left, she clutched my wrist. "You're killing me. Tell me before I explode."

She let go of my wrist and I stirred my spoon around my coffee trying to work out where to start. "So, I wasn't going to do it—"

"Have sex, you mean?" She nodded eagerly.

I rolled my eyes. "Right. I hadn't intended on having sex. Anyway, I decided not to go to this guy right after my shift like I normally do. This time, I went to him in the afternoon and something about that, something about him . . ." I shrugged my shoulders. "I don't know . . . it was just right."

"Good on you, babe. It's about time. So did it blow your mind?"

"He was amazing. So gentle."

"What? So it wasn't like he fucked your brains out?"

I laughed her. Lolita never held back; she really was a piece of work, but in the nicest possible way. "It wasn't like that. Besides after three years without a man inside me, I didn't want to be split in half."

Lolita tilted her head back and laughed so hard I saw right down her throat. "Jeez, babe, you're a riot."

"It's true. If you saw what the Jamaican drummer had, you'd be scared too."

She wriggled her eyebrows. "I'm sure Memphis could take it."

I slapped her on the arm. "Don't make me sorry I told you that name." I'd kept the name of my naughty alter-ego a secret from Lolita for fourteen weeks. *I hope she doesn't make me regret telling her.*

She tapped her nose. "Don't worry. Your secret's safe with me."

"Don't even tell Calvin."

She looked up to the right and tugged on her lip.

"You already told him? Lolly!"

"Cal and I don't keep secrets. You know that."

She gave me one of her cute little smiles that seemed to allow her to get away with murder. I knew her and her husband shared everything and Lolita thrived on gossip. It was one of the other reasons I loved her—our conversations were never boring.

My mind drifted to my last bedroom romp, and how I'd considered keeping it a secret. Knowing that Lolly told Calvin everything, cautioned me against sharing this one with her. I couldn't stand her husband knowing.

"Oh my god," she said it loud enough that half the diners in the café turned to her.

"What?" I frowned.

"You're hiding something. Tell me."

I shook my head. "No, I'm not."

"The way you're smiling, it has to be bloody good. Come on, cough it up."

I ate the last piece of my cake, contemplating what to say. Lolly had missed her calling; she should've been an interrogator or something. It was inevitable now, I'd have to tell her, I just had to decide how much to tell her.

Lolita leaned forward and placed her hand over mine. "Jane, you know you can tell me anything. Whatever it is, I've probably done it before myself."

She scrunched her nose in the cutest of ways.

"It's just that . . . it happened so . . . so quickly," I stammered.

"It's okay. Start at the beginning. Whatever it is, you must've enjoyed it."

I cocked my head at her. How the hell she interpreted that was beyond me.

"Babe, you can't wipe the smile off your face. Tell me."

"Alright, but please don't tell Cal. It's embarrassing." My shoulders sagged.

"Why? He loves you. Nothing you ever do would stop that."

This might. I stewed over my options, but no matter how hard I'd try to keep it from her she'd get it out of me anyway. "Oh alright." I sighed. "There was this Irish guy. He came into the hotel the night after Savanah's birthday party."

"Last Saturday?"

"Yes. Anyway, he was quite drunk, but he was bubbly and happy. And, well, he was cute. So the next morning, I dressed in the French maid outfit."

"Again?"

I shrugged. "I thought he'd get a laugh out of it. Anyway, I went to his room and I did my usual spiel, you know, letting him know I was horny and that I didn't like to be alone. And I was down to underwear when a woman walked out of his bathroom, practically naked."

"Holy fuck!" Lolly eyes bulged. "What'd you do?"

"I didn't know what to do. I stood there like a stunned mullet. Then they invited me to join them.'

"Oh shit. You lucky bitch."

My jaw dropped.

"What? There's nothing wrong with a threesome."

I lowered my eyes to my coffee and rolled my spoon around the rim, catching the chocolate powder.

"You didn't join them, did you?"

I shook my head. "I watched them.'

She let out a breath. "I bet that was fucking hot."

I grinned at her and leaned forward. "It was so hot. To see their expressions and what they did to each other . . . it was out of this world."

Lolita licked her lips. "Oh shit, I'm so jealous." She palmed her chest. "I've never even done that."

It was my turn to bulge my eyes. "Really? You mean I've had a sexual experience you haven't?" That was completely unexpected. Having known Lolita for three years, I would've sworn she'd have done just about everything there was to do with sex.

"Looks like it. You should've joined them, though."

"I couldn't. I couldn't do it. I just stood back and watched." I paused to look at the surrounding tables, then I lowered my voice. "I think I liked it."

"Of course you did, babe. It'd make me as horny as hell too. And let's face it, you've become a bit of a voyeur."

I nodded as I stewed over her comment. Since the first of January this year, I'd watched fourteen men get their rocks off. Each man had offered something different to the experience. Watching was fun, and with it came knowledge. I was discovering what gave me sexual gratification, and along the way, I was learning a heap about how to please a man.

However, I still wasn't sure if this would ultimately help or hinder me finding a man. This was the big question.

"You're frowning."

I licked the chocolate off the spoon and then huffed. "I was just wondering if this whole . . . situation would help me find the man of my dreams."

"Jane . . . in the last fourteen weeks, you've got your rocks off fourteen times. Sure, you've only had sex once in that time, but you've had mind-blowing orgasms, and the guys have, too. You've met more men this year than you've met in your lifetime." She placed her hand over mine. "Okay, babe, here's my prediction. By Christmas this year, you'll be head over heels in freakin' love."

I cocked an eyebrow at her. "Yeah right! And where am I going to find this love of my life?"

She grinned her gorgeous smile at me. "I think he'll be one of your sexual conquests. He won't be able to stay away from you. Just like your horny cowboy."

My thoughts shifted to Billy, my hunky urban cowboy. So far, he was the only man who'd come back. If I was going to find the love of my life, then I needed to get to know these men better. That concept was very appealing—I just had to figure out how to do it.

* * *

It was my day off and the only interesting thing I'd done today was go shopping for a new disguise.

I'd started at the costume shop and tried on everything from a nurse's uniform, teacher's outfit, hooker's lingerie, and a naughty nun's habit, plus a dozen or so others in between.

In the end, I went out to the dress shops in the plaza and searched for the perfect dress to suit my sexy twin, Memphis.

It was now four o'clock in the afternoon and I was out on my balcony, enjoying the amazing view over the beach, savoring a glass of Shaw & Smith wine with a packet of corn chips. So, it was a lovely coincidence that, as I pictured myself in that sexy new red dress, the perfect man to help me christen it put on a show on the grass strip between the walking path and the beach in front of the Hot Horizon Hotel.

He wore tight little shorts and running shoes. His body glistened with sweat as he went through an exercise routine right before me.

Squats, crunches, lunges, push-ups and a few other exercises I'd never seen before. He worked his legs, arms, back, abs and all the muscles in between. The guy was a machine. It was a punishing workout, showing off his strength and stamina. When it was over, he reached for a towel and headed toward the ocean. I thought that'd be the last I'd see of him, but I was wrong.

Half an hour later, the sexy fitness fanatic strolled back up the beach and headed right into my hotel. It was my lucky day. I jumped up, grabbed my master security card and raced out my door to the elevator. I leapt in when it arrived and punched the button for the lobby. My timing had to be perfect to make this work.

The blood in my veins pounded in my neck as the elevator pinged open at the lobby floor. He was there, standing right in front of me, and he was so much hotter that I'd been able to witness from four floors up. He smiled at me, and god damn if that wasn't the most glorious smile I'd ever seen. As we passed each other, I smelt sea salt and coconut-laced suntan lotion.

The second I stepped out of the elevator, I spun on my heel. "Oh, hold the elevator please." I shoved my hand forward, blocking the doors from closing.

I stepped back into the mirrored cube and nodded at him. "Sorry, I forgot my bag." It wasn't a lie; I'd grabbed nothing but my keys.

He'd pressed the button for the fifth floor and, using my master security card, I pressed the button for the penthouse floor. *I could dream a little, sometimes.*

"Lovely day," he said.

"Yes, it's beautiful." He didn't know the half of it.

"See ya later." He stepped out of the elevator.

I wanted to say, '*Yes, you will, in about half an hour or so,*' as I held the door open to see what room he went to.

Room twenty-nine.

I rode the elevator up to the penthouse suites and back down to my floor again, then returned to room thirteen, my home.

I poured myself another glass of Shaw & Smith, and as I showered and applied the abundant makeup required for my disguise, I sipped the lovely sweet wine and wondered what the rest of my afternoon would hold.

My dress was blood red, fitted me like a second skin, and stopped high on my thigh. From the moment I put it on, I continually tried to pull it down. It was a very unsexy habit that I needed to stop. I chose the cute blond wig that fell just below my ears and had a huge struggle getting my long dark hair into it. Once it was in place, however, one look in the mirror was enough to confirm my sexy twin, Memphis, was back. It never ceased to amaze me how confident I felt as Memphis, but as Jane, I was a bumbling mess when it came to men.

My only hope was that some of Memphis's bravado would rub off on me soon.

Today's choice of stiletto was a pair of very high Mollini shoes with lace crossover straps at my ankle. I matched their simple black finish with one of my large black bags, dabbed on my favorite Bobbi Brown red lippy and did my final check in the mirror.

Convinced that all traces of my boring self were gone, I smiled at my reflection and then headed for the door.

I rolled my hands down the silky fabric of my dress as I rode the elevator to the hunky gym junky's floor. At his room, I paused to swallow back my nerves, and when the door suddenly opened, my conquest just about barreled me over in his rush to get out.

"Oh, sorry," he said, as he found his balance by gripping the doorframe.

"Oh, no, no. I'm sorry. I must have the wrong room."

He was obviously heading out, so my game was over. I turned toward the elevator.

"Don't go."

My heart leapt to my throat as I turned back to him. "Sorry?"

"I mean . . ." He ran his hand through his wavy blond hair. "Do you have to go? I was just heading down to the bar; maybe you could join me. If you're not busy, that is."

I tugged on my bottom lip as my heart said *'hell yes'* by my head said *'don't be a fool.'* "Oh umm, I really should be—"

"Have you got a date?"

I huffed. "Pfft, no." Then realizing how automatic that was, I closed my eyes and turned away again, ready to sprint to the elevator, even in my eight-inch heels.

"Good," he said. "Let's at least have one drink and see where the night takes us."

Before I knew it, he'd shut his door and sidled up beside me. Together, we made our way to the elevator, and he pressed the down button. "I'm Hunter McCall." He held his hand toward me.

My palm was lost in his firm grip. "Memphis."

"Memphis . . .?" He said it like he was expecting a surname.

My heart leapt at my throat. Why, oh why, hadn't I thought of a surname for Memphis? At a loss, I just shrugged and smiled. "Just Memphis."

He nodded, as if accepting that was all he was going to get out of me. "Okay then, Just Memphis, what brings you to the Gold Coast?"

His questions already had me regretting my decision not to make a run for it while I'd had a chance. "I'm taking some time out."

"Well, you picked a beautiful spot for it. Marriage break-up?"

My jaw dropped as I glared at him.

"Wow, okay, not that. Boyfriend then?"

"You're a nosey one." Even though I frowned my horror at his suggestion, I decided to go with that. At least I could draw on some real emotions if needed. "Cheating bastard ex-boyfriend, to be exact."

"Ahhh, well good on you for taking this holiday then," he said, as the elevator door pinged open.

With his hand on my lower back, he guided me toward the Triple H bar, and I was torn between letting him know I was a green belt in karate and looking out for Marjorie, who'd be sitting behind the lobby counter.

This was going to be a huge test of my disguise. Every person who worked in this bar and in the whole hotel for that matter, knew me. Well, they knew Jane; none of them knew about Memphis. I'd lose my job if ever anyone found out. If Tania the barmaid even glanced at me twice, I'd probably pass right out.

Hunter and I slipped onto stools at the far corner of the bar, and he asked me what I'd like to drink. That was when I remembered my next mistake. I had no money. "Oh shit, I'm so sorry but I don't have my wallet." Feeling like a complete idiot, I slipped off my stool, ready to leave.

"Stop." He held his palm toward me. "It's my shout. There's nothing better than killing a few hours with a beautiful stranger."

It took all my effort not to bulge my eyes. His words could have come straight out of my mouth. Hunter was easily the beautiful stranger amongst us.

"So what would you like to drink?" He smiled at me. The wicked glint in his light blue eyes begged me to stay.

How could I resist? "I'll have a glass of Shaw & Smith Sauv Blanc, please."

"Perfect. I'll have one too." He wandered to the counter, and as he placed our order with Tania, I admired his sinfully handsome face. He was guy-next-door hot in a Chris Hemsworth kind of way, with a nicely trimmed two-day growth that culminated at the dimple in his chin. He had blond hair and pale pink, perfectly kissable lips. The white T-shirt tucked into his low-slung jeans failed to hide the contours of his torso; if anything, the tight fabric enhanced the six-pack that I already knew was there. I pictured him as an outdoorsy type of guy. If I was lost in the jungle or something, Hunter would be the man I'd want to save me. Even his name suited a man who'd be capable of catching my dinner with his bare hands.

He looked after himself. The question was, other than his lovely offer to buy me a glass of wine, how else would he look after me?

I was ready to find out.

Mr. Fitness returned with our glasses, and we chinked them together.

"Perfect strangers," he said.

I laughed at that; his toast totally hit the mark. "Perfect strangers," I replied.

If I was going to get through this, I'd need to dominate the conversation. I couldn't have him asking me any more tricky questions. "So you know why I'm here—what're you doing on the Gold Coast?"

He held up two fingers. "Two reasons, actually. I competed in the Cooly Classic open swim on Sunday, and I extended my stay to do some business."

"How did you do in your swim?"

He ran his thumb over his stubbled chin. "I didn't win; I didn't lose either."

"Just finishing must be an achievement."

"It used to be, but now I want more. I thought this was to be my year. But . . ." He rolled his eyes and had another sip of wine.

"And what do you do for work?"

"I'm a chocolatier. I have my own range of specialty chocolates, and I'm trying to crack the Queensland market."

I raised my eyebrows. "You make chocolate? Wonderful."

"Oh, not just any chocolate. My mother was a Swiss pastry chef and my father a French chef, and I grew up with them competing for my approval of their culinary masterpieces. I live and breathe chocolate. It is, in my opinion, the most diverse, complicated, yet divinely simple treat on the planet."

His passion captured me. I leaned forward on my elbow. "Carry on."

"Chocolate is no longer just the block of Cadbury's you buy at the supermarket. It's made with love and care, exquisite and complex flavors, and an impressive eye to detail."

"What's the name of your chocolate?"

"I branded it The Sweet Spot."

My jaw nearly dropped as I realized Hunter would definitely be exploring my sweet spot later. I chuckled at my naughty little thought. "Fabulous name."

"Yes, I thought so. It conjures up all sorts of indulgent promises." He raised an eyebrow at me.

"Really?" I said it with the skepticism it deserved.

"Yes, really." His voice had become deeper in the space of seconds. "How about you come back to my room and I'll introduce you to heaven?"

I cocked my head at him, wary of his cheesy comment.

"What?" He palmed his chest in mock hurt. "It's the name of one of my chocolates."

I giggled at him. His offer sounded perfect and before I knew it, we'd finished our drinks and were walking arm in arm toward the elevator. This never happened to me. Never. First date jitters normally threatened to crippled me. As the elevator rose the six floors, I had to remind myself I was Memphis.

Sexy, confident, in-control Memphis.

We laughed as we entered his room, but I didn't miss him squeeze my butt. I turned to him and pointed my finger, with every intention of scowling at him. But he wrapped his hand around my finger and kissed the tip of it. "Sorry," he said. "I couldn't help it."

"You will be sorry." I chuckled. "I have a green belt in karate, and I'm not afraid to use it."

His tongue flicked out over his bottom lip, leaving a slick of moisture in its wake. "You're a fascinating woman, Just Memphis."

Hunter was very cute, and although I had every intention of getting my rocks off with him, it was nice to play hard to get for a change. "You're not bad yourself Mr. Chocolatier."

"Right." He placed his arm around my waist and led me to the dining table where he pulled out a chair. "Would the madam like a seat?"

I placed my bag over the back of the chair and sat down.

"Give me a moment," he said. "I'll be right back." The perfectly formed globes of his ass glided up and down beneath his jeans as he walked to the kitchen. Normally, this interlude would be where I'd take my dress off, but today I decided, I wanted this sexy stranger to do it for me.

After a couple of minutes fussing about, Hunter returned to the table with a black presentation box, which he centered on the table. "Don't touch," he said, before he raced off to the kitchen again.

When he returned, he held a bottle of wine and two glasses. "Shall we?"

I nodded, grateful this was my day off, because saying no to him would've been impossible. It was shiraz though, and aware of my poor tolerance for red wine, I promised myself I'd only sip it.

With our glasses topped up, he held his toward mine and we clinked them together. "Cheers."

"Cheers."

The wine was delicious, and I guessed, probably expensive. I imagined it would be perfect for sitting by a fire and sampling chocolate with, which is no doubt why he chose it.

He sat at my side, tugged the black box toward us, and lifted the lid. The delicious smell of fine chocolate filtered up from the attractive selection.

"So Just Memphis, let me see if you can tell what this flavor is?"

"Mmmm, what do I get if I answer correct?"

He directed his dazzling blue eyes at me and blinked. "Oh, I don't know . . ."

"How about if I answer correct, you take off a piece of clothing. If I'm wrong, I'll take something off."

He rubbed his hands together and whistled. "Perfect." Then he reached into the box, removed a chocolate, and held it toward my hand.

I opened my mouth and with a cheeky grin, he popped the delicacy onto my tongue. I closed my eyes and savored the delicious chocolate.

It was heaven.

The perfect amount of sweet and flavor. If Hunter truly had made this, then he possessed a very special talent.

I opened my eyes and he had his elbow propped up on the table, his chin on his palm, and a look of intrigue on his face. "Okay, Just Memphis, what is it?"

"I believe that was hazelnut praline." I gave it my best guess.

His jaw dropped. "I'd hoped you'd get it wrong." His stood up and whipped his T-shirt off in a flash.

I couldn't believe I was right, then I wondered if he was just trying to charm me. "You're not cheating are you?"

"Are you kidding? I'd much rather see you naked than me."

I stood up. "Then how about you help me out of this dress." I turned my back to him.

Hunter stood up behind me, and as one of his hands glided to my hip, his lips found my neck and he cruised little kisses up and down my flesh. His breath was hot and heady. I closed my eyes and leaned back against him. I smelt chocolate and expensive wine. I smelt the ocean and complex cologne. I smelt hot, sexy man.

I felt the release of my dress as Hunter glided the zip from my shoulder blades to my lower back.

He reached in through the open zipper, and as his warm hand caressed my waist, the bulge in his pants grew against my lower back. A delicious pulse between my legs struck up a steady beat. I reached up to my shoulder strap, and as I tugged my dress down, Hunter sucked his breath in through his teeth.

Goose bumps prickled my flesh as I stepped out of the dress, kicked it aside and turned to him. Hunter's cock was a hard lump in his jeans, begging for release.

"You have an exquisite body," he said.

The way he said it turned my bones to jelly. Hunter was one of the fittest men I'd ever seen, and to have him impressed with me, made me want him even more. I reached behind my back and flicked off my bra. No sooner had my lingerie touched the floor than Hunter had closed the distance between us. He bent over and sampled my breast. As I clawed my nails up his back and ran my fingers through his full head of curly blond hair, he sucked and licked my breasts, first the left, then the right. He was an expert, taking my desires to steamy heights.

When he stopped, it was as if my insides had been removed.

"Sorry," he said. "But I, umm . . ." He looked down at his groin.

"Oh, here, let me help." I reached for his belt, unbuckled it, tugged it from the loops and tossed it aside. With my eyes trained on his, I glided the zipper down. Without warning, he whisked me off my feet and carried me to the bed. He placed me down and stripped out of his remaining clothing. His cock was full and proud, pointing at me, begging me to touch it. I swiveled on the bed, placing my stilettos on the floor, and urged him to step forward.

He did.

I inhaled his manly scent. God, he smelt good. I clutched his balls in one hand and as he spread his legs, giving me all there was to give, I wrapped my other hand around his cock and glided it up and down his shaft. Hunter groaned, and I groaned with him.

After the few wines and idle chitchat, this moment with him now seemed so perfect. I was ready to go all the way with this perfect stranger.

That thought had my clit pulsing like static electricity. I wrapped my lips around the crown of his penis, slowly drawing the hot muscle into my mouth. His groans of approval had my insides clenching and a wave of bliss heating up inside me. I held onto his cock, and I glided my tongue up his length from his balls to the very pink head. Hunter clutched at my shoulders, his nails digging in.

I fed my hand into my panties and flicked my throbbing clit with my finger. The sensation was like a slingshot, shooting waves of desire through me.

I flopped back onto the bed and raised my hips. "Take my panties off."

Hunter obliged and in a flash they were gone, and we were two perfect strangers admiring each other's bodies. I was in voyeur heaven. As Hunter's eyes traveled up my body, I spread my legs and reached down to touch my clit. It was at the heightened peak of sensitivity. I couldn't keep my eyes open a second longer and as I closed them I drove my finger into myself. Suddenly Hunter was between my legs, his rough chin stubble at my pussy, his hot tongue gliding up and down my velvet folds. As I rubbed my clitoris, his tongue probed my pulsing hole.

His finger joined mine, exploring my most sensitive region, and his tongue continued to lick me. An orgasm built within me like no other. I raised my hips, offering all I had, begging him to fuck me, but he kept going, licking, sucking, probing with his fingers. My insides wound as tight as a spring. I cried out, clawing at the sheets, and as I ripped them from the bed, my orgasm ripped through me.

Wave after wave of ecstasy took me to another world. It was a long moment before I was released from its glorious grip.

When I finally opened my eyes, I saw the magnificent smile on Hunter's handsome face as he looked up from between my legs.

"Do you have a condom?" I said.

He nodded and as he dashed off and as his cock bounced up and down in time to his pace, my mind bounced from devil to angel and back again, over what I was doing.

I'm about to have sex with a stranger.
A fucking hot stranger.
But still a stranger.
Who cares?

Shit. My brain was saying one thing, my body was saying another and I wanted to smack all the disrupting thoughts away. I didn't have to though. Because from the moment Hunter and his stunning body stepped from the bathroom, the only thing I wanted was my perfect stranger's cock inside me.

The second Hunter arrived at the bed he tore open the silver foil. Maybe he was worried I'd change my mind. To show him I wanted it as much as he did, I glided my hands over my breasts, squeezed my nipples, threaded my fingers over my torso and then spread my legs further apart. My high heels made this awkward, tilting my knees at a weird angle, and I wished I'd taken my stilettos off.

A sudden memory hit me. It was of me being bent over the photocopy machine and my first serious boyfriend, Ryan, taking me from behind. It had been good but our sex had always been forbidden, so consequently, every time was rushed. We never even undressed.

Right now though, I had all the time in the world. I stood up, turned my back to Mr. Fitness, spread my legs, planted my heels on the carpet and bent over the bed.

Hunter didn't miss a beat. He eased up behind me and placed one hand on my hip, and with his other hand, he glided his cock up and down my pussy.

I reached down between my legs to feel what he was doing. He let me take over, and I used his rock-hard muscle to punish my clit. Rubbing up and down, another orgasm built inside me, taking me to the edge of the world.

I glided him into me, pushing back until I was completely full and his balls were flush against my pussy. When he withdrew, he created a void that made me feel so empty that I leaned back, pushing my butt toward him, telling him I wanted more.

He drove into me so fast and deep that I gasped and clawed at the bed. He did it again, slowly out, and rammed full-tilt all the way into me.

It was pleasure and pain. Perfect and corrupt. And I wanted it over and over.

"Yes," I cried out as he did it for the fifth time. Hunter cried out too, and he rammed me again and again with perfectly timed trusts that matched my primal groans.

"Yes. Yes. Yes." We both matched identical cries of pleasure.

My body clenched around him with each charge and he became faster, harder, and I couldn't believe it, but he grew bigger by the second. He pounded me, and it was fucking wonderful.

He took me to the limit.

My orgasm shuddered through my body and I saw stars, the moon, nothing at all. It was just me and my body being pleasured by the most incredible cock ever.

Finally, he fell forward onto my back, and I rode out his ragged breathing until he slipped out of me and onto the bed at my side. I flopped onto the bed too and turned to him. As I watched him gather his composure, I admired him all over again. Hunter, my fitness fanatic, was an exquisite example of a man in his prime.

I couldn't believe how much my life had changed this year. Men like Hunter never crossed my path. Now though, it was like I was a heat-seeking missile, and I found my target every week.

"Just Memphis, you're incredible."

"As are you, my perfect stranger."

He smiled a smile. *That smile*—the one that said the world was perfect.

With that lasting look forever imbedded in my mind, I slipped off the bed and found my dress on the floor. I stepped into it and as I zipped it up, I spied the box of chocolates.

I plucked a triangle-shaped dark chocolate with white chocolate drizzled in perfect stripes over the top. I showed it to Hunter before I popped it into my mouth. It truly was delicious.

"Can you guess it?" He propped up on his elbow, looking at me with a cheeky grin.

I gathered my lingerie and shoved them into my bag. As I hooked the strap over my shoulder, I turned to him. "I'd call it Cointreau White Chocolate."

His jaw dropped, and I laughed as I made my way to the door. He didn't need to know I'd seen the description on the box lid.

"Will I see you again?"

I paused at that question and turned to him. "If you did, then we wouldn't be perfect strangers."

"I'm willing to take that risk."

I laughed as I left Hunter still lying naked on the bed.

I made my way to my room, riding a euphoric high that floated me home and into a long hot shower.

Afterwards, I reached for my diary, turned to 6th April and wrote *Mr. Hunter McCall, Room 29, The Perfect Stranger.* I wrote in elaborate detail all about the sexy chocolatier and how comfortable I'd been with him at the bar. Sex with Hunter was incredible, and I wondered if it was because I'd taken the time to get to know him a little before we jumped into bed together.

Of course, it could also be attributed to the fact that he was one of the sexiest, athletic, yet relaxing guys I'd ever met.

I put the diary on my bedside table and slipped beneath my sheets.

As I rolled onto my side, I played pictures through my mind of my new lover doing exercises out in the golden sun, only this time he was completely naked and his body was slicked with sweat, highlighting all his glorious muscular contours.

I giggled at that thought and let sleep take me to a wonderful new world.

Kitty Kendall

10TH APRIL
RISKY ROLE PLAYING
Room 8 - Hot Horizon Hotel

One of the greatest advantages of working and living on the Gold Coast was the diverse range of people I saw and met. Today though, was proving to be one of the most fascinating days for people watching. The convention center, just around the corner from the Hot Horizon Hotel, was hosting the annual Supernova once again. As my hotel was one of the closest, it was fully booked with people dressed as everyone from Superman to Sailor Moon. It was comic addict's heaven.

The costumes alternated from full-body suits to barely anything at all. Most of the women's costumes ensured plenty of skin showed. A bit like my naughty twin, Memphis's, choice of clothing. I sat forward on my chair as a thought blazed through my brain. This was my chance to go out in public dressed as sexy Memphis.

I checked my watch. I still had seven hours until work.

A commotion coming from the walking path below caught my attention, and I stood up to look over my balcony. As I leaned on the railing, a group of guys shuffled out of my hotel all dressed in costumes, and talking and laughing so loudly I could almost hear everything they said, despite being four floors up.

I spied Spiderman, a pirate who was the spitting image of Captain Jack Sparrow, a Star Wars Storm Trooper, and four different-colored Power Rangers. As they shuffled up the walking path, one last guy raced to catch up to them—Batman. His cape shifted from side to side with his gait. He was taller than the rest of the men, and his broad shoulders filled the costume perfectly. When he reached the group, not one of them acknowledged his late arrival and I wondered if they would've left him behind. For some inexplicable reason I felt sorry for him.

I knew what it was like to not fit into a group. Growing up in small-town Australia meant that my choices for friends were limited. My school had less than one hundred and sixty kids. Being the chubby one of my year meant I was always good fodder for picking on, mostly by boys, but the girls could certainly bring on the bitchiness when it suited them.

The insults didn't usually bother me. I guess I always knew I'd leave Mildura and move somewhere more exciting, so making life-long friends never seemed that important. It was ironic that the only true friend I'd had, Chelsea-Lee, turned out to be the greatest bitch of all when she stole my fiancé from me.

With that shitty thought driving me, I grabbed my things and hiked downstairs to catch a cab to Pacific Fair Shopping Center. I made my way to the costume shop that I'd already frequented a couple of times for disguises for my Memphis alter-ego.

Costumes On The Coast was a hive of activity, and I had a sinking feeling that I may have left my purchase too late. I strolled up and down the aisles without any clue what I was looking for. A Batman costume fitted to a mannequin in the window gave me an idea. I sought out a staff member.

The small Asian woman behind the counter greeted me with a weary smile.

"Hi, can you help me please?" I said. "My boyfriend is going to Supernova as Batman; is there a costume that would go with that?"

Her eyes glanced over my body, sizing me up, I guess. "For you, lovey, I have a few options." Her English was so perfect I imagined she'd lived in Australia her whole life. "Hopefully I haven't sold out. It's been a crazy couple of days."

She was quick on her feet, and I raced to catch up with her as she dodged the people down the crowded aisle.

"We had some Batgirl . . ." Her voice trailed off as she flicked through a rack of clothes. "No, sorry, they've all gone."

"What else is there?"

"I think Poison Ivy is made for you." As she toddled off, I wondered who or what she was referring to.

In the middle aisle, she plucked out a plastic bag and held it toward me. "You're in luck. The change rooms are back there; go try it on."

I walked where she'd pointed, then slipped behind the curtain and tugged the costume from the bag. The green boned corset was the feature of the costume, but there was barely anything to it. I doubted my boobs would fit. The other bits and pieces were green fishnet stockings, green satin underpants to match the corset, elbow-length green gloves and a green mask. The only thing that wasn't green was a fiery long red wig, which was of poor quality compared to the almost human-hair wigs I'd bought the other week. Fortunately, one of my wig purchases was a striking copper color that fell to my shoulders. If this costume fitted me, not only would it be a miracle, but it seemed I had the perfect wig to go with it.

Holding the corset against my torso, I judged it for size. This was going to be tight. "Oh, what the hell?" I said to myself as I began to undress.

I was an expert with the fishnet stockings, having worn them several times in my Memphis disguise over the last couple of months. The corset, however, was a different story. It had multiple bones that ran in parallel lines up my torso and to do it up, I had to wriggle tiny hook-and-eye clips into place at my front. The battle came at my boobs, where the fabric finished halfway across my nipples. To get my breasts in, I had to tuck my nipples downward, and at the same time plump the bulk of my breast upward. The result, when I wrestled the final clips into place, was a very narrow waist and great bulging mounds that threatened to burst from the top.

My first thought was *no freaking way*, but as I turned from side to side in the cubicle, I realized this was exactly the type of outfit Memphis would wear. I put the mask on for the finishing touch and smiled at myself. This was perfect.

"Well hello Poison Ivy." I giggled as admired my reflection.

Once I clipped out of the outfit and could breathe again, I shoved all the pieces back in the bag. The exhausted Asian woman smiled at me as I placed it on the counter. "I knew you'd like it."

"It's going to drive my boyfriend wild." It shocked me how easy it was to lie. Then again, since the first of January this year, my whole life had become a lie. During the day I was mousy Plain Jane, but when the stars were all aligned I'd become Memphis, a cheeky seductress. Thank god, no one but my friend Lolita and her husband knew about my secret, or else they'd have me carted off in a padded wagon.

I caught a cab back to my hotel and ran the gauntlet through reception, hoping Marjorie, the afternoon manager, didn't see me. I'd be stuck with her for at least twenty minutes if she did. I successfully jumped into the elevator and pressed the button for my floor.

In my room, I applied my meticulous makeup to create Memphis and shoved my hair into the fiery copper-colored wig. I wriggled into my new costume again and opened my closet to scour my range of shoes.

I found the perfect pair. They were a similar shade of green to my costume, with wrap-around ankle straps and killer heels. I didn't know what I'd been thinking when I bought them, because they hadn't been worn yet. It was as if they'd been waiting for this very moment.

When I finally looked in the mirror, Poison Ivy looked back at me, and I liked what I saw.

My heart skipped a beat as I committed to doing this. So far, the only time Memphis had gone outside was when a series of unfortunate events had me running from the hotel like a crazy woman. This time, I planned to stride through the lobby like I owned the place.

I grabbed my bag and keys, thrust my chin forward, and headed out my door. In the elevator, I jiggled on my toes to check my boob wobble in the mirror. It was a wonder they didn't pop right out of the corset.

At the lobby, the elevator doors slid open and I nearly walked straight into Needledick, my boss.

My legs just about crumbled to jelly at the sight of him. He'd finished work hours ago. What he'd be doing here now was beyond me; he usually spent as little time in the hotel as he possibly could.

When his jaw dropped and his eyes zoomed in on my bulging cleavage, I knew he didn't recognize me. Needledick and I didn't get on at the best of times—he'd thrive on the opportunity to get one over me, instead of ogling my breasts.

I glared at him. "Are you right there?"

"Sure am." He licked his lip.

"Creep," I said with satisfaction, as I pushed past him and out the elevator.

I felt his eyes burning into my ass as I strode across the lobby like a superhero on a mission. I sensed Marjorie, the afternoon manager, at the counter, but didn't turn to look at her. Instead, I threw my bag over my shoulder and headed straight for the double glass front doors and the blazing sunshine.

Once outside, I had two choices—walk to the convention center, which was about half a mile away, or catch a cab. As I pictured the cranky cab driver taking me such a short distance, I decided to walk. Normally, this wouldn't be a tough decision at all; I walked everywhere. But in eight-inch heels and with both my ass and my boobs hanging out, I was totally out of my comfort zone.

Within twenty paces, I had my first horn toot from a car. By the time I got to the corner, I'd had seven. I couldn't recall a time in my life when I'd had a wolf whistle.

Damn it felt good.

It reminded me of a time as a teenager when my best friend, Chelsea-Lea, and I walked from her house into town. We were about fifteen years old and dressed up for the quarterly Blue Light disco that took place in a large barn. A group of guys had driven past in a beat-up old Cortina and whistled at us. Of course, Chelsea-Lea assumed it was just her they were admiring, and for some inexplicable reason, she took offense at it, whereas I would've been thrilled had it been me they were interested in. Back then though, I was well out of my league hanging around a girl like Chelsea-Lea; she and I had completely different agendas in life.

Now though, with the rush of blood driving through my veins, I'd take any admiration sent my way.

At the traffic lights that controlled the crossing over the main Gold Coast highway, I stopped and pressed the button. As I waited, I was joined by seven other people who, based on their over-the-top costumes, were heading to the Supernova expo, too. I was promptly flanked by Wonder Woman and a terrible impersonation of Peter Pan.

"Hey Poison Ivy, how you doing?" Peter Pan wiped the sweat from his brow.

"I'm excellent."

"You been to one of these before?"

"First time."

"Oh, you're going to have a blast. Hey, stick with us and we'll show you around."

Wonder Woman glared around me at Peter Pan, and I didn't miss her clenched jaw. Clearly, she wasn't impressed with his offer.

I waved my hand. "Thanks, but I'm catching up with a few friends in there." Another lie—damn, I was getting way too good at these.

It was a surprisingly hot day for early April, and thankfully, I wasn't wearing much. I really felt for Peter Pan though; his full-body Lycra suit would cook him alive pretty soon if he didn't get into the air-conditioning.

We crossed the four lanes of traffic and two railway lines as a group, and the moment we hit the path on the opposite side, Wonder Woman took Peter Pan's hand and headed off toward the convention center ahead of me. It was the first time in my life where I'd had a woman threatened by my looks. I chuckled at that little glory.

The closer I came to the convention center, the more people joined me and struck up conversation. It seemed like everyone but me knew who Poison Ivy was. Some of the costumes were incredible—so much time and effort had been put into designing them. Many disguises I recognized, but just as many I didn't.

The instant I climbed the steps of the convention center and walked into the spacious air-conditioned foyer, I was struck by the fun vibrant atmosphere. Clearly, everyone was here to have a great time. It wasn't like any expo I'd ever been to or been involved in. My hotel held conventions regularly, and one aspect of my job was coordinating them so they ran smoothly.

Compared to this one though, the conventions I'd managed were utterly boring.

I waited in line to buy a pass, sandwiched between The Thing from The Fantastic Four and a six-foot Chewbacca. My view was blocked the whole way, but once I'd bought my ticket and passed through the entrance gateway, from that moment on, I was caught up in a whirlwind of chaos.

I wasn't quite sure what the purpose of Supernova was, but if it were about showing as much skin as possible while maintaining your disguise, then this expo was a winner. My outfit was skimpy, but some of the women barely even covered their nipples.

I saw Xena Warrior Princess and Captain America kissing, and burst out laughing. As I glanced around, it seemed like I was the only person that was here by myself. Not that I minded—I'd been by myself for a few years now. A big line-up of people caught my eye, and I went over to see what the commotion was. As I neared, I realized Jack Gleeson, who played Joffrey Baratheon in Game of Thrones, was at a table at the head of the queue, signing autographs. Whilst I loved Game of Thrones, that character was one of my least favorite. I had no intention of lining up for him. If it had been Daenerys Targaryen, the Dragon Mother, on the other hand, I would've lined up until the blisters on my feet were large enough they'd need their own zip code.

I ambled my way around one crazy impersonator after another, and the smell of food had me heading toward a group of rowdy people in the seating area. My stomach growled as I joined the line that threaded toward the counter. As I waited my turn, I scanned the crowd and spied my Batman from earlier today. He stood back from his group of mates who were sharing a joke that Batman didn't seem privy to. He glanced toward me, and our eyes met. I nodded at him, and I couldn't believe he actually looked around to see if it was someone behind him that I was indicating at. When he turned back to me, I smiled, and when his jaw dropped I laughed. Batman didn't know it yet, but he'd just become my next potential sexual conquest.

I ordered my food and carried my serve of hot chips and gravy over to him. He hadn't taken his eyes off me since I'd smiled. Maybe he thought I'd vanish if he did.

As I neared him he tugged out a chair, and when I sat, he sat beside me and the first thing I did was check his left hand. No wedding ring. Perfect.

"Hi. I'm Poison Ivy," I said, as I did my best to eat a hot chip dipped in gravy in the sexiest way possible.

"I'm Batman." He ran his tongue over his lips and I admired his nicely trimmed two-day growth and square jawline.

"I can see that."

The blue Power Ranger came to Batman's side. "Hello. Who do we have here?"

I chomped away on my chips, deciding not to give the newcomer any attention.

"This is Poison Ivy."

"Yes, you are," Power Ranger actually purred, and I looked at him with uninterested eyes.

"Have you been to this before?" Batman asked.

"First time."

"Then maybe you'd allow me to show you around."

I pushed back on my chair. "I'd love that."

With my tub of hot chips in one hand, and my other hand hooked into Batman's elbow, we started to walk away. Batman turned over his shoulder and said, "I'll catch up with you guys later."

We left his group of mates with stunned looks on their faces, and I returned to nibbling on my chips. As we strolled side by side, up and down the aisles, Batman explained each of the stalls to me. His fascination with the comic scene was right up there as obsessive. More than half of the things he talked about were beyond me. It seemed to go on forever.

A deep voice came over the loud speaker announcing the expo was finishing in ten minutes. I glanced at my watch; it was four-fifty p.m., still four hours away from the start of my shift.

I tossed my leftovers into a bin and turned to Batman. "Do you want to go back to your place?"

His mouth nearly fell to the floor.

"I'll take that as a yes." I tucked my arm into his again and directed him toward the exit. "Let's go then."

I released my hold on him once we reached the stairs and reminded myself that I had to let him lead the way.

Batman placed his hand on the small of my back, and like a true gentleman, led me across the congested Gold Coast freeway. It wasn't until we were on the opposite side of the street that he spoke again.

"So what's your real name?"

I quickly debated what to tell him. Was I Jane Nichols, Memphis, or Poison Ivy? I really did have a few screws loose. "Tonight I'm Poison Ivy." I grinned up at him and when he smiled, I noticed faint laugh lines beside his eyes, and that had me guessing him to be about my age or maybe just over thirty.

"Excellent," he said. "I'm staying at the Hot Horizon Hotel; it's only a couple of streets away."

"Okay."

Large high-rises blocked out the western sun so the beach and walking track that ran parallel to the sand was now bathed in shade.

A light breeze drifted off the ocean, and the sounds of the waves crashing into the shore perfected the scene. It couldn't get any better if it tried. "It's lovely along here at this time of night," I said.

"Sure is. Are you here on holiday?" His voice was a sexy baritone.

"Yes, I'm from Mildura." A lie and a truth mingled together. Did that count as bad? I couldn't decide.

"I'm just from Brisbane. We've come down to Supernova for the last three years."

"Sounds like fun."

"It is. How long are you here for?"

"Just a couple of days." I cringed at my never-ending lies.

"By yourself?"

"Yeah. I needed to get away for a bit."

He sighed. "I can relate to that."

It was almost dark now, yet the white cresting waves crashing into the shore were still visible. I breathed in the salty sea air, and despite my jiggling boobs and exposed ass, felt completely comfortable with this situation. That admission was as powerful as a dose of adrenalin. "What do you do?"

"I'm an emergency dispatcher."

I sucked the air between my teeth. "I bet that can be stressful."

"Yes. Very." Batman's shoulders slumped.

The look of genuine anguish on what little I could see of his face made me decide there and then that I was going to give him the perfect escape from real life. And what better way to do it than a little role-playing. "Well, Batman, maybe tonight we can rescue each other."

He smiled down at me, and I liked what I saw. "Sounds like a plan to me."

The solar-powered lights that dotted the walking path flickered on, casting a golden glow over his profile. Batman was head-to-toe in costume; the only parts of his body that were visible were his lips, chin, and eyes. His two-day growth indicated he had dark hair; his strong jaw line had me believe he was handsome; and he was very tall, at least eight inches taller than me. My heels had us matching in height, though.

From what little I saw of Batman, he was the epitome of tall, dark, and handsome.

Before we entered the lobby, I made sure I was positioned on Batman's right-hand side. This ensured that when we crossed the marble expanse, his broad frame would hide most of my body from Marjorie's inquisitive gaze.

We rode the elevator in silence and arrived on the second floor moments later.

The instant we entered his room, he was on me. Suddenly, my hands were pinned above my head and his tongue was down my throat. The speed of it shocked me, and it was a few frightful seconds before my brain kicked into gear and my years of Karate training took over.

I kneed his groin, and with a howl he released my hands. Back in control, I wriggled out from his embrace, bent over, and karate chopped the back of his knees so he tumbled to the floor. It had all happened so quickly.

He rolled to his side and clutched his groin. His eyes bulged at me, showing he was in as much shock as I was. "What the hell was that for?"

I decided that maintaining my character was the only way to get through this, and put my foot on his hip. "I'm in charge here, bad boy."

"Jesus, you could've told me."

By the horrified look in his eyes, I'd completely ruined it. There was little chance I'd be getting my rocks off with Batman now.

He groaned and tucked his knees higher. "How'd you learn to do that anyway?"

I shrugged. "I'm a green belt in karate."

"Shit, really?"

I nodded. "Three years of training."

A smile curled at his lips. "I think I'm in love."

I burst out laughing. *Holy shit, I hadn't expected that.* Men were strange creatures.

Just when I wondered if I should leave, he eased up onto one elbow. "So, Miss Ivy, what do we do now?"

I nudged him with my foot so he lay flat on the floor. "Mmmm, do you think you can behave yourself now?"

He nodded with the eagerness of a teenage virgin.

"Okay then. Take your gloves off."

With a flick of a couple of Velcro straps, he peeled his gloves off and made a show of tossing them onto the bed. It looked like my Batman had lovely supple hands with very long fingers. An image of those fingers plunging inside me had my insides clenching with want.

It was time to get naked with my superhero.

Using my teeth, I plucked at the fingertips of my gloves to release them a little, then I held my hand toward him. "Would you mind?"

I heard him swallow before he reached up and glided my green gloves down my arm. Once they were removed, he tossed them over his head onto the carpet.

"What's next?" He grinned.

"Your shoes."

Batman sat up, zipped out of his heavy leather boots, and made a show of tossing them aside, too.

I glanced down at his feet. "Socks are not sexy!"

"Oh right." He bent over, whisked them off in a flash, and threw them away.

Batman remained in a seated position on the floor as I stepped over his legs and planted my high heels on either side of his hips. I towered above him.

"Are your balls okay?"

He huffed and looked up at me. "Probably not."

"Maybe I have something that'll help." I squeezed my fingers into my corset and popped by boobs out above the boned satin. It wasn't difficult—they were about to burst out anyway. Batman leaned back on his hands and stared at my breasts, openmouthed.

As I pinched my nipple between my thumb and finger, I watched for his reaction. Batman cleared his throat and rolled his tongue over his bottom lip, leaving a light sheen in its wake.

"Feel better?"

He shrugged. "A little."

I squatted down in front of him. "Here . . . your turn."

He squinted at me as if this were a test. "You promise not to knock me out?"

I chuckled. "I promise."

Batman leaned forward, and being so tall meant his mouth was the perfect height for my breasts. He paused and our gaze met. Batman's eyes were intense green, as if his superpowers were drawing the pigment out of my costume. I don't think I'd ever seen such a vibrant iris color. The dark lashes circling his eyes enhanced the attraction.

"Go on," I said. "I won't hurt you."

He reached up with his left hand and ran his smooth fingers over my perky nipple. Next second, he flipped me onto my back and had me pinned beneath him.

His glorious grin was the only thing that saved him from a karate chop to his Adam's apple.

"Gotcha!" He grabbed my hands and held them to my side.

"I guess you do, bad boy. What do you plan to do with me now?"

He blinked a few times, and I could see his mind churning.

"How do you get out of that costume?" I asked.

"There's a zip up the back."

"Can you take it off, but leave your cape and mask on?"

"Yeeeessss." He dragged the word out. "Only if you keep your corset and mask on."

"Deal," I said. "Help me up."

Batman stood and launched me to my feet.

With sneaked glances at each other, we both plucked at our costumes, and within a minute or so I'd stripped out of my unnecessary apparel and wore my mask, my corset with my boobs still peaking over the top, and a pair of French knickers that I'd purposely worn beneath my costume underpants.

Batman was down to his blue jockey underpants, his cape, and mask.

What was hidden beneath his costume should never have been concealed. Batman had a body that'd make any woman swoon and most men jealous.

A thick swirl of hair covered his pectoral muscles and gathered in a line that ran all the way to his jocks.

I stepped forward and ran my fingers through that tussle of coarse hair. I'd never had a lover with so much chest hair before. With my shoes now off, his nipples were the perfect height for sucking. So as I drove my fingers through his glorious pelt, I leaned forward and flicked his nipple with my tongue.

Batman sucked the air through his teeth and placed his hands on my shoulders. As I rolled my teeth either side of his hardening bud, careful not to hurt him again, his hands roamed to my plumped up breasts. He had soft yet firm hands that massaged my breasts and manipulated my nipples with expert skill.

My wandering hands found his groin, and I ran my palm over the length of his hardening rod. Batman groaned and crumbled at his knees a little with my touch. I slipped my hand into his jocks and tugged his cock out over the elastic.

Batman sucked in a deep breath and stepped back. He glanced down at his growing erection and then at me. A lustful glaze glistened in his green eyes. "I feel like I've fallen into a dream."

"Let's make it a reality then." I hooked my thumbs into his jocks and lowered them to his ankles, and when he stepped out, I tossed them aside.

He swallowed, hard, then he stepped forward and repeated the process with me.

Suddenly, all measured control evaporated. His hands were on me, his fingers in me, his mouth sucking my breasts, his tongue lashing my nipples. My knees buckled with the glorious onslaught, and I grasped his cock in one hand and his balls in the other and stroked him until his rock hard muscle stood to full-blown attention.

At one point, I glanced at the bed, and upon seeing two singles I realized Batman shared a room. My only hope was that his roommate didn't return any time soon.

Then again . . .

I smacked that naughty thought away and turned my attention back to the lovely specimen at my fingertips.

As I worked my magic on his rock-hard shaft, I spread my legs farther apart and Batman slid two fingers inside me, spreading me and filling me all at once. From the angle he had, each thrust grinded over my clitoris and punished it with exquisite rhythm. In and out he went, repeating each thrust with the same intensity as the last. If he could do this all day, I'd let him. The heavenly movement ticked all the boxes. From the perfect pressure gliding over my sensitive clit on the outside, to teasing the greedy erogenous zone deep, deep on the inside.

My building orgasm had my insides squirming with impending release. I clutched my arms around him, clung onto his cape, and bent my knees so Batman could go as deep as his fingers could go. I cried out as an explosion of senses rocked my world. My orgasm was long and sweet and wet as it rolled through me again and again.

Panting with exhaustion, I stepped back on wobbly legs.

Batman's cock stood up between his legs like a flagpole. He didn't have the biggest cock I'd ever seen—that victory went to the Jamaican drummer I'd met a few weeks ago. But the man before me was certainly well endowed, to the point where I wondered if this solid member would fit inside me. Right now, with my still throbbing pulses rocketing from my insides to my clit, I was willing to give him a go.

"We need a condom." My unsteady legs took me to my bag, and I dug around for the foil packets I knew were in there. I plucked one out and handed it to him. He tore the foil open with his teeth, and as he rolled it onto his cock, I glanced around the room. The kitchen counter caught my eye, and I strode over and turned with my back against it.

My reflection in the large glass doors made my decision perfect, and I beckoned Batman over. His cock stood up, bold and proud as he crossed the distance between us. I turned, placed my hands on the counter, spread my legs, and thrust my ass toward him.

"Look." I indicated toward the glass door to our right. "We can see ourselves."

A primal groan released from Batman's throat, and as I watched the reflection, I both saw and felt his mighty cock nudge at my pussy. I put my hand between my legs, grabbed onto his shaft, and guided him inside me. I eased back, pushing on his cock until Batman filled me all the way to the hilt. He stretched me like no man had stretched me before. It was a little uncomfortable, touching something deep inside me that didn't want to be touched.

"Stay still," I urged, and he stiffened. "You're very big."

He groaned again and squeezed his hands on my hips.

I analyzed the reflection. Here I was, Plain Jane, Memphis, and Poison Ivy all rolled into one, getting fucked by a masked superhero. If I thought this year was crazy before, it had officially hit insane now.

And it felt so fucking good.

I slowly pulled forward, dragging his glorious member out of me. But at the very tip I stopped and pushed against him again. His fingers were a vice on my hips as I drew him in with exquisite slowness. It didn't hurt this time. In fact, it was the opposite. Whatever the head of his penis played with inside me, begged for more.

I repeated the move, and drew out and back in, a little faster this time.

Again I did it. Soon, I planted my feet and let Batman take over. In the reflection I watched my breasts thump back and forward against my corset and his cape swish with each thrust. He tilted his head upward, clenched his jaw, and rammed me again. I reached up onto my toes, giving him a deeper plunge that hurt like hell but felt so fucking good at the same time.

Our rhythm grew faster, and I clutched at the counter and squeezed my eyes shut as he pounded me. My second orgasm was a shuddered explosion that rocked me to my core. I cried out, and Batman joined me in grunts of primitive pleasure.

"Yes," he yelled. "Yes. Yes. Yes." He continued to thrust until he began to soften inside me.

Batman peeled his fingers off my hips, and I pushed up from my bent over position. I turned to look at my sixteenth sexual conquest for this year. He opened his eyes and smiled. It was that glorious smile that showed complete satisfaction.

"That was amazing," he said.

"I agree." I nodded. "Do you always come here as Batman?"

He shook his head. "First time." He licked his lips. "Although I think I will every time from now on."

"It suits you."

"Thanks." His eyes shifted, and a look of concern clouded them. "Nobody will believe this happened. Not with a woman like you."

I'd had this comment from men a couple of times already this year, and I had the perfect solution. I tucked my breasts back into the corset and set about gathering my bits and pieces off the floor. I found my French knickers that had been tossed aside in haste and held them toward him. "Will these help?"

His eyes lit up. "Sure will. Thank you."

I put on my green costume undies and sat on his bed to strap on the high heels.

"Are you going to tell me your real name?" Batman had moved to the dining table and sat with his cape over his groin.

"Masked crusaders never reveal their true identity." I strode to him, gave him a kiss on the cheek, and made my way to the door.

"Wait," he said as I gripped the handle. "How will I find you again?"

I glanced at him over my shoulder. "The most priceless gifts in the world are the ones that can never be recreated."

As I walked from his room to the elevator, I wondered where in the hell I got that saying from.

Thankfully, I didn't run into another soul on my way to my room, and I was just about exhausted when I finally hopped into my hot shower.

Refreshed again, I reheated a slice of pizza that I found in my fridge and took it and my diary out to my balcony.

At the top of the page for 10th April, I wrote, *Batman, room 8 - Risky Role Playing.*

As I detailed everything that I did with my superhero, I wondered if it was the anonymity of his disguise that'd made him so sexy.

I guess I'll never find out.

As I ate my pizza and watched all the faceless people walk along the beach down below, I realized it was the anonymity of my Memphis disguise that made me feel sexy. As Memphis, I could say and do anything I wanted. I could also be any person I wanted to be.

It was ultimate freedom.

22ND APRIL
FOREPLAY BY THE FULL MOON
Room 47 - Hot Horizon Hotel

Friday morning announced its arrival with a glorious display of gold over the dark indigo ocean, and just as the rays touched the marble expanse of the lobby floor, I grabbed a cup of green tea and headed out to my favorite spot in the hotel. The sun lounge was the perfect place to welcome in a new day. Spears of light pierced a scattering of clouds, making them glow from the inside. As the minutes ticked by, more and more people joined me in the open air. Most of them performed some sort of exercise. Dozens of walkers and joggers trotted along the designated path that wove along the grass strip, and the surfers hit the early morning waves by the bucket load.
"Where's the Iced Vovos?"
I gasped as I turned to the voice. "Henry! What're you doing here?"
Henry's handsome grin lit up his face, highlighting the wrinkles around his eyes. "I'm staying for a couple of nights."
I couldn't stop staring at him. I never thought I'd see my suave stranger again. My heart fluttered as I contemplated his return. At first, I thought he must be here for work, and had no choice in where he stayed. But then . . . could he be here to see me, Jane Nichols, meek and mild hotel manager, or maybe, Memphis, my sexy alter-ego?

Henry was the only one of my male conquests who knew my secret. Up until now, it hadn't bothered me, because I'd never thought I'd see him again.

"You didn't think I'd be back, did you?" He must've noticed my confusion.

I shook my head. "Ah, no."

"Why not? You're the most fun I've had in years."

"Pfft, really? What about your wife?"

"Soon to be ex-wife. I filed the papers not long after I left you last time."

"Oh, jeez." I covered my mouth. "That's not good."

"Are you kidding? It's great. I'm happier than I've been in years, and she's off traipsing around the world with my ex-golf buddy. They're made for each other—both self-centered twats. Besides, she was never any fun. She spent much more time focusing on her hair or nails than she did on me."

I paused with my teacup near my lips. "That's a shame."

He raised his eyebrows at me. "You think?"

I chuckled. "Yes, I think."

Henry ran his hand through his grey-peppered hair. "That's the nicest thing I've heard all year."

I sipped my tea, listened to the crashing waves and tried to ignore the sexy heat emanating from the suave Mr. Addison.

"So you finish your shift in about"—he glanced at his watch—"an hour. Is that right?"

"About that."

"Want to join me for breakfast?"

Oh god, did I really want to do that? Henry was good looking, kind and considerate, fun to talk to, and he'd taught me some incredible moves, but did I really want . . .

"Okay, not breakfast." He must've sensed my hesitation. "How about lunch?"

I shook my head. "I don't know Henry. It's just a little too—"

"Okay. Here's the plan. You have a nice relaxing day. I'm staying in room forty-seven; I couldn't get the penthouse this time." He tilted his head at me. "Why don't you come up to my room after sunset and we'll have a wine together and . . ." he waited until our eyes met, "see what happens."

My insides clenched as I remembered the incredible orgasm he'd given me on his rooftop terrace last time.

"You're smiling. So is that a yes?"

"It's a maybe."

"I'll take the maybe." He stood. "I'll be waiting. Oh, and don't worry about Memphis; she can stay home."

My jaw dropped.

Did he really want me as me?

"Bye Jane. See you this evening." Henry strode back across the lobby, and I admired his broad shoulders and toned bottom. For a man just over twice my age, he was incredibly fit.

I could've stayed on that lounge and contemplated my crazy situation for hours, but the *ding* of the reception bell had me racing back to my job.

The minutes whizzed by and before I knew it, Needledick, my shithead boss, had arrived, and after the customary shift handover to him, I headed for the elevator. Thoughts spun through my head like a tornado, and I knew I wouldn't be able to sleep.

When I stepped into my room, the sun cast a long golden stripe through the break in the curtains. I tugged them farther apart, opened the glass sliding doors and stepped onto the balcony.

The Gold Coast had put on a magical day.

I made a snap decision to go for a run along the beach. Five minutes later, I was back downstairs and jogging along the path that ran parallel to the breaking waves. I headed away from the bustling Surfers Paradise mall, and with the sun burning into my left cheek, I picked up my pace and concentrated on my body rather than my scrambled mind.

The waves were quite big today, and that meant surfers were out in force. Every shower station I ran past had young men with supple tanned bodies that smelt of suntan lotion and sea salt.

Last year, I wouldn't have given the men so much as a glance, but now, after sixteen weeks on my crazy sexual challenge, I found myself actually perving on them. Still, I admired a man who looked after himself as much as the next girl, but I'd learned that the quality of his body didn't always translate to his prowess in the bedroom.

My mind drifted to Mr. Henry Addison. He was one year shy of sixty, and yet I found him very appealing. Not just his body either. There was a confidence about him that screamed sexy. And if our last session together was anything to judge by, he was an expert at knowing how to please a woman.

A hot flush hit my neck at dangerous speed, and it had nothing to do with the intense pace I set. I took a wooden pathway down to the beach and tiptoed across the soft sand so I didn't get any in my shoes. Once I hit the firmer sand from the outgoing tide, I picked up my pace again.

Ahead of me, an elderly couple walked together in the shallow water. They were holding hands and looked about as relaxed as any couple in love possibly could. The woman said something that had both of them laughing, and I found myself jealous of what they had.

I picked up my pace yet again and sped past them in a blaze of arms and legs.

In the near distance I spied yellow flags, and realized I was approaching Mermaid Beach Surf Lifesaving Club and that meant I'd run about two miles. As I slowed my pace, I checked my watch and nearly died. I'd only been running fourteen minutes. That was a record for me. Lolita, my best friend, always told me exercise and sex were the prefect remedies for anger. But were they also good for confusion?

I stopped at the surf club and sat on a park bench that'd been made from old surfboards. As my body ebbed with exhaustion, the young men around me provided a lovely distraction. Based on their bodies, it was obvious surfing was the consummate workout. These men had muscles in all the right places. They were trim, toned, and tanned, and all wore genuine smiles. People watching had become my new hobby and right now, I was in voyeuristic heaven.

A woman joined the group in a colorful bikini that showed off her sexy figure. She slotted in amongst the men as if she were meant to be there. I envied her. Over the years, my friends had dwindled away to just one— Lolita. But she was married with a family, so we rarely shared any social time together. Not that I'd be able to anyway. With my permanent night shift, how was a woman like me supposed to find fun?

Mr. Henry Addison.

The fact that it was his image that popped into my head had my thoughts spinning.

I slipped off my shoes and socks and headed down to the water. As I walked knee deep in the surging waves, the water crashed into my lower legs as I made my way back toward home.

Before I was even half way back, I decided I'd take Henry up on his offer. It wasn't until I left the beach that I decided to meet him as me, Plain Jane, and not Memphis.

The idea both horrified and thrilled me at the same time.

I showered, ate a couple of pieces of toast with peanut butter, and crawled into bed.

As I counted the waves crashing into the shore below, I drifted off to sleep.

* * *

Five o'clock came around very quickly, and as I rolled to my side and turned off my alarm, I noticed my little black and white cow ornament that my Aunty Ann had given me. *'Time to look for greener pastures,'* she'd said after I'd unwrapped the cute little gift.

On impulse, I picked up my mobile and dialed her. Aunty Ann was my mother's sister and while my mom and dad's never-ending attention had been on my brother and his successful football career, Aunty Ann had focused on me.

It was so wrong that I hadn't spoken to her since Christmas.

The phone rang just once before it clicked. "Jane! It's so nice of you to ring."

"How are you, Aunty Ann?"

"Much better for hearing your voice. How are you?" I imagined her sitting in her favorite chair, with her enormous boobs resting on her lap as she sipped on her first or second beer of the day.

"I'm great."

"Tell me you have a new man."

My mind flipped as I debated what to say. I'd never lied to her before. "Actually, I have a few on the go at the moment."

She laughed until she coughed, and I waited out the noise. "Good for you, darling. I bet they're all spunky."

"Yes, yes they are."

"I'm so glad you gave that Alexander the boot. He was an ass."

"It took me long enough." We'd dated for three years before I'd found out he was cheating on me. It took me a further three months to work out he'd had sex with nearly every woman in Mildura. Despite all that, I'd still been heartbroken when I broke off our engagement.

Not any more though.

"At least you did it. Hey, I went to their wedding you know?"

"Did you?" Alexander had married my ex-best friend just six weeks ago. I still couldn't believe she did that to me. "Did you throw up on their wedding cake?"

Aunty Ann broke up into fits of laughter again, and I chuckled along with her. "Oh, that would've been perfect. No, I behaved myself, but I tell you what—they've both got nice and chubby since you last saw them."

"Really?"

"Yep. Chelsea-Lee doesn't have that sparkle like she used to."

"Good. There is justice in the world." I was always the chubby kid growing up, and I'd suffered more than my share of torment over it from both boys and girls, Chelsea-Lea included.

"Anyway Aunty Ann, I have to go. I've got a hot date."

"Oh, tell me, is he tall dark, and handsome?"

I grinned. "He's suave, sophisticated, and sexy."

"Ooooh, sounds delicious. Give him a smooch for me."

We said our goodbyes, and I was still laughing as I hung up the phone. From what I knew, Aunty Ann had been single her entire life. She was likely to remain that way until the day she died. I truly hoped that wasn't a destiny for me.

I had a long hot shower, which included shaving my legs, and cleansing and toning my face. All the makeup I'd been using lately for my Memphis disguise was probably messing with my pores.

Henry's suggestion that I leave my naughty alter-ego behind was an interesting one, because it was Memphis that he'd met last time. Memphis was sexy and sassy, and knew exactly what she wanted—sex. I, on the other hand, was usually shy and dorky when it came to men.

Hopefully some of my Memphis traits would come out to play.

I still put on a touch of makeup—just enough foundation to cover the scattering of freckles across my nose, plus mascara and a touch of lipstick. That was it. It was a refreshing change from my usual get-up.

I blow-dried my hair and styled it using my curling wand. The result was loose curls that fell over my shoulders and down my back. It was rare for me to wear my hair down; usually I couldn't be bothered messing with it, so it went up into a ponytail or bun.

The decision of what to wear was much harder. Over and over I dragged clothes from my closet, tried them on, and then returned them because they were too old, too conservative, too skimpy, or just plain ugly. Although I wanted to look and feel sexy for him, I wanted to ensure it was me he was seeing, and not Memphis.

In the end, I settled on a Bohemian maxi skirt that fell to the floor and a white linen top with elasticated sleeves that could either sit up on my shoulders or down on my biceps. I wore nice chunky earrings in a bold pattern to match the skirt, and selected a pair of flat comfortable sandals. I glanced in the mirror.

Is this what a twenty-eight-year-old single woman should look like on a hot date?

I had no idea, but I was about to find out.

With another dab of lipstick, I grabbed my bag and keys and headed for my suave tutor's room.

Henry opened the door after I knocked just once.

"Welcome." He leaned over and pressed his lips to my cheek. His aftershave was a delicate blend of floral and spice. "You look stunning."

A tingle crawled up my neck as he placed his hand on my lower back and guided me into his room. A couple of candles flickered inside two large wine glasses set up on the balcony table. It was a clever idea to stop to wind from blowing them out. *I'll use that myself sometime.*

"I thought we'd have a drink outside. Would you like one?"

"Yes please." Although I'd have to watch how many I drank, because in a little more than three hours I had to go to work.

"Perfect. I took a guess that you'd like champagne?" He pulled out a chair, and he guided it in as I sat.

"That'll be lovely."

He poured a generous amount of bubbles into both our glasses, then held a bowl of strawberries toward me. "Pop it into your champagne."

I did as instructed, and the bubbles attacked the fruit as it bobbed and spun at the top of the glass.

Henry sat down and held his glass toward me. "Here's to perfect strangers."
I nearly crumbled at his toast, because Perfect Stranger was the nickname
I'd given to Hunter McCall, the chocolatier I'd met just two weeks ago. I
sipped my drink, hopeful that it wouldn't come straight back up again.
"Are you hungry? I took the liberty of putting together a nibble plate, if
you're interested?"
My stomach growled at the very thought. In my haze to get ready, I'd
completely forgotten to eat. "Sounds great."
"Good. I'll be back in a second."
I nibbled on another strawberry, and as I heard Henry fussing about in the
kitchen, I spied the edge of the moon beginning its glide up from the ocean,
hundreds of miles in the distance. Thousands of stars lit up the night sky,
tiny pinpricks in a blanket of black.
Henry returned carrying a large plate topped with an abundant selection of
nibbles.
"I didn't know what you liked, so I've covered all bases."
"Wow, lucky I'm hungry."
"Yeah, I got a bit excited." He wriggled his eyebrows.
"Oysters and strawberries, I see. Looks like you're trying to get me excited."
"Well, that too. I'm just pleased you came." He ran his tongue over his
bottom lip. Clearly he didn't miss his sexual innuendo. He sat again and
offered me a small plate. "Please eat."
Our fingers touched when I reached for the plate and I glanced at the
handsome older man beside me. Henry had perfect features to be an aging
movie star. With just the right amount of grey hair and wrinkles, he
appeared to be maturing gracefully. He could sit right alongside George
Clooney or Pierce Brosnan and look like he was meant to be there. Right
now though, he sat with me and that made me feel wanted. What I really
wanted though, was for him to do to me what he'd done last time. And any
other special tricks he'd like to teach me while he was here, too.
He topped my plate up with a few oysters and a dollop of pink sauce.
I'd had oysters a few times in my life, but couldn't say I'd really enjoyed
them. Unlike Lolita; she raved about them. She was convinced fresh oysters
were a sign of a great restaurant. Using a tiny fork, I scooped it into my
mouth and after a moment's hesitation, I chewed. The slightly tangy pink
sauce and the fresh oyster were the perfect combination. It was delicious.
"Yum," I said, as I forked another into my mouth.
"I agree. These are Cape Hawke oysters. Bought them fresh this
afternoon."
The creamy, buttery texture was exquisite, with just a touch of lemon.
Although I could've eaten a dozen, I resisted, and scoured the selection for
what to have next.

"Try these," Henry suggested. "It's just come out of the pan." He reached for a spear of asparagus with his fingers. "Here."

He held it toward me, and the head of the vegetable bobbed up and down, begging me to bite it, so I did.

Henry grinned. "You are hungry."

"Always."

We ate in silence for a moment or two as the moon continued its grand entrance up from the horizon. The silvery orb dominated the inky black sky.

"Have you ever had sex by the moonlight?" Henry's deep baritone was that of a man in his prime.

I cleared my throat. "Ummm, no."

"Good. Here, try some mini bruschetta."

He diverted the topic so quickly. I couldn't resist the portion he held toward me.

"It's buffalo mozzarella, fresh tomato, seasoned with salt and pepper. Simple, yet delicious."

Henry seemed to have planned this so well, I wondered if the timing of the full moon was also intentional. Until this year, I'd always had sex with the lights off. The idea of having a man touch me by the light of the moon set my insides into a frenzy.

The bruschetta was so delicious I reached for another one.

"I love watching you eat."

I brushed some crumbs off my lips. "Seriously?"

"Yes." He nibbled down an asparagus spear. "My wife was so finicky about her food, always so worried about the calories or sugar content that each meal became a mathematical equation. Just watching your eyes light up with each new taste is a refreshing change."

"I don't think you can see my eyes light up out here."

"On the contrary, under this moonlight and the flickering candles, you're bathed in an exquisite glow." He reached over my shoulder. "Do you mind?"

I shook my head, and Henry glided a lock of hair to my back, reached for my sleeve, and tugged it down my shoulder. "That's better. I can see more of you now."

I swallowed another sip of champagne as the delicate tendrils of the ocean breeze drifted over my bare skin. Henry's eyes were intense, and when he licked his bottom lip the urge to lean over and kiss him was excruciating.

"Would you like anything else?"

Just your hands all over me. I cleared my throat. "No, thank you. It was all delicious."

Henry stood and cleared the table, taking the large plate inside. He returned with two bowls—one with strawberries, and the other with whipped cream. He topped up our champagne, placed the bottle on the floor, and then reached for my hand. "I want to show you something."

I allowed him to help me stand, and then turn me so I faced the moon. Henry eased my second sleeve off my shoulder. He guided my hair aside and ran delicate kisses down my neck and shoulder. The combination of his breathing and hot tongue drew my arousal out quickly, and I moaned.

"Jane," he whispered.

My eyes snapped open; to hear my real name tumble from his lips was a shock. I'd been Memphis with so many men, I'd literally forgotten what it was like to be me.

"You're exquisite." He wrapped his arms around me, and as each of his hands cupped my breasts, he continued his kisses.

The cool breeze mingled with his hot tongue created shivers across my skin. "See the moon?"

I opened my eyes. "Yes."

"It's going to watch your body sing over and over tonight."

I melted into his touch, and a groan tumbled from my throat.

"Shhh. If you keep quiet, you'll enjoy it even more."

Once again, Henry was my teacher, and I was his very willing student. He raised my arms and lifted my top up over my head. In a flash, my strapless bra was gone, and his hands were back on my breasts. I should've been worried about being seen. I should have been worried about a whole heap of things. But I wasn't. Right now, nothing mattered but my pleasure. With that thought came a glorious sense of intoxicating freedom.

It was time to feel his flesh. "Take your shirt off, please."

He stepped back, and as I stood there, topless in the moonlight, I felt like Henry and I were the only people in the whole world.

The heat of his skin caressed my back as he held his body against me. His kisses continued up and down my neckline, and the moon continued its rise above the ocean. It was now a complete full moon, bold and bright and showing me the way.

I turned to Henry, and as I threaded kisses up and down his neck, I reached for his belt buckle. His hands clutched over mine.

"I keep my pants on remember?"

I blinked and frowned at him.

"I want this to be about you."

He seemed so sincere that I couldn't object. Why would I anyway? The first three lovers I'd had in my life were selfish and inconsiderate. To have a man who wanted my sexual pleasure to be about me and only me was a dream come true.

"Do you trust me Jane?"

"I trust you."

"Good."

He turned me toward the ocean again and undid the button and zip at the back of my skirt. I stepped out of the flowing fabric and closed my eyes, riding the wave of lust coursing through me.

Henry came up behind me again and nestled his body to mine, and as his lips traced kisses over my shoulder, he spread my legs apart with his foot. I was his willing puppet.

His hands glided from my upper thigh to my breasts, to my neck. His fingers found my lips, my stomach, and my hardened nipples.

He was gentle and excruciatingly slow, and I wanted him to touch me lower. I bent my knees, silently begging him to tear my panties from my body and thrum my clitoris like he did last time, but he resisted. My breathing became deep and loud as we writhed together in a sensual dance that had me shuddering all over.

My eyes shot open, as I realized I'd just had an orgasm that rocked me from out of nowhere. I turned to him, openmouthed.

"Shhh," he said, knowing.

"How did you . . .?"

He touched his finger to my lips and I hushed.

"Would you like to lie down Miss Nichols?"

With the way I was feeling right now, I would've cartwheeled the length of the Gold Coast naked if he'd asked me. Henry was a master magician.

I nodded, and Henry raised my hand to his lips and kissed my palm.

"Wait right here." He placed the strawberries and cream on a seat, then whipped a towel from the deck chair at the side of the balcony and spread it out over the table.

He turned to me and hooked his thumbs into my panties. "May I?"

Hell yes. I wanted to scream it from this eighth-floor balcony. I wanted the whole world to know that I'd just had a fucking incredible orgasm. And I wanted to do it all over again.

Henry could do whatever he wanted to me.

He slid my panties down my legs and at my pussy he paused to sniff, loud and deep. He let his breath out right at my sex, and while I couldn't be certain, I thought he'd deliberately blown his hot breath over my clitoris. Henry did it again, inhaled in through his nose, and blew a long deep, hot breath over my sex. I ran my nails up his bare back and spread my legs. Henry didn't miss my signs and did it again.

God damn, sex with an older man is a glorious thing.

When my panties fell to my ankles, I stepped out of them and Henry stood up, brought the blue lace to his nose and inhaled again. "Yum," he said, before he tossed them through the open glass doors.

He turned his attention back to me, put his hands on my hips and lifted me onto the table with ease. The bulge in his pants was unmistakable, and I felt sorry for him. Twice now Henry had remained dressed from the waist down, while I, on the other hand, was completely naked.

"Do you . . ."

"Shhh." He reached for my breasts, curled his fingers beneath them and took their weight into his hands. His eyes glazed with the movement, and to my relief, I realized he was enjoying this as much as I was. That was the acknowledgement I needed to completely let go.

"Lie back," he said, and I eased back onto the towel and closed my eyes. "That's it; keep your eyes closed."

The breeze tantalized my skin until my already rock-hard nipples peaked even more, begging to be touched. I arched my back and breathed in deep as I waited to learn whatever glorious technique Mr. Henry Addison was about to teach me.

A touch to my lips had me open my mouth. I tasted cream on my tongue, and I bit down into a juicy strawberry. As I chewed on the delicious fruit, a new sensation had me arching my back again. Henry had touched the other half of the strawberry to my nipple. I couldn't hold back and opened my eyes.

Henry was at my side, using the strawberry as his brush and my body as his canvas.

He bent forward and sucked the cream from my breast, drawing out my nipple until it snapped from his tongue, and I gasped.

"Shhh," he said, grinning.

"I can't." He was being completely unreasonable if he thought I could be quiet while my body was receiving this much action.

He dipped the strawberry in the cream again and held it toward my mouth. "Yes, you can." Henry teased me with the juicy fruit before I bit it in half with one aggressive bite.

The moon was a magical orb high over the balcony, providing enough light to see my sex guru. His squared out jaw and intense eyes were the picture of eternal concentration as he drew out my pleasure.

As I savored the delicious berry, all my other senses hit sensation overload. Fingers of cool breeze danced over my skin as Henry dabbed the strawberry from my left breast to the right, and then licked the cream off with a mixture of delicate tongue-lashings and intense sucking.

I writhed beneath his touch, and just when I thought I couldn't handle any more, his hand glided between my legs, and his finger tapped my clitoris. My eyes shot open as shudders of exquisite pleasure rolled from deep inside me, all the way up to my bulging nipples.

Henry sucked my breast and continued to tap my clit. Tap. Tap. Tap.

He rubbed his palm over my pussy, then returned to the tapping.

Tap. Tap. Tap.

With a light twist of his fingers, he tweaked my clit, then tap, tap, tap.

I spread my legs as far as they would go and raised my hips, begging him to finger me, but he continued with the tapping. Continued with the sucking. I bucked beneath him, then grabbed his hand and shoved it between my legs.

"Now," I yelled.

Henry answered my cry and shoved his fingers into me. My orgasm was instant, driving great waves of unparalleled pleasure through me. Over and over, hot juices spilled from my body. I clutched at the sides of the table, raised my hips, and begged him to keep going.

He did, and I experienced the best fucking multiple orgasm ever.

Suddenly, I hit sensation overload. I snapped my knees shut, trapping his hand in me so I could ride out the new phenomenon that rendered me useless. I couldn't breathe. I couldn't move. It was exquisite and special and amazing. I wanted it to last forever.

It was a long moment until I was able to focus again, and when I did, it was as if my body had completely liquefied.

A blanket of utter satisfaction smothered me. It was glorious, and with the glow of the moon, the tickle of the breeze, and a suave, sexy man at my side, I could've stayed right there all night.

I rolled my head to my side and gazed at my teacher. Henry Addison had a dark stain in his pants, and a light sheen covering his upper body. The moonlight carved out each defined muscle in his torso, highlighting his obvious fitness.

Henry was the picture of a satisfied man.

"Thank you," I said, as I pushed to sit up.

"No, thank you."

With the towel between my legs, I slipped off the table, and when Henry went inside his room, I used the solitude to discreetly wipe myself.

Sex had become very messy business.

Henry returned wearing a fresh pair of pants.

"Henry," I said, and he ran his hand through his thick hair as he turned to me. "Why didn't you let me undress you?"

A small smile curled at his lips. "Because I don't want this to be over."

I frowned at him, confused.

"I have a lot more to teach you, Jane."

I couldn't stop the broad smile forming on my face as I nodded at him. "I look forward to it, Henry."

Now that the inferno heating up my insides had subsided, I realized how cool the breeze had become as goose bumps shivered across my skin. I found my clothing and quickly re-dressed.

As I readied to leave, Henry came to my side. "You don't need Memphis, Jane."

I debated that comment in my mind until finally, I had a response. "Without Memphis, I would never have met you."

A beautiful smile lit up his face. I'd just made him a very happy man and that made me happy too. Mr. Henry Addison was handsome. He smiled with his whole face. His dark irises dazzled, and the lines around his eyes and mouth deepened. He nodded. "I like her then."

I kissed his cheek and headed for the door.

"Jane," he said, as I pulled down on the handle. "I'll be back."

I looked at him over my shoulder. "I'll be waiting."

My wobbly legs were driven by the air of satisfaction coursing through my veins, and I somehow managed to walk to my room.

After a long, hot shower, I wrapped a towel around me and with every muscle in my body unravelling; I crossed the room to my bed. I sat cross-legged, reached for my diary, and turned to 22nd of April. At the top, I wrote, *Mr. Henry Addison, Room 47 – Foreplay by the Full Moon.*

I described in great detail how I'd had an orgasm while he'd barely touched me. It proved that my ability to climax was as much about my mind as it was about my body.

Henry had taught me something very powerful about myself tonight.

I'd be forever grateful to my suave tutor.

26TH APRIL
SILENT BUT DEADLY
Room 25 - Hot Horizon Hotel

"So you're trying to tell me you had a fucking mind-blowing orgasm without him even touching you?" Lolita's eyes bulged at me, and I glanced around the Blue Haven coffee shop to see if anyone had heard her. She could be so loud sometimes.

Satisfied that her excitement had gone unnoticed, I shook my head. "He was touching me."

"Yes, yes, but not your vajayjay?"

I nodded. "Correct."

"Holy fuck, babe, that musta been intense."

"Like you wouldn't believe."

Matt, the cranky-ass waiter arrived with our drinks and my lemon butter cake, and as we waited out the interruption, I watched Lolita's face form into a scowl, no doubt itching for him to go. She'd have a dozen questions for me by the time he sauntered away.

The instant he left, she leaned forward and tapped her long pink fingernail on the table. "Tell me how he did it."

"That's the thing . . . I don't know. He told me the moon was going to watch my body sing over and over, and then he glided his hands all over me and whispered stuff in my ear." I shrugged at how lame it sounded now. "It was crazy."

She picked up her green tea and paused with it near her lips. "I'm so fucking jealous right now."

I shook my head. "No, you're not." Lolita was married to one of the hottest men in the world and to top that off, the two of them were crazy stupid in love with each other.

"I am too. Calvin'll have to pick up his act or I'll—"

"You'll what?" I laughed at her.

She rolled her eyes skyward, thinking. "I'll make him come to our Tuesday morning sessions so he can hear what you've been up to."

"Like hell you will. I'm not telling him what I do with these guys."

"He already knows."

"Yes, but it's not *me* telling him."

She pouted at me. "Now you've had two sexual experiences that I haven't."

I grinned at her. If I'd had a decade to think about his, I could never have predicted how my life had turned around this year.

"So you're still on track, hey?"

"Sure am. Seventeen men in seventeen weeks."

Lolita sat back on her chair. "I'm proud of you, babe."

I was too. Taking my sexual gratification into my own hands was easily one of the best decisions I'd ever made.

"So do you think Mr. Suave and Sophisticated will be back?"

"Henry told me he would be."

"Really? And you're happy with that?"

I frowned at her. "Why wouldn't I be?"

She shrugged. "I don't know. Because he knows your secret. Because you've already had him twice. Because he's a hell of a lot older than you."

I rolled her questions around my head and I nibbled on my lemon cake. "First, let's get this out of the way. His age has nothing to do with it. He's more fit than half the men I've been with. And with age comes experience."

"True." Lolly nodded, as if knowing what I was talking about.

"Regarding him knowing my real identity, there was something . . . oh, I don't know, it was . . . it was really special to be with a guy who knew my real name."

She laughed. "Not many girls get to say that."

I chuckled with her. "I guess not."

"So you've had him twice—will you have him a third time?"

"Lolly, if he keeps doing this stuff to me, I'd have him a hundred times a week."

"Holy shit, babe." Lolita shifted back on her seat and thrust her arms in the air. "I want what she's having." She yelled it out, and this time people did turn around to look at us.

We laughed together and finished off our drinks.

"So what's next?" She cocked her head at me.

I held my palms out. "Number eighteen, of course."

* * *

Number Eighteen introduced himself to me fourteen hours later. I'd been at work for just half an hour when Mr. Corben Willis swaggered to the reception counter with a full duffle bag thrown over his shoulder. He was tall, tanned, and bulging with muscles like steel, and a steely gaze to match. Corben was nothing like the men I'd had so far this year, and that made him appeal to me.

"So what's brought you to the Gold Coast?" I wouldn't normally enquire, but a few weeks ago, I'd decided that getting to know Memphis's conquests a little better was a significant part of my year-long challenge too.

"I'm a security guard. I was here for the Anzac Day parade yesterday."

"Oh right, that's cool."

He nodded and waited out my attention to the paperwork in silence.

"Here's your room card." I smiled up at him. "You're in room twenty-five on the fifth floor."

"Thanks." Maybe idle chitchat wasn't his thing.

As he wandered to the elevator, I inhaled the lingering scent of his cologne and admired his sexy butt. I wanted to blow him a kiss and tell Corben I'd be seeing him soon.

That fleeting meeting with Corben was the only highlight of my night. Not that I was surprised; Tuesday nights were never busy. The only good thing about Tuesdays was that I had the next day off.

I whiled away the time doing the staff rosters and other tedious paperwork. Then, completely bored out of my brain, I hopped onto the computer, and as if my fingers were possessed, I was suddenly looking at pictures of Mr. Corben Willis.

Apparently, Number Eighteen qualified for Mr. Universe in Sydney two years ago, and according to the pictures I was now drooling over, he totally deserved to be there. Holy smokes, Corben was a beast. And Memphis was the perfect beauty to tame him. My insides purred at the prospect.

Three hours later, I started yawning. Twenty minutes after that, I began toying with the idea of putting the 'back in five minutes' sign on the counter and tackling Number Eighteen head on.

The second the clock ticked over to one in the morning, I hit crazy mode. Without a single soul in sight and nobody to answer to, I left my post at reception and raced to my room on the fourth floor. With the images of Corben's pumped up body whizzing through my over-excited brain, I transformed myself from mousey Plain Jane who he'd met downstairs, to smoking-hot Memphis.

After seventeen weeks of doing this, applying the over-the-top makeup had become second nature, and I did it in record time.

I chose a flowing backless pink dress with a peek-a-boo cut-out showing just the right amount of cleavage. It was impossible to wear a bra, which was perfect, because this meant one less piece of clothing to remove. Time was of a premium.

It took an excessive amount of time to wrestle my hair into my long blond wig, but I eventually did it. Then I tugged on a pair of white court shoes with eight-inch gold spike heels that I could use to poke his eyeballs out should the need arise.

I glanced in the mirror and, satisfied that all traces of Jane were gone, I grabbed my bag, double-checked that the condoms were in there, and headed for the door.

The Hot Horizon Hotel was very quiet as I rode the elevator up to Corben's floor and then strolled to his room. I put my ear to his door and was surprised to hear yelling. It took me a moment to realize it was the television. Number Eighteen was awake.

This was a rare treat for me; many of the men I'd groped so far this year had been fast asleep when I'd forced myself into their room.

I flicked some of my long wig over to my front, careful not to cover my cleavage, thrust my shoulders backward, enhancing my boobs, and knocked three times on the door.

The television was adjusted down in volume and a moment later, the door opened.

My second impression of Corben didn't disappoint. He wore a pair of black track pants that hung loosely on his hips; a white drawstring was the only thing keeping the pants in place. Even in this relaxed state, his muscles screamed for my attention.

I cleared my throat. "Someone told me there was smoking-hot guy up here." I made a show of glancing up and down his body. "They were right."

He chuckled and ran his hand over his thick black hair. "Really?" He said it sarcastically.

"Yes." I cocked my head. "Really."

"Well now that you found him, what's your plan?"

I flicked my hair over my shoulder. "I was hoping this smoking-hot guy would like some company."

He stepped aside. "That could be arranged."

I strode past him and noticed the lingering scent of his cologne was still there. Some kind of football match played out on the television but thankfully, the volume was low enough that it wasn't painful. I flung my bag over the back of his dining chair and turned to him.

Corben stood between me and the now closed door, hands on hips, legs slightly apart, a cocky grin on his face.

"I've got an offer for you," I said, as I bent over and grabbed his stubby of beer off the coffee table.

"Go on."

"May I?" I indicated at the beer.

He nodded, and I took a sip. It was bloody horrible, but I tried not to pull a face. I had no idea why I did that . . . beer was not my thing.

I put the bottle back down and looked at him again. He still hadn't moved.

"You don't say much, do you?"

"I don't think you're here for conversation." His eyelids lowered, and he gave me a cocky, knowing look.

"Okay then. Here's the deal. I have ten minutes; do you think you can fuck me stupid in that time?"

Holy shit. I can't believe I said that.

"I reckon I can." He strode to me.

I palmed his chest as he neared, feeling the concrete abs beneath his hairless torso. "I have some rules though."

"Of course." He rolled his eyes.

"I don't like rough. I don't kiss. And I'm in charge."

He played with the drawstring below his navel. "Demanding. But okay."

Aware of the ticking clock, I peeled out of my heels. Time to start this.

I reached for the flawless skin covering his bulging pectoral muscles. Beneath his right nipple the word *trust* was tattooed in simple cursive writing. I traced the ink with my finger.

It reminded me of Henry Addison's question just four days ago. "Do you trust me?" I asked.

Corben looked down at me and cleared his throat. "I don't know you."

"Right." In light of the situation, my question had been a dumb one. A blaze of heat at my foolishness threatened to have me self-combust.

I had to remind myself I was Memphis. Sexy, sassy, in-control Memphis.

I tugged at his drawstring and weaved my hand into the elastic of his track pants, seeking the beast hidden within. To my relief, he wore no underpants. Quick, easy access. Exactly what a speed date should be.

He wasn't anywhere near hard yet, so I cupped his balls and leaned in to suck his nipple. Corben just stood there, hands at his sides, breathing casually, as if what was happening right now was an everyday occurrence. Maybe for hot guys like him it was.

As I manipulated my hand from his balls to his penis, I flitted my tongue from his left nipple to his right. He began to grow at my touch, and as his cock thickened and hardened, my insides clenched with the thrill of it.

I'd never experienced the growth of a man's cock in my hand before and damn, if it wasn't the sexiest thing ever.

Within a surprisingly short amount of time, he'd tripled in size.

I had to see it.

Pushing my thumbs into the elastic of his track pants, I then tugged the pants down to his ankles. I stepped back to look at this glorious creature.

Corben just stood there, muscle on muscle, with a mighty erection, hard and waiting. Waiting for me. It was nice to be waited on. No, it was better than nice; with his glorious member reaching out for me like that, it was fucking hot.

I tugged my bag from the back of the dining chair and rummaged for a condom. It took way too long, and I made a mental note to put them into a zippered pocket next time.

Found at last, I handed one to him. "You'll need this."

He tore the wrapper in half with his teeth, and as he rolled the rubber on like an expert, I reached up, undid the button at the back of my neck and let my dress fall to my waist. As he ogled my exposed breasts my nipples peaked, hardening and pulsing out a wanton beat. I undid the zip at the side of my dress and the flowing fabric fell to the floor.

Suddenly, Corben was on me. He placed his hands on my hips and hoisted me up so I had no choice but to wrap my legs around him. At the kitchen counter, he shoved things aside, and the crash of crockery didn't horrify me like it should have—in fact it was the opposite.

My panties were torn from my body, and the sound of shredding fabric excited me like I would never have believed. The fact that a man with a body like Corben wanted me set my insides pulsing like crazy.

At his insistence, I leaned back, and he manhandled and sucked my breast, drawing out my nipple until it snapped from his lips. I put my weight on one hand and reached around to rub my throbbing clit. Next second his finger was in me, plunging in and out of my pussy as I plucked and played my clitoris. I looked down to see not one but two of his thick fingers glide into me, each slick with my juices.

It drove me wild and I rubbed my clit harder and harder, punishing it in time with his finger-fucking. Our breathing grew to fever pitch, and I screamed as an orgasm shuddered through me.

Corben reached behind him, grabbed a kitchen chair and placed the seat behind his knees. He clutched my butt and tugged me forward on the kitchen counter.

"Wrap your legs around me and put your feet on the chair."

I did as instructed.

"Put your arms around my neck."

Done.

He picked me up and cradled his hands around my butt cheeks. "Use the chair for support."

I dug my toes into the leather cushion.

"You ready for this?" His dark eyes penetrated my lust-filled haze.

"Yes."

He held me with one hand and with the other, he reached between my legs and nudged the head of his penis to my already wet opening. We stayed there, poised, ready for action, and as I studied his dark eyes, I wondered what he was thinking. Was he hesitating or drawing out the excruciating expectancy?

My answer came when the head of his cock pushed upward, spreading me apart as he lowered my hips onto him, filling me with his manhood.

I hung suspended from him, and with his hands clutched to my hips, I used my leverage on the chair for support. He raised my hips up, and I pushed with my legs and soon understood what do do. Rather than him thrust in and out, in this position I was to glide up and down. I was in charge. Exactly how I liked it.

So I moved up and down, slow at first, finding a rhythm, but it wasn't long before my pace increased.

Tightening my clutch at his neck, I bounced up and down while he barely moved. He was trapped at my orgasmic mercy. I took the rapid-fire bouncing action to the limit. This position was new to me, but why the fuck hadn't I discovered it before?

As our eyes locked, my mouth fell open with uncontrollable gasps. He gritted his teeth, drawing out the tendons in his neck like high-tensile wires. His rock-hard cock clawed at my pussy, driving right up inside me.

"Arch your back," he demanded.

I nodded, ready to do whatever he said. I readjusted my grip behind his neck and thrust my breasts forward. If I thought this would only increase the sensation for him, I was so wrong. This slight adjustment had his cock nudging something deep inside me that may never have been touched before. It was pleasure and pain. Exquisite. Mind-blowing. Out of this fucking world.

I closed my eyes and bounced up and down until my heart was set to explode.

Somehow, Corben had released one of his hands from my butt and attacked my clit with his thumb.

His cock remained upright as I pummeled him. He thumbed my clit. I bounced up and down. Faster. Harder. Deep, deep, deeper still.

I was in sensation heaven.

My orgasm burst through me, every muscle in my body vibrating as I screamed out the release. A guttural growl erupted from Corben. He clutched at my hips, driving his fingers into my flesh and bouncing me up and down in time to his final thrusts.

I opened my eyes to watch the glorious spectacle.

His teeth were clenched; steely muscle lined his jaw. His biceps, now glistening with sweat, bulged with each thrust. His eyes flitted beneath his closed eyelids, occasionally showing a flash of white.

After several deep, slow thrusts, his grip on my hips released and he opened his eyes.

I licked my lips and swallowed. "Wow." I nodded at him, and he nodded back.

Man of many words.

He stepped forward, plonked my butt on the kitchen counter, and slid out of me. It was as if my insides had been removed. Without a word, Corben strode off toward the bathroom, and I hopped down from the counter. My wobbly legs could barely hold me up, and I clutched at the back of the dining chair as I gathered my dress from the floor. One glance at my panties was enough to know they were ruined. At the rate I was going, I'll have none left soon. *Mental note to self . . . go shopping for underwear.*

Without any underwear to worry about, I was redressed and had my shoes on quite quickly. I was contemplating making a silent getaway when Corben emerged from the bathroom with a towel slung low on his narrow hips. There was no doubt his glory in the Mr. Universe competition was justified. The man was a muscle warrior.

"You're over your ten-minute time frame."

Oh shit. I'd forgotten all about that. "Yes. Yes, I am. Must go." I made for the door.

"What's your name?"

I turned to him and admired that glorious body one last time. "I'm Memphis. What's yours?"

"Corben."

I nodded. "It was nice to meet you, Corben."

"I'm here until ten, tomorrow. Knock on my door any time you want."

With that lovely comment, I strode from his room and made for the elevator.

Back in my room, I was shocked to see I'd been away from reception for forty minutes. I yanked my clothing and wig off and jumped into the shower. The imaginary ticking clock reverberated through my brain as I refreshed and redressed back in the clothes I'd had on earlier. I didn't bother to moisturize or reapply any makeup. I brushed my teeth, gulped back a glass of water, and left my room to head for the elevator.

My body was still a lust-filled inferno as I rode the agonizingly slow elevator to the lobby. I wiped the sweat from my forehead, pushing my annoying fringe to one side. I adjusted my ponytail at the back of my head and tried to force some calm into my still racing heart.

When the elevator door pinged open, my heart hit panic mode. Four adults, five children, and an abundance of luggage filled the lobby.

I raced to my position behind reception.

"About bloody time," said one of the women as she bounced a baby on her hip. "We've been waiting over half an hour."

"I'm so sorry. We had an emergency upstairs."

"Yeah, right. What were you doing? Taking a nap?"

"Rebecca!" the man at the counter with a serious three-day growth said. "Let it go."

"No. I won't let it go." She spun to him. "We've had a shit day, and the last thing we needed was to be left hanging at this time of night."

Oh shit! I'd been so caught up in satisfying my stupid libido that I hadn't even thought about the late check-in register. "What are your names, please?" I tried to ignore the acid burning in my stomach.

Two kids began fighting over a ball, and the other woman went to sort them out.

"Thompson and Higgins," the man said.

The woman sat the baby on the counter and leaned over to look down at what I was doing. "We rang the number on the door you know."

I shot a glance at her.

"That's right." She thrust her chin at me. "We spoke to your boss. He said we could have a discount."

Oh crap. This wasn't good. They'd called Needledick.

"He's on his way here now."

I gasped and covered my mouth.

Her eyes glinted. "Now you're worried, aren't you?"

Worried was a freaking understatement.

"Leave her alone, Rebecca." The man dragged her from the counter. "I'm sorry about that; we've had a pretty stressful day."

"No, I'm sorry. I should've been here." I felt ill. Close to throwing up.

Bile shot to my throat when the glass sliding doors at the front of the hotel opened and my shithead boss strode toward me. His clenched jaw highlighted his anger.

I couldn't believe how quickly he'd got here. I was only gone for about fifty minutes. How did this happen? How did *I* let this happen?

"Jane," he barked my name. "Where the hell have you been?"

"I'm sorry Mr. Karwatsky, there was an emergency up on the fifth floor."

"Really?" His skepticism was unmistakable. He turned his attention to the guests and smiled sweetly at them. "I'm so sorry for this inconvenience. I'll make sure Jane takes twenty percent off your accommodation." He turned to me and sneered, and I knew that money would be coming out of my next paycheck.

I deserved it. My stupid libido was bound to get me into trouble sooner or later.

With their paperwork sorted, I handed the couple the cards to their rooms and helped them load their luggage onto a couple of trolleys. "I'm so sorry." I apologized for the umpteenth time as they took turns bundling into the elevator with their luggage.

Once the guests had vacated the lobby, I turned to Needledick, and knew my trouble was only just beginning.

"Right, miss." He slapped his hand on the counter. "What was this supposed emergency?"

I swallowed as my mind raced for an answer. "The guest in room twenty-five smashed a pile of plates by accident and needed a dustpan and brush. I went up to help him."

"Is that right?" He waggled his head, seeing through my lie.

As I nodded with conviction, a trickle of sweat rolled down my lower back. "It's the truth."

"Let's go see him them."

My eyes bulged. "Pardon?"

"Let's go see if he was happy with your service, shall we?"

"Oh, god. Um, there's no need for that."

He spun to me. "Yes, Jane. There is. I think you've been up in your room instead of manning the counter."

My shoulders slumped as I shook my head.

He snatched his keys off the shelf. "Come on."

"Me?" I palmed my chest

"Yes, you." He shook his head at me as if I were a crazy person.

We awaited the return of the elevator in silence and stepped in together. My mind was a fucked up scramble as I tried to picture how this would play out.

On the fifth floor, Needledick strode ahead of me and knocked on room twenty-five. Corben opened moments later with a huge grin on his face.

"Sorry to bother you, sir, but I just wanted to check that Jane helped you with the broken plates."

I reached up onto my tiptoes so he could see me better and mouthed please to Corben.

He frowned at me, then cocked his head to the side. "Come and look for yourself." He stepped aside, and Needledick strode into the room and headed to the kitchen.

Corben's eyes pierced me. As I stepped past him, he squeezed my butt. "Well hello, Jane."

I wanted to vomit. Again I mouthed *please,* and he winked at me.

He turned to Needledick. "As a matter of fact, I've never had such good service in a hotel before."

My boss turned to look at me. Shock registered on his face.

"That's right. Not only did she help clear up broken dishes, but because I'd dropped my dinner too, she offered to buy me pizza."

Needledick turned to me. "Oh, did you?"

I nodded, unable to speak.

"I believe she intended to pay with her own money, as well. You should look after staff like this." Corben placed his balled fists on his hips.

"Oh yes. I do, of course."

"Does he, Jane?" Corben's question caught me off-guard.

I had enough ammunition to bitch about Needledick for a week. But I wanted this job. *Needed it.* I decided to avoid the question. "I really like working here."

Corben's eyes twinkled. "I bet you do."

Needledick held his hand toward Corben and they shook. "I hope you enjoy your stay."

"It's been amazing so far." Suddenly, Mr. Silent had a lot to say.

Needledick headed toward the door, and I turned to Corben. "Thank you." He wriggled his eyebrows then reached over and squeezed my butt again. "Thank you, Jane."

I just about died as I left him and joined Needledick in the elevator.

"I guess I owe you an apology."

I nodded and straightened my shoulders. "Yes. Yes, you do."

He glared at me. This was the second time I'd put him in his place.

He cleared his throat. "Jane, I'm sorry for not believing you."

"Thank you."

"We seem to be heading in the wrong direction, don't we?"

I frowned at him. "Pardon?"

He shifted his feet, and I hated this excruciatingly slow elevator for the hundredth time. "You and I. For the first year or so, we got on really well. Things have changed."

"You never used to be late for work." I couldn't believe I'd blurted that out.

Needledick nodded. "You're right. It's been a bit of a juggling act since mom got sick."

I frowned at him, wondering what the hell he was talking about it.

"Oh." He raised his eyebrows. "I assumed Marjorie told you; she loves her gossip."

"Told me what?" Marjorie truly was a gossip queen, so I couldn't image what she'd held back.

The doors pinged open, and we stepped across the marble expanse to reception.

"Mom moved in with me about a year ago when her treatment became too much for her to handle. Nights are the worst time." He heaved a heavy sigh.

Oh god. I felt terrible. "I'm so sorry. I had no idea."

"It's okay, you weren't to know, and besides, it's no excuse for me being late."

For the first time in years, I saw a human being in Mr. Karwatsky, not the asshole boss who'd hired me.

"Anyway, I better get back to her. Enjoy the rest of your night."

As he walked toward the front door, I crumbled onto the office chair, completely shattered.

My brain was a fucked up roulette wheel of thoughts for the remainder of my shift, and it was a huge relief when the sun cast its morning rays over the horizon. I made a green tea and poured it into my favorite teacup, decorated with black-and-white cows. With the cordless phone in one hand and my tea in the other, I went outside to enjoy the view.

The beautiful beach scene was perfect therapy. Waves crashed into the shore with repetitive harmony. Rainbow lorikeets flitted from one Pandanas palm to the next, and the sun pushed up from the horizon, bathing a warm glow onto the golden beach in front of me. My tea too was light and delicate, exactly what I needed. I finished it, placed the cup beside me, closed my eyes, and breathed in the fresh sea air.

"Morning."

I spun to the deep voice and gasped. Corben walked toward me in tiny black shorts and a white singlet top that highlighted his nipples as rock-hard pebbles. His muscles flexed and bulged with his stride.

I covered my face with my hands, and as I felt him sit beside me, I peeked at him through my fingers. "Hi."

"So . . . do I call you Jane or Memphis?"

"Oh god."

"No, not God, I'm just Corben."

I chuckled and lowered my hands.

"You nearly got sprung, huh?"

I huffed. "Yeah."

"Would it have been worth it?"

I tucked my hands under my knees, and swung my legs backward and forward as I contemplated his question. Sex with Corben been absolutely mind-blowing, but was I willing to lose my job over it? For his sake, I had to say yes. "It was worth every one of those ten minutes." I smiled at him.

"It was more than that, you know."

"I know."

As I studied the crashing waves, I felt his gaze, and wished I'd put on at least some makeup to cover my freckles.

"You're by far one of the hottest women I've ever met."

I chuckled, disbelieving. "Thanks." As I ran my hand over my ponytail I wondered what he thought of me now. Plain Jane was in full view in the blazing morning sunshine and with not even a lick of lipstick to beautify me.

"I mean both you and Memphis."

I glanced up and our eyes met. Words escaped me.

"It's the truth." He leaned over and kissed my cheek. "I come to the Gold Coast all the time. From now on, I'll be checking into this hotel." He stood up, and I admired every lump of his exquisite physique. "Don't lose your job."

I shook my head and rolled my eyes. "I don't plan to."

Corben leapt down the stairs two at a time, and I watched him run along the path that ran parallel to the beach until he disappeared in the distance.

I went back inside, and an hour or so later, Needledick arrived to take over from me at reception.

"Good morning," I said. "I'm sorry again about last night. Did you get back to sleep?"

"No need to say sorry. It wasn't your fault that woman rang me. I'd actually forgotten my number was the emergency contact on the front door."

"I didn't know it was either. It should be mine, really. After all, I'm the one who lives here."

His eyes brightened. "Are you sure?"

"Of course. Makes sense to me."

He nodded and smiled. I was stunned at how nice his smile was, and wondered if it was the first time I'd seen it.

After he did the standard checks for shift changeover, I headed back up to my room.

I stripped out of my clothes and put on a cotton short and T-shirt pajama set. Then I sat on the bed and reached for my diary. I turned to 26th April, and wrote *Mr. Corben Willis - Room 25* at the top. As I thought about how he was a man of very few words, I wrote, *Silent but Deadly.*

I went on to detail that wonderful position we did while he held me in his arms and how I managed the depth of the penetration for a change. It was a glorious thing to have that much control.

His question over whether or not the risk had been worth it rolled through my brain.

I'd taken on this challenge from Lolita without fully understanding how it was going to affect me. Not just physically, but mentally too. So far, in eighteen weeks I'd had eighteen sexual encounters. Each one had been unique and amazing, and had completely blown my mind.

Jobs could be replaced; this challenge, however, was my once-in-a-lifetime opportunity.

I, Plain Jane, was having the ride of my life, and I decided there and then that even if I lost my job, I'd carry on this crazy sexual journey until the tick of midnight on the 31st of December. *Bring it on.*

I slipped under my bed sheet, rolled onto my side, and as I pictured Corben's rippling abs, I pretended he was lying naked beside me, dozing. It was a glorious image to help me drift off to sleep.

2ND MAY
THE CONSUMMATE CASANOVA
Room 40 – Hot Horizon Hotel

For a Monday morning, it'd been unusually busy with preparing the finishing touches for The Mighty Pen conference that was booked just two days ago. Apparently, the original venue, which was just four blocks away, was shut down by authorities after an outbreak of salmonella. Lucky for my hotel, we had an available conference room that could accommodate the two hundred delegates at short notice.

I finished preparing the nametags and sorted them into alphabetical order, then hopped onto the computer to summarize the enormous list of people with food allergies. I'd been organizing conferences here for a little more than three years and I was fairly certain food allergies were becoming more prevalent. Thank god I didn't have any problems like that. I loved my food.

I completely lost track of time, so I was surprised when the sun began its morning crawl across the marble lobby. As I looked out at the stunning sunrise over the ocean, a man strolled through the sliding glass doors, glanced around, and then headed toward me. He was silhouetted against the blazing daybreak, but based on his lively step I had him pegged at about my age—twenty-eight.

"Good morning. Welcome to the Hot Horizon Hotel." I shoved my annoying fringe away from my eyes and smiled at him. It wasn't until he reached the counter that I spied the streaks of greying hair at his temples and realized he was much older than I'd originally thought.

"Hi, my name's Benson Cooper. I have a room booked for tonight."

"Oh." I frowned and checked the clock on the computer. At six a.m., the chances of his room being ready were minimal.

"I know I'm really early. I'm here for the conference and I can check in later, but I thought I'd try my luck." His frameless glasses reflected in the lobby lighting and made it hard to see his eyes.

"Let me see." I rummaged through the check-in index cards for his name, pulled it from the pile and keyed his room number into the computer. "Oh, fortunately that room was vacant last night."

"Must be my lucky day." He grinned at me, and I was struck at how genuinely pleased he seemed. I was a sucker for a great smile.

"Have you come far?"

"Just flown in from Perth for the three days. Caught the red-eye. I'll sleep well tonight, that's for sure."

He was a chatty fellow—much different to the hunky Mr. Silent But Deadly, who I'd had a quick romp with last week. I guessed Benson to be about forty-five or so, but that didn't worry me. Not since I'd met Henry Addison, anyway. Despite being nearly twice my age, Henry was a master at pleasing a woman. I stifled a smile at that naughty thought.

"Can I have your license please?"

Benson handed it over, and as I photocopied the card, I noted his age as forty-seven. Benson was fast becoming my next sexual conquest. I really should stop thinking of them like that; I sounded like a predator.

Then again, maybe I was.

"So what do you do?" I needed to change my focus.

"I'm a journalist for *Spice* magazine. We specialize in articles on functions and special events, like product launches, conferences, exhibitions, etcetera etcetera. I'm always looking out for the latest trends."

I cringed. "This conference hasn't started off well then—having to change venue at late notice."

"True, but they seem to have landed on their feet."

I nodded. "They were lucky we didn't have the conference room booked."

"Sure were. I'm happy though. I'd much rather stay a bit farther from the center of Surfers Paradise anyway. I'm looking forward to a bit of R and R."

He smiled again, and I loved how his whole face lit up. Benson seemed to be a man very comfortable with himself. Compared to some of the men I'd met this year, this was a refreshing change.

"So, here's your card for room forty. You're on the seventh floor." I checked Benson's ring finger as he reached for the card. It was unadorned.

"Perfect," he said. "I hope I have a great view."

"It's amazing. You'll love it."

Benson grabbed the handle of his suitcase, and as he made his way to the elevator I admired his figure. Older men were quickly reaching the top of my hit list—although I had to wonder if Benson was just as amazing in the bedroom as Henry was. The orgasms I'd had with Henry were stuff dreams were made of. But was it just him, or did all older men possess this wonderful gift?

I had to find out.

Benson didn't know it yet, but there was little chance he was going to get all the R and R he wanted.

As I giggled at that thought, Needledick arrived to take over my shift, and I wiped the smile off my face.

"Morning, Jane."

"Morning."

"Been busy?"

"Yes, but mainly with getting ready for the conference."

"Oh, that's right. I forgot about that."

My jaw nearly dropped. He was the hotel manager; he shouldn't forget important things like that. "Right, well everything's sorted. About one third checked in last night; the rest will be in this morning. Hopefully it goes smoothly."

"I'm sure it will. You've done an amazing job."

My jaw actually dropped. Needledick never complimented me.

He grinned at me, and it was just a little bit creepy. I said goodbye and dashed for the elevator.

Men were weird creatures.

I opened the door to my room, went straight to the bath, and turned on both taps. I poured in a generous dose of Moroccan Rose Otto Bath Oil. According to the bottle, by the end of my bath, not only would I smell lovely, but my mind would be free of stress and notably relaxed. I'd like to see that miracle. I didn't think my mind ever relaxed—too much shit swirling around for any vacant space to survive.

My growling stomach had me heading to the kitchen. I glared into my sparse fridge until I decided on peanut butter on toast yet again.

With my toast in hand and a bottle of water under my elbow, I opened the glass doors and stepped out onto the balcony. May had brought the cooler weather with it, but I wasn't complaining—this was my ideal temperature. Not too hot that sweat would break out of every pore the moment I stepped outside, and not too cool that I'd need to carry a jacket everywhere. If you asked me, which nobody ever did, this was the best time of year to hit the sunny Gold Coast.

Knowing the bath took forever to fill, I slipped into a chair, and as I ate my simple breakfast, I admired the view. The sky was a beautiful blue, dotted with several puffy white clouds. Down on the beach, seagulls swooped and ducked as they fought over their breakfast and dodged the waves. It was such a peaceful setting, reminding me of how lucky I was to live right on one of the most beautiful beaches in the world.

My phone rang, and as I headed toward my handbag, I contemplated who'd be on the end of the line. Only two people called me—my mother and my best friend, Lolita. And only one of them made me smile by the end of the call.

I glanced at the number on the screen, and my heart leapt to my throat as I pressed the green button. "Aunty Ann, are you okay?"

"I'm fine, dear."

"Oh, it's just you never call me."

She tutted. "That's not true. I call you occasionally."

Okay, I'll give her that. "Are Mom and Dad okay?"

"Yes, yes, everyone's okay. Will you let me talk?"

"Sorry." The worry evaporated in a flash and I sat on the edge of my bed. "What's up then?"

"Just a bit of juicy gossip."

"Ooooh, do tell." I could count on Aunty Ann to keep me up to date with what was happening back in my home town.

"Turns out Chelsea-Lee's pregnant."

I sucked the air through my teeth. "Really?"

"But, there's been a few rumors that Alexander may not be the father."

"Holy shit! Are you serious?"

"Sure am. Apparently, she's four months pregnant, but if that's true, then her conception coincides with Alexander's annual trip to Singapore for work."

"Oh my god. That's gold."

Aunty Ann broke into laughter that was quickly followed by a coughing fit. As I waited for her to catch her breath, I pictured Alexander, the man I was once puppy-dog in love with. He'd never shown any remorse after I found out he'd cheated on me with dozens of women while we were engaged.

"You know what Aunty Ann? This's Karma."

"It sure is, sweetie. Karma's a bitch that bites."

I chuckled at that. Aunty Ann was the queen of interesting sayings.

"Now, tell me." She grew all serious. "Are you getting a bit?"

Getting a bit was an understatement. This year, I'd been getting a lot. "I have men lining up."

"Good. Have a root for this old duck, will you?"

We laughed together, and after a bit more idle chit-chat we said our goodbyes. I'd spent the first twenty-five years of my life in Mildura and Aunty Ann was the only person I missed from back home. Including my parents.

Did that make me a bad person?

I decided it didn't. There must be a million people out there who can't relate to their parents. One of Aunty Ann's favorite sayings was, "You can choose your friends, but you can't chose your family."

She always seemed to understand the angst I had with mom and dad, and I'd always love her for that.

The sound of tumbling water had me dash to the bathroom to turn off the taps. I managed to prevent catastrophe by about four inches. I lifted the plug to let a little bit of water out, then I went out to the balcony to grab my cold toast and water. I put them on the edge of the bath, then stripped off and slipped into the warm water.

"Chelsea-Lea, pregnant!" I tried to picture her with a bulging belly but couldn't. The woman I knew three years ago was all about tight clothes and partying. I could easily recall one of our conversations where she'd declared she'd never have kids.

The possibility that she'd screwed around on Alexander was the best news I'd heard from home in years. Now the two of them had a taste of what they'd done to me.

I truly did believe in Karma. Although, if Alexander hadn't done what he did, then I would never have moved one thousand miles away from home. I wouldn't have met my best friend, Lolita, and I certainly wouldn't be participating in the challenge of my lifetime. Fifty-two sexual experiences in fifty-two weeks.

As I slipped under the water, I inhaled the lovely floral scent, and my thoughts drifted to Benson, just four floors above. I wondered if he were doing the same as me. Rest and relaxation. A flutter of excitement rolled through me at the thought of going up to him after this bath.

Would he generate the same kind of mind-blowing orgasms Henry did? Damn, I wished I could stop comparing them. It wasn't fair on any of the men to be compared to someone they didn't even know.

My hand fell between my legs, and after a moment's pause, I touched my clitoris. It was hard to believe this tiny piece of my body could give me so much joy. I applied pressure with my finger and rolled the little nub around. Instantly, tingles of excitement twitched inside me. It seemed that each time I was with a man, I learned something new about me and my body. Or was I becoming easier to please because I wanted it so bad? I dipped my finger into my pussy. It was hot in the bath, but it was even hotter inside those velvet folds.

I squirmed at my own touch, delighted at my ability to draw out this simple pleasure.

Alternating between playing with my clit and plunging into my hole, I closed my eyes and tried to clear my head of any thoughts other than my own sweet touch. From this angle, every drive into my pussy rolled my finger over my clit.

Unlike the beautifully scented Moroccan Rose Otto Bath Oil, this was a guaranteed way to clear my mind.

I thrummed my sensitive bud, rolling it between my thumb and finger and then applied pressure until it just began to hurt, then I plunged my finger into myself again.

Spreading my legs, I raised my hips out of the water and glanced down to see what I was doing. I really had become a voyeur; I just wished I could see better. I adjusted my hips, and that was when my feet slipped and fell back into the bath. My ass hit the bottom of the tub, hard and as I banged the back of my head on the rim, a wave of water barreled onto the floor.

As I rubbed the back of my skull, certain I'd have a lump the size of an egg in a few minutes, I glanced at the floor. A significant puddle was promptly being soaked up by my black-and-white cow-patterned bath mat. I sighed at the mess and winced as I ran my fingers over my new painful lump.

"Shit. What am I doing?" There was a perfectly good man waiting for me in room forty.

With that thought, I gave myself a quick wash, hopped out of the bath, and dried off with a towel. I set about transforming myself into Memphis. As I'd spent some time talking to Benson this morning, I took an additional precaution by applying extra makeup to disguise my eyes. It occurred to me that I may be able to buy colored contact lenses. I made a mental note to look into that. In the meantime, electric blue eyeliner was the ideal choice for distracting from my green irises, and foundation ensured my freckles were well and truly covered.

Satisfied with my makeup, I chose the short blond wig. This was the first time I'd worn it, and it was quite a wrestle to get my long hair all tucked up in place. Once my hair was in, I checked for stragglers. All good.

Now for the outfit. My wardrobe really was a disaster. If I was going to get through the rest of the year in this challenge, then I needed to plan some serious shopping.

I tugged my trusty French maid outfit from the closet and held it against my body at the mirror. A handful of men had seen me in this slutty costume, and that was exactly how I felt holding it—slutty. Plus, it was daytime, so wearing my trench coat over it would not only look ridiculous, it would appear suspicious.

I cast the costume aside and dived back into my closet. After procrastinating for about ten minutes, I chose a simple shift dress in ivory and navy that had just one zip up the back. Quick and easy to get in and out of. I matched this with a pair of navy Louboutin stilettos with a pencil-thin six-inch heel.

I glanced in the mirror touched Ciaté Liquid Velvet lipstick to my lips, and I was ready to go.

With my bag clutched over my shoulder, I made my way to the seventh floor. While I waited for the elevator, a brilliant idea for why I'd be knocking on Benson's door hit me.

As I rolled the idea around, the doors opened to five people inside, so I was instantly grateful I'd decided against wearing my French maid outfit.

Thankfully, the seventh floor was deserted. At Benson's room, I plumped my boobs up in my strapless bra, sucked in a quick breath, and then knocked on the door.

After a couple of moments, the door opened, and my heart skipped a beat at the sight of him. He wore a hotel-supplied waffle weave bathrobe that was peeled open to the tie around his waist. I instantly wondered if that was the only thing he was wearing.

"Hi," he said, and flashed his gorgeous smile at me.

"Hi." I tilted my head, trying to emulate a sexy come-hither pose.

"How can I help?"

"I'm here for the conference." It was scary how good I was at lying these days. "I overheard you checking in with that lady downstairs and when you scored this room, I thought maybe my room would be ready, too." I shrugged. "No such luck for me."

"That is unlucky." He had a cockiness about him that said he knew where I was going with my story, but he refrained from elaborating on it.

"Exactly, and as we have a couple of hours to kill . . . well, I was wondering if you'd like some company."

Even with his glasses on, I saw his eyes light up. "Yes, yes of course, come in."

He stepped aside, and I strode across the carpet as if I were a runway model. I tossed my bag on the back of a dining chair and turned to him as the door clicked closed. Benson had a neatly trimmed three-day growth that failed to hide a cute dimple in his right cheek that deepened with his grin.

"My name's Benson." He held his hand toward me.

"Yes, I know. I overheard downstairs." I nearly giggled at my clever role-playing prowess.

"Well . . . can I get you a coffee?"

"Oh, no thank you."

He rubbed his hands together as he walked toward me. "So which newspaper do you work for?"

Oh crap. I hadn't thought my harebrained idea through that much. "*The Country Times*." I blurted out. "Yep, I'm a country girl." *Who is a complete idiot.* "You could've fooled me."

I scrunched my nose up at him. "That's sweet of you to say." Damn, this idle chit-chat was hard work.

"Are you here for all four days?"

"Maybe. I always find these conferences so boring."

He nodded. "Some are. It just depends on the speakers and the other guests." A small grin curled at his lips.

"Boredom makes me horny."

He swallowed loud enough for me to hear, and that was my cue to get moving. "I'm going to be straight with you, Benson. I find you really attractive and well . . . would you like to . . . you know, get naked?"

His eyes bulged. "I . . . I . . ." He blinked.

"First though, are you married?"

He shook his head. "Divorced. Twice."

"Hmmm. Do you have a current partner?"

He rolled his eyes to the ceiling.

"Don't lie to me. I'll know."

He rubbed his hands together. "I don't have *a* partner."

I squinted at him. "You have more than one partner?"

His smile this time wasn't quite so bold—it was more like cheeky.

"How many?"

A quick glance at the ceiling again. "Three."

"Oh shit. So you're a bit of a player then? Are these women married?"

"Not all of them."

Holy crap. Benson was a lady-killer. And not in the body-in-the-trunk kind of way. I frowned. "You must be pretty good in bed then."

He adjusted his glasses. "It may've been mentioned a few times."

Older men were quickly becoming the most intriguing, and I was ready for a piece of that lady-killer action.

"It's getting hot in here." It truly was, and it wasn't just the sun penetrating through the open curtain. I turned around. "Would you mind unzipping me?"

Benson's hands brushed against my neck, soft and supple, then the zipper glided all the way down to the top of my buttocks. Shrugging the dress off my shoulders as I turned to him, I dropped it to the floor and stepped out.

Benson licked his lips and tugged on the cloth belt around his waist. I thought he was going to remove it, but he didn't.

"Should we at least have a drink or something?" His voice was shaky.

"No need," I said, as I reached behind my back and unclipped my bra. I caught the lacy fabric over my breasts. "Do you want me to carry on?" I winked at him, trying to look sexy.

He nodded and cleared his throat.

As I gradually lowered my bra, he ran his tongue across his lips and my nipples began to harden. I flung the lingerie at him, and he caught it with one hand and nudged his glasses back up his nose.

As he glided the lacy fabric between his fingers and watched me, I gently twisted my nipples, stirring up lovely sensations from between my legs that then blazed through my body.

I stepped my feet apart and dug my stilettos into the carpet, and with Benson watching me, I ran my hand over my sex. My panties were soft lace, providing little resistance to my pressure.

I put my finger in my mouth, slicking it with moisture. With a slight bend in my knees, I curled my hand over my torso, tugged my panties aside, and flicked my clit with the tip of my finger. Everything clenched up inside me with this touch. I did it again. Just a quick flick of my clit.

Then I remembered what Henry had done a few weeks ago, and I tapped at my delicate bud. I did it a few times—tap, tap, tap—but it had nowhere near the same amount of appeal that it had when Henry did it, so I abandoned that idea and went back to rubbing.

In my lust-fueled haze, I glanced over at Benson. He still remained at a distance, but now, protruding from the gap in his robe, was his cock. His resistance to cover it proved he was happy with my show.

I hissed at the tingling sensations running through me, and Benson hissed with me. As I dragged my finger out, I applied pressure to my clit. With another bend of my knees, I delved deeper into my pussy. With each probe of my velvet folds, another layer of lust stacked inside me.

Rubbing harder and faster, I closed my eyes and explored my hot oasis over and over. But today, for some reason, it wasn't enough. I couldn't quite get there.

Snapping my eyes open, I strode to Benson and tugged his bathrobe apart. "Oooh, what have we here?"

His gaze flitted from his cock to me, drawing attention to the flagpole that I couldn't miss if I tried.

Mr. Lady-Killer looked lost for words.

"Let's take this off?" I undid the knot at his waist and pulled the belt out slowly until it was a long fabric bridge joining the two of us together. And that was when I had my second awesome idea of the morning.

I twirled the belt around like a lasso. "Okay, Casanova. Ready to show me what all these women rave about?"

Before he answered, I placed my hands on his hips, guided him to the bed, and shoved him so he fell backwards. He landed diagonally across the covers, which was perfect for my plan. I stepped to the head of the bed, and kneeling on a pillow, I weaved the belt around the wooden rungs. Now I had two loose ends ready to attach to something. Preferably his wrists.

I looked down at Benson. He hadn't moved. But his eyes were filled with lustful expectation, and his rock-hard rod showed his willingness to play. His cock had a decent curve to the right, but it was still very impressive. It wasn't the biggest member I'd seen, nor the smallest. I didn't know whether to giggle or hate myself at my insistence on comparing my conquests' body parts.

I patted the pillow. "Up you come, bad boy." God, I'm a diva!

Benson willingly wriggled up to the pillows and placed his hands above his head. I reached for his left wrist and knelt over him to tie one end of the belt.

Suddenly, Benson was on my breast, sucking it into his mouth with feverish moans. I braced with my hand and lowered to him, giving him all of me. He rolled his tongue and sucked my nipple with expert skill. His free hand roamed up and down my waist, and I raised my knee to straddle him, giving him something truly special to play with. He didn't waste a second. Benson's finger glided over my already throbbing clit and into my pussy. I gave up my intention to tie up his other hand and concentrated on the horny beast beneath me.

As I grinded my pussy back and forward, his fingers plunged into my hot depths. His mouth continued to lavish my breast, sucking, nipping, and rolling his tongue around my now very sensitive nipple. The orgasm that I'd started in the bath earlier came back with a vengeance, creating a tidal wave of pleasure that rolled from my very core right up through my body.

His cock thumped into my backside, seeking an audience, and I pulled my breast from Benson's eager lips and curled my fingers around his shaft. He groaned in time to my movements as I glided my hand up and down the solid muscle.

One of his hands attacked my breast while the other ravished my pussy. Benson didn't need any lessons; he truly was a lady-killer. As I rocked back and forward, pumping his cock with a repetitive twisting motion, the climax inside me built to fever-pitch.

I let go of him and leaned back so my hands were on his knees, and he had full view of my vagina. Benson's thumb punished my clit with swirling pressure, and with his other hand, two fingers plunged into my throbbing hole, hard and fast.

I screamed as I came, riding out the exquisite wave of lust that barreled through me. As I gasped for air and rocked my hips back and forward, my juices spilled onto Benson's stomach over and over.

It was a long moment before I pushed up from his knees and sat on his torso to look at him. His glasses were slightly fogged over, but his smile was glorious. The long white belt trailed from his wrist and up over his shoulder.

"My knot didn't hold, hey?"

"Honey, nothing would've held me back."

I giggled at that. "I'm glad."

"I know you were." His still rigid cock bounced into my buttocks.

I grinned. "Really?"

"That was one of the most incredible orgasms I've ever witnessed."

"I thought you were an expert."

"I never said that, but a woman has to be willing to let go to have what you just had."

I smiled at him, knowing exactly what he was talking about. "Are you ready to let go then?" His cock thumped me again. "I'll take that as a yes."

I slid off him and off the bed, removed my stilettos, and headed to my handbag. Thanks to my intentional planning, the condoms were in a zippered side pocket, and I reached in and removed one.

I turned back to Benson, and his spread-eagled position offered a full view of what he had to offer. For a man close to turning fifty, he was still very much in his prime.

As I walked back to him, I admired both his nicely formed abs and the sexy arrangement of his chest hair that ran between his nipples and in a neat line down his torso to his groin.

I handed over the condom, and when he reached for it, I noticed the robe belt still hanging from his wrist. I contemplated tying him up again, but decided against it; I wanted Benson's hands both on me and in me.

With the condom now in position, I straddled his waist again, leaned forward, and offered my breasts to him. He didn't complain, and the tongue-lashing I received soon had my insides squirming.

His cock, nudging at my butt, was begging to be saved, so I eased back, and using my hand, I guided the head of his penis to my opening. Benson strangled the bed sheets with his clutched fingers as, ever so slowly, I lowered down onto him. When he was fully inside me, we remained locked for a moment, savoring each other as only two complete strangers can do.

His jaw dropped, and a gasp tumbled from his throat as I glided up again. I stopped at the very top, just prior to release, and without warning, plunged full-tilt, hard and fast, ramming his cock right up inside me. Benson gasped and yanked the sheets from the mattress.

I did it again, slowly up and hard down. Whatever he touched inside me protested the first couple of times, feeding me both pleasure and pain, but soon the scales tilted to just pleasure—one hundred percent, mind-blowing pleasure.

I put my hands on his chest for support and repeated the movement over and over, each time getting just a little faster.

"Turn sideways." His voice was barely a whisper.

"Hey, what?"

"Twist around to my right. My bent cock is supposed to be amazing."

I blinked at him, but eager to experience this sexual miracle, I obliged. Twisting so his cock remained inside me, I now faced sideways with my feet on one side of his legs and my hands on the bed on the other side.

"Now sit up and squat on top," he instructed, and I pushed up from the bed to sit atop him.

I turned to glance at him and with a nod of his head, I braced my hands on his thighs for support and pumped up and down. It was a glorious move. The head of his bent cock pressed against my vaginal wall, grinding up and down my inner core. In this position, the angle of his cock provided the perfect amount of friction and strength to please my eager pussy.

Holy shit. Mr. Lady-Killer may've found my G-spot.

I bounced up and down, determined to please him as much as this position pleased me. With Benson pinned beneath me, he was unable to move, but by his clenched jaw and fisted hands I could tell he was loving every minute of it. I was close now, riding the knife-edge between building arousal and exquisite release.

Benson clutched at my arm, digging his fingers into my bicep. I stopped moving as his breath hissed through his teeth. His eyes were closed, his jaw clamped shut, and I knew he was on the knife-edge too.

Suddenly his eyes shot open, it was time. I pumped up and down, riding out an orgasm that ripped through me like a tornado, tearing every shred of pleasure from my body again and again. We both cried out with the elation of release.

Completely exhausted, I fell sideways onto his chest, and his cock popped out of me. I rolled to his side and my head fell to the crook of his shoulder. He wrapped his arm around me as if we were long-time lovers.

As I lay there, listening to his racing heart and inhaling the tangy odor of our sex, our simple embrace nearly brought me to tears. I realized this was what I'd been missing. Sure, I was having amazing sex, but sometimes all I wanted was a man to hold me, to share a cuddle and assure me that the world would soon be round again.

Lying in a man's arms after sex was a little slice of heaven. It was also something I'd rarely experienced.

And not just with the men I'd met this year.

Will, the guy I'd lost my virginity to, had launched out of bed after we'd had sex as if his dick was on fire. Ryan, the man I'd shared a secret relationship with, had always pulled up his pants and walked away from the photocopier he'd bent me over, as if the walls would start talking if he'd stayed. And Alexander, the man I'd once pledged my heart to? He was always in the shower within seconds of rolling off me. It was like he couldn't wait to get my scent off him.

Maybe this after-sex cuddle was the one thing I'd been missing since I'd lost my virginity.

Maybe it was as important as my sexual pleasure.

Maybe, if Lolita's prediction that I'd find the man of my dreams this year was to come true, then this after-sex moment was something I should put a little more effort into.

It was an interesting concept, and obviously something I needed to explore more.

When my breathing returned to normal, I pushed up from his embrace and turned to sit on the side of the bed. "Thanks for that."

"Thank you." He tugged the sheet over himself. Benson was probably the first one of the men I'd been with to do that. Except for Batman that is, but he'd used his cape. I nearly giggled at that mental image. All the other men seemed quite happy to show off their jewels. Maybe Benson was actually embarrassed by his bent member.

I stood up and gathered my bits and pieces off the floor.

"Would you like a shower?"

I turned to him, curious about his comment. Then I remembered my lie about why I was here.

"No thanks. I'm sure my room will be ready now."

I tugged on my dress, zipped it up, and slipped into my shoes.

"So, I guess I'll see you downstairs."

"I guess so." I slung my bag over my shoulder.

He propped up on his elbow. "You know, you never did tell me your name."

I pushed an annoying hair out of my eye. "It's Memphis."

He nodded, as if he'd expected me to say that. "Well, Memphis, I have a feeling this is going to be the best conference ever."

I laughed as I headed out his door.

Back in my room, I removed my abundant makeup and had a long hot shower. I was completely exhausted by the time I sat on the side of my bed and reached for my diary. I turned to the 2nd of May and wrote *Mr. Benson Cooper – room 40, The Consummate Casanova.*

I detailed at length his wonderful curved cock and how it touched places inside me that no man had played with before. Benson sure did know how to use that oddity to his advantage—and mine, for that matter.

Once I'd finished writing, I placed the diary on my bedside table and rolled to my side. As I lay there listening to the waves crashing into the shore below, I imagined a hunky guy lying next to me. I'd be snuggled up to his side, feeling his warmth, and listening to his heart as he trailed his fingers up and down my arm.

Lolita's comment rolled through my conscience. '*By the end of this year, you'll find the man of your dreams.*' As I pictured all the men I'd had so far, and imagined the thirty-three men that were yet to be explored, I wondered what the man of my dreams would look like.

As those glorious images accompanied me to sleep, I welcomed the notion that maybe, just maybe, Lolita could be right.

13TH MAY
PLAYING WITH PLEASURE
Room 3 – Hot Horizon Hotel

I groaned at the sound of my alarm, turned to my bedside clock and couldn't believe I'd slept for four hours. It felt more like ten minutes. With reluctance, I dragged myself out of bed and tugged open the blinds. It was an overcast day and the dark clouds shimmered silver in the midday sun. Squinting against the glare, I opened the door and welcomed in the delicate sea breeze.

With images of Lolita yelling at me, running through my mind, should I be late, I made my way to the bathroom and had a quick hot shower. Refreshed, but still in need of a few more hours of sleep, I went through the motions of blow-drying my long hair and messing about with it until I was satisfied. Instead of my usual ponytail, I clipped some of it back from my face, and the rest I let fall down my back.

I applied a touch of makeup to cover my freckles, darkened my eyelashes and dabbed on some Ralph perfume.

At my wardrobe, I scanned my clothes for the ideal outfit to wear to lunch at the marina.

It was an excruciating process and in the end I chose a simple sleeveless white dress that fell just above my knees. The delicate cut-out pattern on the upper chest and over my shoulders was an interesting feature, and I added a cute pair of pearl-drop earrings that my Aunty Ann had given to me one Christmas.

For a touch of color, I chose a mandarin-shaded handbag and wasn't surprised I had a pair of shoes to match. If I had an outfit to match every pair of shoes I owned, then I'd never have a dilemma over what to wear.

I glanced at the clock. *Twenty to twelve.* Provided there was no traffic, I'd make it to the marina with minutes to spare. Clutching Calvin's birthday present, I headed out my door and to the elevator.

Needledick, my boss, was hunched over the computer keyboard when I stepped from the elevator and into the lobby, and I deliberately maximized the distance between us.

He glanced up, and I saw the whites of his eyes. "Hey Jane." He actually waved.

"Hi Mr. Karwatsky."

"I told you to call me John."

"Right. Hi John." I much preferred to keep it all formal with him.

"You look lovely. Have you got a date?"

My insides squirmed at his inquisitiveness. We rarely had a conversation, and that was exactly how I preferred it. "Lunch with a girlfriend," I said as I continued my stride across the marble expanse, praying my six-inch heels didn't have me face-planting on the shiny surface.

"Okay, then. Have fun."

I felt his eyes on me even as I progressed through the sliding glass doors.

A taxi arrived within seconds of me reaching the sidewalk and I slipped into the backseat.

"Marina Mirage, please."

The driver had distinct odors of garlic, sweat and stale cigarettes emanating from the front seat, and deciding I'd rather have wind-blown hair than suffer the nasty stench, I wound down the window.

I inhaled the fresh sea breeze. The smell of the ocean was one of the simple pleasures I'd enjoyed every day since I'd moved to the Gold Coast. Having grown up on a farm, surrounded by cow paddocks pockmarked with yesterday's meals covered in swarming flies, it was a wonder the smell of manure wasn't permanently etched into my sinuses. Many people loved the scent of the country. Not me. Give me the ocean any day.

The taxi's arrival at the marina was greeted with the elegant symphony of ropes clanging on giant ship masts. The extensive marina berths were occupied with all manner of boats ranging across a wide variety of price brackets. A couple even had their own helicopter riding atop their sleek lines.

Scents of carefully prepared meals drifted from the abundant restaurants begging for my attention via overzealous waiters in crisp white shirts. As I made my way to Sunset Waterfront restaurant my heels clicked along the boardwalk that hovered over the water by some clever architectural miracle. I heard Lolita's laugh long before I saw her, and I grinned as I climbed the stairs to the restaurant. A quick glance at my watch confirmed my perfect timing. It was right on midday. As I arrived at the top of the steps, loud drumming rumbled from a three-piece band set up on the stage in the corner.

The smile fell from my face and my stomach just about hurled out of my mouth when I saw the man on the drums. It was my Jamaican hunk, Mr. Hot Chocolate. His body glistened with a fine sheen, showing off both exquisite biceps and the intricate tattoo of the dreadlocked woman that I already knew was there. His voice sang a lover's song, drawing me in with its beautiful melody. The man was a god.

"Jane. Jane, we're here." Lolita waved at me from a table to my left, and I lifted my mandarin-colored bag to shield my face as I made my way past the stage to her table.

I expected Lolita and Calvin to be at lunch, but my already tumultuous stomach hit volcano mode at the sight the third person at the table. Clayton, the single dad she'd already tried to set me up with once before, sat opposite them. If I could've discreetly glared at Lolly, I would've. She knew how much I hated surprises, especially the blind date kind.

"Hey babe, you look fucking gorgeous." Lolita hugged me and kissed both my cheeks. She frowned, and fearful she'd already sensed my shock, I mentally slapped myself into gear.

"Hey Lolly, how are you?"

"Look who's here. You remember Clayton?" She said it like it was a surprise to her too. But knowing her obsession with solving my 'single' status, I was convinced it wasn't.

"Yes, of course." I nodded at him. "Hi Clayton."

"Hello. You look lovely."

"Thank you."

The way they were seated, it was clear I was to sit next to him. It was also clear that Lolita was attempting another matchmaking session with us. I stepped around the table and leaned over Calvin to kiss his cheek. "Happy birthday." I placed his gift in front of him.

"Awww, you didn't have to." Calvin paused for barely a second before he ripped open the wrapping like an excited child would.

He plucked the miniature silver guitar cufflinks from the velvet box and twirled them in his fingers. "These are great. Thanks, Jane."

"You're welcome." I arrived at my chair and Clayton rose to his feet and reached for my hand, and when he leaned in to kiss my cheek I smelt his delightfully scented cologne. He tugged my chair out to help me sit.

"Thank you," I said as he returned to his seat at my side.

As Calvin poured me a glass of wine, the music picked up its beat and I could easily imagine Dontrel's dreadlocks dancing about his face as he pummeled the taut leather drum.

I gulped back half a glass of wine before I managed to drag it away from my lips. Lolita's intense blue eyes drilled into me, and she frowned.

Our waiter arrived, and within a minute we each had our serviettes draped across our laps, our water glasses filled, the menus handed out, and the daily specials explained with great flamboyance. The dour waiter who served us at our coffee shop each Tuesday sure could use a lesson from this guy.

Once he left, and as Calvin and Clayton scanned the menu, Lolita cleared her throat. I glanced at her and she mouthed, *are you okay?*

I shook my head.

She bulged her eyes and nodded over her shoulder, a sign that we could go to the ladies.

I nodded.

Lolita didn't hesitate. "I'm busting for the loo," she said as she slipped back on her chair and flung her oversized bag over her shoulder. "Come on, Jane."

It wasn't a question, and I leapt out of my seat. The minute I was at her side she tucked her hand into my elbow and led me to the restroom.

The heavy door slammed behind us as we entered, and she tossed her handbag on the bench, turned to me, and clutched my wrist. "Holy shit, babe, I didn't know you hated him that much."

"Who?" I frowned.

"Clayton. You look like you've already chucked your oysters."

I shook my head. "It's not Clayton. Dontrel."

"Who?"

"The drummer out there. It's Dontrel, my Jamaican guy."

Her eyes bulged. "The hot black guy with the fucking huge cock?"

"Lolly!"

Someone giggled from behind a closed cubical door and we both burst out laughing. I tugged Lolly's arm, snatched her handbag off the bench and together we squeezed into a cubicle. I locked the door and we stifled our laughter as we waited a ridiculous amount of time for the mystery person to flush, wash their hands and leave. Once the door banged shut again, we burst out laughing and returned to the sink area.

Lolly unzipped her bag and rummaged through its vast contents. "Are you sure it's him?"

"Of course."

"Let's go say hi."

"What? No! He'll recognize me."

"No he won't. Remember, you were in disguise." She turned to the mirror and applied another layer of lipstick.

I chewed over what she'd said. Yes, I'd been in disguise, but did I really want to risk it?

As if on cue, the band kicked into another song, and Lolly practically dragged me out the bathroom.

"This's going to be fun." She pulled me to the dance floor. While Lolly broke out into groovy moves that had her boobs in a jiggling frenzy, I tried my best to keep my back to the band, my stomach contents contained, and dance like a normal person. Lolly stared at the musicians, no doubt checking out Dontrel with her oversexed eyes.

"He's gorgeous," she yelled over the tribal beat.

"I told you."

"I wish I could see it."

I frowned. "See what?"

"His cock."

My jaw dropped and I glanced around, horrified that someone may've heard her. Satisfied that the pulsating beat had drowned her out, I turned back to my crazy friend. "Well you can't."

She flicked her head and wriggled her hips in flexible moves that'd make a seasoned pole dancer jealous, then she leaned in. "Hey, you can take a photo for me."

"What?"

"Take a photo of his . . ." She put her hands to her groin and moved them to symbolize a penis, then wriggled her eyebrows at me.

My eyes just about lunged out of my sockets. "Have you lost your mind?"

"A sneaky one, when he's not looking."

"No!" I slapped her shoulder. "Don't be ridiculous."

"Geez, you're such a party pooper."

"And you're crazy."

"No I'm not. I'm curious. You can't tell a woman that you've seen the biggest cock in the world and not prove it."

My jaw dropped. "You don't believe me?"

She shrugged and gave me that cute smile that allowed her to get away with anything.

"I'm not taking a photo his penis—" The music stopped mid-sentence and a violent heatwave flashed up my neck and cheeks as the entire restaurant turned to me. I was set to self-combust as Lolly burst into fits of laughter. She bent over, clutching her stomach in hysterical agony, leaving me exposed to the world in the center of the dance floor.

I slinked back to our table. Calvin's cheeky grin made it obvious he, along with everyone on the Gold Coast, had heard what I'd said. Clayton cocked his head and had a curious look on his face that I couldn't read. Was it pity? Disgust? Either way, I was fairly certain his interest in me had just nosedived.

Lolly was still cracking up with laughter when she joined us.

"So . . . we know what you two were talking about. The question is who?" Calvin was just as forthright as his wife.

Lolly reached over the table and placed her hand over mine. "You okay?"

"Ahhh, no."

"Don't worry. It was hilarious."

"For you maybe."

"So, cough it up. Who were you talking about?" Calvin repeated his question.

"Oh just—"

"Nothing," I cut Lolita off before she blurted it all out. With bulging eyes, I tried to indicate Clayton at my side. With my hand strangling the stem of my glass, I swallowed the rest of my wine in one gulp.

"It's just girl talk." She winked at me and reached for the wine list. "Looks like we need more wine." Lolita managed to guide the conversation away from my gaff with ease and thankfully Calvin let it slide.

A discussion over our wine choices ensued, and before long the conversation kicked off as if the four of us had known each other for years. From my position at the table, I had a side-on view of the band. Dontrel oozed passion for music. When he sang, it wasn't just his voice that I was attracted to—it was his expression and movement. Every ounce of Mr. Hot Chocolate believed in that music. He was glorious to watch.

For entrée, the four of us shared a plate of oysters prepared three different ways, and as Lolita declared they were some of the best she'd ever tasted, I reflected that they weren't as delicious as the ones I'd shared in the moonlight with Mr. Henry Addison, my suave tutor.

I tried not to chuckle. Here I was sitting next to a handsome man who may or may not be keen on me. Barely ten feet away was a man who'd shown me his cock that was, in my inexperienced opinion, the biggest one in the world. Meanwhile, I was thinking about the man who gave me a mind-blowing orgasm while barely touching me.

I really had lost my mind.

Clayton's hand was suddenly on my leg, and I nearly jumped through the table.

"Oh sorry," he said. "I was just asking if you were ready to order mains."

"Oh, um, no." *Smooth, Jane. Really smooth.* I was such a pathetic fading flower when it came to men, and yet put a wig on me, ply on the makeup and name me Memphis and suddenly I became a sexual diva. As I attempted to hide behind the oversized menu, I forced myself to act normal. *Just be me.*

But even that was impossible. I didn't know who I was anymore.

We ordered our meals, and as the band took us through songs from around the world our conversation flowed. Clayton was pleasant and the topics flitted from food to travel to kids.

When there was a lull in the conversation, I turned sideways to Clayton and asked him the question I'd been dying to ask all afternoon. "Tell me about your daughter?"

He placed his wine glass down "Okay, well Telitha is seven; she's a little tomboy. She'd much prefer to climb trees and kick a ball than go to ballet."

She sounded like my type of girl, and for some reason it made me wonder what her mother had been like. "What happened to her Mom?"

He cocked his head at me and sighed with a sorrowful look. "Her mother ran off when Telitha was just four years old."

I regretted being so nosy and was beginning to feel the pressure to change the subject when he carried on. "We went on a cruise, the three of us. Four days into the holiday, Bella hooked up with a young German man. When we disembarked in Turkey, she announced she was leaving and we haven't seen her since."

My hand went to my mouth. "Oh dear. That's terrible."

Clayton shrugged. "It took us a few years to get over it, but things are better now. Thanks to Lolly. She's the mother Telitha doesn't have."

I glanced at Lolly and she glowed that motherly glow that suited her so much. *When I grow up, I want to be just like her.* I felt sick at how I'd judged Clayton. The poor man had been through hell.

Our meals arrived, and as I enjoyed a delicious barramundi, crumbed in macadamia nuts and smothered in a buttery cream sauce, I tried to follow the conversation that was centered around the parents at ballet class. Clayton, apparently, was the only dad who turned up regularly to dance practice, and if I were to believe Lolly, then every other woman who attended was trying to get into his pants.

Clayton shrugged off the suggestion with a coy grin.

"You should see it, Jane." Lolly pointed at me with half a prawn loaded on her fork. "These women practically drool at the sight of him. And most of them are married."

"You're exaggerating." Clayton shook his head.

"No I'm not." She turned her eyes to Clayton, growing serious. "You wouldn't know flirting if it slapped you over the head."

Our laughter was drowned out as the band took up a new song with gusto. Dontrel attacked the drum with heightened intensity, and his song described a lover's dance. It was impossible to talk, so we ate the rest of our meals in silence.

I finished my fish just as the band announced a small intermission. To my horror, I watched Dontrel step off the stage and head straight to our table. In a flash, I tugged the clip out of my hair and tussled it around my face in a feeble attempt to hide. I seriously considered diving under the table

"'ello," he said, as he arrived at Lolly's side. "I hope you're enjoying our little band."

Lolly grinned up at him as if he were a male stripper. "Oh, it's fabulous." She held her hand forward, and for a horrible second I thought she was going to touch his abs. "I'm Lolita."

Dontrel swallowed her palm within his hand. "Dontrel. Nice to meet you."

"This is Clayton, Calvin, and over there is Jane." I wanted to poke her eyeballs out.

"'ello. We play here every Friday lunch. And 'ere's my card; I'm available for private parties, too."

"I bet you are." Lolly actually smirked at me.

I grabbed his offered card, though I needn't have, as I already had one of his cards in my empty fruit bowl at home.

Lolita giggled herself stupid when Dontrel finally moved to another table. Calvin just shook his head, not even bothering to ask what she found so funny.

I breathed a sigh of relief when we finally stood to leave.

With lots of flamboyant kisses, Lolita left with her hand on Calvin's ass after she practically shoved him out the door. Clayton and I were left standing in their wake.

"Shall I give you a lift home?"

"No. No. I'll just catch a cab."

"Don't be silly. I'll take you."

Knowing Lolita, I was pretty sure this was yet another one of her cunning pre-laid plans. As we walked along, I forced myself to relax, and I was surprised at how easy it was. Clayton was comfortable to be with. By the time we were in his black Audi, I was beginning to question what my problem was. Clayton was handsome, pleasant, funny, considerate, and based on his fancy car, he was doing okay financially. Plus, according to Lolly, women were falling at his feet. Maybe I shouldn't disregard him so quickly.

We made idle chitchat as we drove along and I learned that he'd been working at the jewelry store at Surfers Paradise for eight years and was now the store manager.

A quick fifteen minutes later, we arrived at my hotel and after a moment of awkwardness, I leaned over to kiss his cheek. "Thank you."

"Would you like to have dinner sometime?"

"Oh, ummm. I work at night."

"Yes, but Lolita said you get Wednesdays off. Is that right?"

I nodded. Lolita sure was a chatterbox. I squirmed on my seat as I pre-empted what Clayton was about to ask.

He blinked at me, obviously expecting my answer to his unasked question.

"So can I take you to dinner next Wednesday?"

Butterflies flitted through my stomach. "I have to warn you, I'm not very good company."

"I think you're delightful."

The butterflies did a little dance and before I knew it, I was agreeing to him picking me up outside the Hot Horizon Hotel at six p.m. next Wednesday.

I had a distinct bounce in my step as I walked into the hotel lobby, and my brain was so pre-occupied that I didn't do my usual gallop across the marble expanse to avoid getting trapped by Marjorie, the afternoon manager.

"Hey Jane."

I was too late to realize my mistake and idled toward her. "Hey Marj, how are you?"

I hugged her bony shoulders to my chest. The poor woman really needed a good steak. "It's been busy. I swear this place is increasing its occupancy rates every week."

"That's a good thing. Keeps us in a job."

"Yes, but I liked it better when I could at least do my nails occasionally." She chuckled.

"Are we full tonight?" May was usually a bit quieter, and the average occupancy sat at around seventy percent

"Nearly. It's weird."

I frowned. "Hmm, it is weird." I had no answer for this strange occurrence. "Anyway, I'm off to get a little sleep. See you in six hours."

"Sure thing. Have a good nap."

After a quick hug goodbye, I made my way to my room. The wine I'd consumed at lunch had me a little sleepy. I tugged open my blinds and stepped onto the balcony to suck in the lovely sea air, hoping the fresh breeze would clear my fuzzy head. As I leaned on the railing, I heard voices coming up from the road below.

I looked down and couldn't believe my eyes. Dontrel had just stepped out of a large black van with his drum tucked under his arm.

It was a little difficult to hear what he was saying, but I thought he'd agreed to be back there at nine p.m. He laughed at something, then he slid the sliding panel door shut and the black van glided away. Dontrel did his sexy swagger into my hotel.

Suddenly wide awake, I seized the opportunity. Dontrel had unwittingly declared himself my twentieth passion partner. I just had to figure out which room he was in.

I waited out ten minutes, confident Dontrel would have vacated the lobby before I went downstairs.

"Hey Jane," Marjorie said the moment I stepped into the lobby.

"Hey, did I leave my phone down here? I haven't been able to find it all day." I hated how good I was at lying these days.

"Oh, I haven't seen it." Marjorie's eyes went straight to the computer desk.

I arrived at her side and made a show of looking in the drawers.

I needed her to leave for a couple of seconds. "Can you check the store room for me?" I felt ill over my sneakiness and yet I continued my ruse all the same.

"Sure."

The second she disappeared into the room at the back, I attacked the index cards. My fingers worked at superhero speed as I scanned through the deck for his last name. Within seconds I pinched it out. Dontrel's driver's license photo didn't do him any justice at all. His skin was so much more luscious than the picture showed. He was in room three.

I shoved the cards away and went in search of Marjorie. "Any luck?"

"No."

"Me neither. It must be upstairs. Don't worry, I'll find it." I touched her arm and felt appalled at my ability to lie to her so easily. My crazy double life was making me extremely devious.

I returned to my room, and with thoughts of Mr. Hot Chocolate undressing two floors below, I hopped into the shower to refresh.

The image of his enormous cock bounced into my head. *Was I really planning on trying to fit that monster inside me?* I wasn't entirely convinced it was a great plan. But then I began to wonder if I'd exaggerated his size. Maybe it wasn't anywhere near as big as I remembered. Just the thought of seeing it again . . . . seeing him in all his chocolate glory too, was enough to set my insides squirming.

I applied my makeup and took extra care with shades of color on my eyes. Not that I thought he took much notice of me at lunch, but I didn't want to risk it. Dontrel would probably remember my black bobbed hair, so once again, I tucked my hair up into that wig.

Now for choosing an outfit. The idea of wearing black seemed appropriate, because not only was it Black Friday, I was also about to have a steamy sexual encounter with a black man. Or at least that was the plan.

My sequined dress was out of the question; it'd already proven a poor choice because of its inability to slip off at a moment's notice. I tugged dress after dress from the hook and finally settled on a classic little black dress.

And for a little fun, I spiced it up by wearing sexy red lingerie underneath.

The dress slipped over my head and glided easily down my body. It fell just below my knees, but the plunging neckline failed to hide my red bra. I tugged at it, trying to conceal the red lace, but each time it bounced back. I was on the verge of whipping it all off and starting again when I realized that this look, with the hint of things to come, suited my cheeky Memphis.

With that settled, I applied my trusty Bobbi Brown red lipstick, grabbed my bag, and headed toward Mr. Hot Chocolate.

I checked my appearance in the elevator mirrors and could hardly believe it was my own reflection. What I did with my eyes changed me completely.

Makeup was a miracle worker. And I was on my way to meet another miracle. With that thought I grinned, and when I liked what I saw in the mirror, I grinned some more.

As the door opened and I strode like a model on a Paris runway toward Dontrel's room, I felt damn good. With a quick fiddle to plump my boobs up, I knocked twice on his door.

The door eased open and oh my god, I nearly passed out at my first glimpse of him. I'd officially walked into heaven. It appeared that the yummy Dontrel had just stepped from the shower as he wore a white towel, slung low on this hips, and his wet body shimmered in the discreet entrance lighting.

"Well 'ello, if it isn't Miss Memphis."

Holy shit. He remembered my name. "Dontrel." I said it with confidence as he stepped aside. As I slipped past the chocolate god, I trailed my fingers across his steely abs. *God damn, the man was solid muscle.*

"'Ave you come back for another game?"

I slung my bag over the back of the chair and turned to him. "I have."

The door clicked shut behind him. "I hope it's not strip poker, 'cause I'm not wearin' much."

I laughed at him and then wriggled my eyebrows. "Neither am I."

His lovely chocolate skin enhanced his brilliant white teeth.

"Let's carry on where we left off, shall we?" I said. "I believe you called it Pleasure Me, Pleasure You."

"Ah, it's coming back to me." He cocked his head. "And we're still not having sex. Is that right?"

A debate galloped through my brain. As much as I was intrigued, one thought of the monster he had concealed beneath his towel scared the hell out of me. The man masterpiece was likely to split me in two, and I didn't want to end up in hospital like those poor people I'd seen on those awful hospital reality shows. "Correct, no sex," I finally said. "But that doesn't mean we won't have fun."

"I'm already 'aving fun," he said, and I saw the movement beneath his towel.

Wow, men really are easy to please.

I slipped out of my red court shoes and with my hands gripped on the hem of my skirt, I lifted my dress up over my head, cautious not to lose my wig, then I opened my eyes.

With the flick of his wrist, the towel was gone and Dontrel was naked.

It took all my self-control not to drop my jaw. His cock was every bit as big as I remembered. Not just in length but in width too. Lolita's comment about taking a photo whizzed through my brain and I smacked the wretched idea away.

"Come on." Dontrel wrapped his fingers around his cock. "You need to catch up."

I'd forgotten how chatty he was. "I didn't know it was a race."

I unclipped my bra and tossed it aside, and as Dontrel glided his hand up and down his enormous shaft, I glided my hand up my torso and cupped my breast. My nipples grew hard and I squeezed them gently. We stood apart, playing with our own bodies in some kind of Mexican standoff. A flutter rippled through me at how sexy this simple act was.

I swallowed, hard, and forced myself to think like Memphis. Confident, sexy, in control Memphis. It was time to take charge.

I strode to him, right up to his side, and while I wrapped my left arm around his waist, my right hand joined his fingers around his cock. He put his heavy arm over my shoulder and tugged me closer. I leaned down and drew his nipple into my mouth. The pebble grew rock hard as I ran my tongue around it. When I nipped a little, he hissed and at first I thought I'd hurt him, but when he bent his knees and his hand moved to his balls, I decided it did the opposite.

As I continued to pump my hand up and down his ever-growing cock, his right hand found my breast and he tweaked my nipple, alternating between gentle and intense.

A small seed of semen oozed from the eye of his penis and I gathered it from his pink head and used it to lubricate his shaft. Dontrel sucked air through his teeth and released our embrace.

"You 'ave to be careful, Miss Memphis, or I'll shoot this load before I've 'ad a play with you."

"Oh. Okay." I was open to his suggestion. I offered him what I hoped was a sexy, I-am-your-plaything smile.

He placed his hands on my hips and hooked his thumbs into my panties. "'Tis time to get you naked."

"Okay." No objections here.

I clutched onto his shoulders, feeling the corded muscle beneath his molasses-colored skin, and he glided my panties down. He fell to his knees, and when his fingers were at my ankles I stepped from my lingerie. Out the corner of my eye, I saw a flash of red as my underpants were tossed aside.

The hot slick of his tongue found my pussy, and I inhaled a shaky breath as my fingers dug into his shoulders and I spread my legs. Dontrel moaned as his glorious tongue flicked my sensitive clit. His finger pushed into my vagina and I gasped and bent my knees, allowing him to push as deep as he could go. A second finger met his first, spreading me apart and moving in an interesting twirling in-and-out motion.

His tongue was as hot as it was hard, flicking and gliding around my throbbing bud with repetitive attention. In and out his fingers plunged with a twisting, grinding action that my body accepted with blind agreement.

I closed my eyes and concentrated on all my other senses. I smelt his soap and the salty sea air. I heard his moans and my heavy breathing. And I felt heaven and earth as my insides slipped into a glorious, lust-filled world. I was on the erotic knife edge, teetering between intense build-up and earth-shattering release.

In a flash, Dontrel removed his fingers and stopped with the tongue lashing. It was like the ground had opened up and swallowed me whole. I snapped my eyes open and looked down. Dontrel was still on his knees, but now he looked up at me with a goofy grin.

"Now, now, Miss Memphis. You can't have all the fun."

He's got to be kidding. My mind struggled to come back from the wonderful world it'd slipped into and I just blinked at him, trying to work out what the hell was happening.

He eased me to sit onto the bed, which was a good plan because I was about to melt into the carpet.

"Okay," he said with a cheeky grin. "I want you to t'ink of a number between sixty-eight and seventy."

I quickly did the math, and then, feeling like a fool, a flush of heat coursed up my neck. As I contemplated his suggestion, that heat flush attacked my cheeks and had me swallowing a lump in my throat. I'd never experienced a sixty-niner before. I'd heard of them, of course, but the concept of sticking my ass in a man's face had never seemed . . . sexy. Nor did the idea of having a man's erection shoved down my throat while I laid at his mercy.

Dontrel suddenly dived backwards onto the bed at my side. His enormous cock hit his abdomen with what looked like a painful slap. His perfect white teeth blazed in a cheesy grin.

"Come on, woman. What ya waitin' for?" He bounced his cock and then tapped his plump pink lips with his finger. "Get your sexy ass up here."

My brain was in devil-and-angel mode as I got onto my knees. What ifs were ruining the lust-filled haze that had consumed me just moments ago. What if my ass was ugly? What if I couldn't fit that huge cock into my mouth? What if this sixty-niner turned out to be the most amazing experience of my new sexual journey?

That last thought had me turning my attention back to my chocolate god. He wanted me. He wanted me to sit on his face. And devilish Memphis wanted to give it a try.

I crawled up to behind his head and turned so my pussy faced him. My heart was feverish tribal beat in my chest as I wriggled forward with my knees either side of his head. One of his hands reached up and grabbed my breast while his other hand sought out my vagina.

As I hovered my pussy over his face, the heat of his breath sent delicious shudders through me. His fingers alternated between punishing my clit and plunging my deepest depths.

Soon, the orgasm that'd stalled minutes ago was right back on track. My insides clenched around his probing digits, driving shivers of ecstasy from the tips of his fingers right through my body.

Without warning he removed his hands, placed them on my hips, and guided my pussy down to his mouth. My heart just about stopped as I eased my knees apart.

His hot breath, his probing tongue, and his glorious cock that pointed at me, begging for attention, had my brain exploding with sensory overload.

I ran my fingers down his torso as I eased forward. Propped up on one elbow for support, I wrapped my other hand around his mammoth cock. It was visual artistry. His black cock, with its glorious pink head and my white fingers wrapped around him, was an erotic masterpiece. I brought my lips to his swollen crown.

He groaned and the vibration through my vagina just about shot me right off the bed. My concentration was like a shattered mirror as it reflected on one incredible aspect of this moment after another.

His tongue slipped in and out of my throbbing hole, as did his fingers, and he sucked on my clit, sending a wicked vibration through every single one of my nerve endings. It took all my focus to continue working on him, and I slowly rolled my lips down, taking each exquisite aspect of his smooth black muscle into my mouth with absolute concentration. Barely a third of the way down, I had to come back up. Dontrel was way too big.

Feeling like I wasn't giving him the justice he deserved, I massaged my eager hand up and down his jackhammer as I sucked him into my mouth again, determined to make it fit. I suddenly gagged, jerked back up, and just about died with embarrassment. But either Dontrel didn't notice or he was too busy to care, because his attention to my pussy didn't waver.

It was at that moment that I let go, and my mind stopped doing its crazy questioning thing. I let my body take over. If Dontrel was happy to carry on doing what he was doing, then I was happy to let him.

It was the trigger I needed, and with a mind of their own, my hips began to glide back and forward. I lost myself in the tongue lashing that ensued, both on me and in me. His breath caressed my pussy in a wave of heat, and his fingers plunged my abyss, playing me with the intensity of the lover's songs I'd seen him perform.

I squeezed my fingers around his cock and glided my lips up and down with increased intensity. Our sex became a frenzy of licking, sucking, and groaning. The orgasm that'd been building for what seemed like days soared to extraordinary heights. I couldn't hold back a moment more. I was there. On the edge.

Ready.

Oh so fucking ready.

And the most glorious thing happened. My orgasm became a full-body experience, rolling through me with waves of red-hot ecstasy. I gasped and eased back at the intensity, and my timing was perfect to witness Dontrel's own miracle.

Semen shot from his cock in a long white stream that landed across his taut black skin. Over and over I pumped him until he was completely spent, and his cock softened in my hand. It was a truly incredible thing to witness.

I leaned forward, easing myself off him at the same time as I quickly maneuvered around to face him so my ass was well away from his eyes. He wiped his lips with the back of his hand, and at first I cringed. But when he smiled, a wicked, happy smile that was a lovely contrast of white teeth on a handsome black man's face, I knew that he wasn't disgusted by my juices at all. In fact, it was the opposite.

"You sure know how to play da game, Memphis."

"Thanks," I said, although I had no idea what game he was referring to.

I eased off the bed and set about gathering my bits and pieces off the floor. Dontrel barely moved as I slipped my little black dress over my head and stepped into my shoes. His cock was no longer enormous as it gradually slinked back into itself.

He propped himself up on his elbow. "You truly are a fascinatin' woman, Miss Memphis."

"Oh." *Was fascinating a good or bad label?* From the look of satisfaction etched onto his face, I decided it was a good thing and grinned at him. "Thank you," I said, as I slung my bag over my shoulder.

"I reckon I'll be back, Miss Memphis."

"I reckon I'll be waiting, Mr. Dontrel."

With one last glance at my chocolate god, I stepped out his door and headed for the elevator.

I floated on an air of bliss as I returned to my room. As I enjoyed a long, hot shower, my body ebbed into relaxation.

After my shower, I headed out to my verandah with my diary and a snack of peanut butter on toast. As I munched away, I opened my diary to 13th of May. At the top I wrote *Dontrel Lewis Room 3*—and as I thought about how much fun he was, I wrote, *Playing with Pleasure*.

I went on to describe my first ever sixty-niner. While the experience was hot, horny, and incredibly satisfying, I felt that I hadn't fulfilled my end of the position to the best of my abilities. It was an interesting acknowledgement.

This journey wasn't just about hot men. It was about learning how to satisfy my body and exploring different sexual techniques. But I'd come to realize that it was just as important to me to please the man who was, in turn, pleasuring me. I'd had inconsiderate lovers before and knew what it was like to be just a vehicle for a man's ejaculation.

With that acknowledgement, I made a promise that I'd explore the magical number sixty-nine a few more times to polish my technique.

I giggled at my cheeky pledge, and as I inhaled the refreshing ocean breeze, I tried to imagine which hunky man I'd perfect this intricate position with. It was a wonderful way to spend the final hour before I started my shift downstairs.

21ST MAY
SURPRISE SURPRISE
Room 27 – Hot Horizon Hotel

At the sound of my bedside alarm, I crawled out of the rumpled sheets and waddled to the toilet. It was that time of the month and not only had my vagina swollen to blimp proportions during my sleep, I felt like my insides were about to disengage and eject through it at any moment.

The last thing I wanted to do was go on a date with Clayton, but of course I would. Lolita would run over me in her mammoth Jeep Cherokee if I wriggled my way out of it. So I turned the bath taps to full and poured in a good slosh of Moroccan Rose Otto Oil to make me smell beautiful. Hopefully ten minutes in the warm water would also sooth some of my cramping.

As I waited for the bath to fill, I glanced in the mirror and immediately wished I hadn't. My freckles appeared to have multiplied and now covered my nose and cheeks with a gazillion dark dots. The bags under my eyes had become puffy dark clouds.

I was going to need some serious makeup to sort this mess out.

After I made a fresh, double-strength coffee, I rested it on the edge of the bath, tied my hair into a top knot and eased into the warm water. As I lay my head back on a rolled up towel, I tried to ignore my throbbing abdomen by thinking of Clayton. He ticked all the boxes for what would be considered a good catch, except for one huge issue. He had a seven-year-old daughter.

I was nowhere near ready to take on someone else's child. I could barely look after myself. One day I'd be a mother, of that I was certain. But not yet.

Would I be leading Clayton on by going on this date? On one hand, I could cancel. Nip in the bud his interest in me before he got too many ideas. On the other hand, it was just a date—nothing serious. It was supposed to be fun, not an outing to assess whether or not I'd ultimately bear his children. The very idea was laughable.

The water was close to cold when I finally stepped out and dried myself. Feeling slightly better, but not quite date-worthy, I decided to sneak in a glass of wine. I was salivating as I poured my favorite Sauvignon Blanc into a wine glass. The first sip was good; the second mouthful was heaven. I sighed deeply and then, with glass in hand, I returned to the bathroom mirror to perform my makeup miracle.

Thanks to my extensive practice in preparing for my Memphis disguises, by the time I'd finished I was actually happy with my reflection. Now for the next dilemma.

My choice of outfit for this date started with underwear. I hadn't realized just how limited my choices had become. In the last twenty weeks, I'd given away several pairs of my sexy underwear to a few lovely men who'd wanted them as 'proof' of our little rendezvous. In addition, some of my favorites had been literally torn from my body. Not that I was complaining—at the time, it made me damn horny. I sipped my wine at this lovely thought.

After a decent rummage through my dwindling collection, and in light of my unsexy feelings at the moment, I chose a pair of skin-tone big-girl panties. They were practical, but extremely unattractive. Should, by some miracle of God, Clayton and I end up getting naked, I'd have to remove these in stealth mode.

The fact that I was even considering getting naked with him was an interesting admission. It showed me that the handsome single dad wasn't completely out of the game, at least from a sex point of view. Oh God, what did that make me . . . a user and abuser? A slut? The angel in my brain wanted to whack me over the head. *I'm just a single woman looking for a little fun.*

"Fun!" That's what I wanted, and that's what I was determined to get.

With my nanna knickers pulled up to my waist I felt nice and secure and turned my attention to my dress choice. I decided on a maxi dress. The colorful flowing fabric was perfect for hiding a multitude of lumps and bumps. I paired the orange and blue dress with a set of dangly orange beaded earrings that matched the dress perfectly.

I gulped down the last of my wine, sprayed on Chanel Chance perfume, applied a lick of lipstick, and with my bag over my shoulder, I headed out the door. Clayton was due to pick me up in five minutes. I waved at Marjorie as I crossed the lobby, grateful that she was occupied with guests, and headed for the sliding glass doors.

The wind whipped at my skirt as I walked down the hotel's front steps and I clutched it at my sides, fearful of flashing my hideous underwear. I spied Clayton immediately. He cut a handsome figure in a white, checkered button-up shirt and navy pants with matching caramel-colored belt and brogues. I was two seconds away from zipping around and running upstairs to improve my attire when he looked up and saw me.

Clayton waved and walked my way. "You came." He sounded surprised as he leaned in to kiss my cheek. He smelt lovely, with hints of floral and leather dominating.

I chuckled. "Of course."

He held his palm forward, and with his hand on the small of my back, directed me to his car.

"I think I'm underdressed," I blurted out as he opened the car door.

"You look amazing."

"Oh, are you sure? I can dash upstairs and change."

"No need, you look beautiful."

I must've looked confused or something because he placed his hand on my forearm. "You can change if you want to. If it will make you feel better. But you don't need to."

"Oh." Little butterflies danced across my stomach. "Okay then." I turned and slipped into the passenger seat and he shut the door.

Seconds later, he was in the driver's seat and he turned to me. The dashboard light cast a pink glow across his freshly shaved skin. "I hope you like a steak."

"Oh, I'm a vegetarian." The words popped out of my mouth before I could stop them, and I had no idea why I'd said that.

His jaw dropped. "Really? Lolita didn't tell me that."

I giggled. "I'm joking. I love steak."

He grinned and laughed. "That was funny. You got me." He turned to the steering wheel and put the car into gear. "So that's how the night's going to play."

"I'm sorry. I couldn't resist." Maybe Memphis's cheeky streak was rubbing off on me after all.

"No. Don't be sorry; it was funny. So have you been to Moo Moo's before?"

I shook my head. "No, but I've heard of it."

"Oh great. You're in for a real treat."

I liked the sound of that. I settled back on the chair and a lovely sense of comfort washed over me as we shared some idle chit-chat on the ten-minute drive to the restaurant.

He parked the car and walked around to open my door. The restaurant was a hive of activity, attacking my senses from the moment the door opened. Flames danced atop sticks that lined the perimeter. Wonderful aromas of chargrilled beef and garlic had my mouth instantly watering. The bar at the front of the restaurant was filled with a throng of boisterous men and women.

Clayton placed his arm around my waist to guide me to the entrance and possibly for the first time in my life, I didn't cringe in response to that move. My stomach growled and my nanna knickers inched unpleasantly up my ass as we were directed past table after table to our seats.

In my inexperienced opinion, Moo Moo's was a great choice for a first date. It wasn't too fancy that I'd feel like a pimple on a beautiful woman's chin. It wasn't too intimate that every pause in our conversation would be excruciating. And if the aromas were anything to go by, I was in for an exceptional meal.

We sat opposite each other, and the waiter filled up our water glasses and explained how the menu worked. Clayton wiggled his eyebrows at the mention of battered onion rings and I smiled in utter agreement with his reaction.

The second the waiter left our side, Clayton picked the leather-bound menu up off the table. "Would you like wine?"

"Absolutely."

"White or red?"

"White please. Red makes me a little silly."

He cocked his head and a cheeky grin curled at his lips. "I like the sound of that."

"Well, unless you want to carry me home, you should stick to white."

"Mmmm, it's tempting."

"Oh stop it."

He smiled and flipped open the wine list. "Do you have a favorite?"

"Sauv blanc. Shaw & Smith, if they have it."

His eyebrows drilled together as he scanned the pages. "Ahhh, we're in luck." He folded the menu over and placed it to his side.

"Thanks for going out with me."

"Lolita would kill me if I didn't." Oh crap, that was a shitty thing to say, and the look on Clayton's face showed it. "Oh, god, I didn't mean it like that." I wanted to crawl under the table. "I'm sorry. I was honestly looking forward to going out with you."

He nodded, and as a heatwave coursed up my neck, the waiter returned.

I was grateful for the distraction. Clayton ordered our bottle of wine and the waiter left.

"Clayton. I really am sorry, I didn't—"

"It's okay. Really. I know how pushy Lolita can be."

I rolled my eyes. "You're not wrong."

"But I'm glad she forced me to ask you out."

My jaw dropped and he grinned a truly charming smile.

"Gotcha," he said.

I couldn't help but laugh. "You're a funny guy."

Our wine arrived and I was quick to swallow a mouthful. This dating stuff was tricky business.

The waiter arrived to place our meals and Clayton talked me into ordering three different sauces and two side dishes to go with a medium-rare eye fillet.

"So, have you been on many dates since you left your cheating bastard ex-fiancé?"

I huffed as I debated my answer. Were my sexual conquests dates? Hunter McCall, the guy I'd actually had a drink with at the bar, was the closest I'd had to a date. But no, I decided that they weren't. "No. None, actually."

His eyebrows shot up. "Wow, that's a shame."

I shrugged. "It's too hard with my job. I work a permanent night shift, six days each week. Nobody wants a girl who can't go out on the weekend."

"I would."

The butterflies in my stomach did a little happy dance, but then I wondered if he was just saying that to charm me. "So, how many dates have you been on?"

"Mmmm, let me see. There was Ellen." He held out his thumb. "Nicole." He thrust out his index finger. "Ronda, Kym." He carried on and on, and with each woman's name he added another digit. I bulged my eyes at him as he passed ten and started on eleven. "Susan, Maria—" Finally, he snuck a glance at me and roared with laughter.

I slapped him on the back of his hand as I realized he was joking. "That was a serious question."

"Well, if Lolita had her way, I would've been on thirty or so dates."

I chuckled at that. She was just as persistent with me. "You still haven't answered my question."

"I've had six dating disasters in two years."

It was my turn to raise my eyebrows as a dozen or so questions bounced to the front of my brain. "What would you call a dating disaster, just so I can have the heads up?"

He grinned at me. "I've had a few shockers."

I leaned forward on my elbow, eager to learn a few tips.

"Actually the biggest problem is how desperate the women are. It's like all they want to do is get me into bed."

Oh god. When I dressed as Memphis, getting a man into bed was exactly what I wanted. I felt as if I'd been punched in the gut, and with the throbbing pain I already had down there, it bloody hurt.

"That's why I was interested in you, Jane."

His comment dragged me from the quicksand I'd tumbled into. "Pardon?"

"You're the first woman I've actually had to pursue."

I scrunched up my nose, not seeing it the same way he did. "You asked me on a date and I accepted. I didn't exactly play hard to get."

"You were certainly harder to get than the other women."

I hope he never meets Memphis then.

Our meals arrived and I used the distraction to stew over his comments. His impression of those women was exactly what I'd been worried about with my naughty alter-ego. If I wasn't sure before whether my experiment would help or hinder me in finding a man, then it shifted straight to the negative now. Clayton had just proved my fears.

One thing was for sure—his comments meant we wouldn't be climbing into bed together tonight. I decided that was a good thing, and not just because I was wearing my nanna knickers either. It seemed right to take this . . . whatever *this* was . . . slowly.

We were silent for a while as we ate our meals. My first mouthful of the perfectly cooked steak smothered in buttery mushroom sauce took me to another world. It was delicious and tender. Having grown up on a farm, where the meat was as fresh as it could ever be, I never thought I'd enjoy such perfection again. I was wrong.

"So you said you've been on six dates in two years. What about before that?"

"I'm a single dad. My focus was on Telitha and we both struggled to get over what Bella did to us."

I knew what it was like to struggle over a nasty breakup, so I understood his comment all too well. "So what's changed?"

"Telitha is old enough now to go on sleepovers." He shrugged and a cloud crossed over his eyes. "I'm lonely."

I could relate to that too, and I nodded.

"How did you meet Lolita?" he asked.

"We both go to the same gym. How about you?"

"Our daughters go to dance class together. Lolita has adopted me as some kind of pet project."

Of course, Lolita had told me about him going to the dance classes. I laughed at his "pet project" comment. "She's made me one of her projects too."

"Oh?" He cocked his head.

"I was an angry woman when I found out my fiancé had cheated on me—"

"With every woman in your home town with a vagina," Clayton finished my sentence. I laughed. I'd forgotten Lolita had filled him in on my disastrous breakup.

"Correct. So she taught me how a good workout could eliminate some of that anger."

He bulged his eyes. "You're game; I've seen her work out. She's obsessed."

"Yep, that's why I love her."

We finished our meals and for dessert shared a giant chocolate brownie smothered in rich chocolate, candied macadamia nuts and vanilla ice cream. I sat back, unable to eat another mouthful, and realized that the throbbing in my abdomen, which had been my constant companion for two days, had finally subsided.

"I'm so full," he said as he eased back in his chair.

"Me too."

"Thanks for your company." His eyes, the color of molten honey, twinkled in the dancing flames.

"Thank you too. It's been fun." It really had. As I thought about all the men in my life, I was horrified to realize that this had been my first ever official date. How could that be? I scanned my brain again, going back twenty-eight years, searching for a candlelit dinner, or a picnic in the park, or anything that would resemble two potential lovers getting to know one another. But there were none. Not even with Alexander. It seemed one minute he talked to me, and the next we were girlfriend, boyfriend.

I'd always been desperate to have a man *like* me . . . or god forbid, love me. The realization was horrifying.

Never again would I be that easy.

This crazy challenge I was on had taught me how much I liked having sex. But it showed me how thrilling anticipation was too. I wanted both. I wanted a man to take me to the limit in a primal, uncontrolled sexual frenzy. But I also wanted to want it so bad that my body was a quivering mess. Each man I'd met so far this year had given me options, Clayton included. With him, I was choosing anticipation. *Let's see where our journey takes us.*

He insisted on paying the bill, but only after I insisted on paying the next one. Which, to my surprise, meant two things. Number one, I'd already accepted there would be a next time, and number two, he wanted to see me again. The butterflies in my stomach hit disco mode.

* * *

It was now Friday night and I still hadn't chosen my twenty-first sexual adventure. My brain slid into desperation mode because I had just forty-two hours to find the perfect man for Memphis or my challenge would be skittled. He didn't even have to be perfect. Just able, single, and staying at the Hot Horizon Hotel.

A potential contender arrived at eleven p.m. and my relief was instant. He was dressed like a runway model in a smart, navy suit that fitted his body perfectly. His white button-up shirt looked as if it'd just been ironed. He had broad shoulders, a narrow waist, and very shiny black shoes. The man screamed attention. My kind of attention. He walked with an interesting shuffle up to my counter and it wasn't until he was very close that I noticed his large diamond earring and the slight acne scarring on his cheeks.

"Hello. Welcome to the Hot Horizon Hotel." I offered him my most wicked smile.

"Hi, I'm Luke Stone, and I'm checking in for three nights."

"Perfect." I set about completing his paperwork. "What brings you to the Gold Coast, Mr. Stone?"

"I'm launching my new fashion line at Myer Pacific Fair on Sunday."

"Oh." I blinked at him. "You're a fashion designer?"

"Sure am." His grin showed off teeth that dazzled nearly as bright as his diamond earring.

"It's lovely to meet you."

"Likewise."

"Here's your access card. You're staying in room twenty-seven." When he reached for the card I gazed at his ring finger and breathed a sigh of relief. It was unadorned. That made Mr. Luke Stone my next adventure.

We said our goodbyes and I watched his tight little butt all the way until he disappeared into the elevator.

The rest of Friday night spun past in a whirlwind of guests coming and going. The Triple H bar was closed to the public for a private engagement party and it was fascinating to watch the guests stagger from the bar in various stages of inebriation.

The bar stayed open for an extra two hours and so, when it all wrapped up at about three-thirty, I only had three hours to kill until my shift was over.

Sunrise brought with it a morning shower. I grabbed my cup of tea and sat outside on my favorite chair to breath in the crisp clean air. The sun speared through the clouds in bright laser beams, creating a full rainbow that stretched the length of the Gold Coast. I wondered if such a spectacle was an omen. Was I finally seeing a light at the end of my relationship wasteland? I had to admit, men really did seem to be coming out of the woodwork.

I thought of Mr. Luke Stone sleeping on the fifth floor, and as I remembered how wonderfully polished he looked in his designer suit, I wondered what the hell I'd wear to meet him. A man like that probably judged people instantly by their clothing.

The *ding* of the bell had me running back to reception before I'd properly considered it.

When my boss arrived to take over from me at six forty-five, I went straight to my room and shuffled through my wardrobe. My knee-high boots caught my eye and I tugged them out. The black leather was soft and silky beneath my touch. Pulling them on, I zipped up the back and then, on a whim, I stripped naked and glanced in the mirror. My lopsided boobs drew my eye and I adjusted my shoulders so they were even. Now my shoulders were crooked and I shuffled them back. My choice was crooked shoulders or wonky boobs. I couldn't decide which was better.

Would Luke find this sexy? Only one way to find out.

I matched the boots with a simple cotton navy and floral dress with a plunging neckline and narrow waist. It stopped midway up my thigh, which was perfect for showing off my boots. It wasn't exceptional but it was cute. It was also the best I could do at such short notice.

After a shower, I fiddled with my makeup over and over. It was ridiculous pressure going to a man who dressed better than I did. Maybe he'd just laugh at me when he opened the door. I blinked at myself in the mirror. So far this year, none of the men had rejected me, and I had no idea what I'd do if they did. Probably return to my room and cry, or masturbate, depending on the mood that gripped me.

Today's wig choice was the fiery red one. Luke would probably recognize a wig when he saw it, so I might as well go with the bold one.

With the final touches in place I glanced in the mirror. I forced a smile, grabbed my black Chanel bag with the gold trimmings, and headed for the door.

My stomach did little flutters as I rode the elevator up to his floor and walked to his room. It wasn't until I had nearly arrived that I acknowledged the annoying knots that had formed in my stomach. I was actually nervous about what Luke thought of my appearance. I wanted to slap myself at this thought. The man didn't even know me, so why did I care whether or not he approved of my outfit? With this silliness sorted out, I knocked on his door.

I quickly plumped up my boobs in my bra as I waited. Time passed as I contemplated that he may be asleep or in the shower or something. I decided to knock one more time before using my all-access key card.

"Coming." His voice seemed a little angry, and I regretted my second knock.

As I waited out in the silent hall, I considered turning around. I decided I'd count to ten and if he didn't show up, I'd go. I got to six when the door opened.

Luke Stone was no longer the fashion designer dressed in the fancy clothes. He commanded attention in a heap of other ways. His skimpy boxer shorts allowed me full view of a body that was a work of art. He was covered in tattoos, bulging with muscles and looked utterly perfect, except for one thing . . . his left leg was missing below the knee.

"Can I help you?" he said.

I swallowed the lump in my throat. "I, um." Words failed to cross over my lips and I wanted to run for the elevator.

"Are you okay?"

The way he said it, with obvious concern for my welfare, was the bitch-slap I needed.

"I was wondering if you could help me."

"Sure, what's up?"

I shrugged one shoulder, trying to look all cute. "I'm a little horny," I said my now well-practiced speech. "And I don't like to be alone."

His eyes bulged and he blinked at me. He cleared his throat, and I realized it was his turn to have trouble speaking. It was time for Memphis to take over.

"May I come in?"

Without a word, he edged aside and I waltzed into the room, placed my bag over the back of his dining chair, and turned to him as the door was closing. Luke may only have one and a half legs, but the rest of his body made up for it. Whatever he did for exercise worked just fine.

I undid the fabric belt at my waist and made a show of twirling it around. "You don't have to do anything." I drew the belt out of the loops and flung it aside. "I'll just pleasure myself and you can watch."

"This is some kind of prank, right?"

I'd heard this a few times already and I shook my head. "No. Just me trying to satisfy my naughty urges."

"What about me?"

I started undoing the buttons down the front of my dress. "You can pleasure yourself too." I peeled my dress open and shrugged it off my shoulders until it hung from my waist. I reached behind my back but paused with my fingers ready to release my bra. "Do you want me to continue?"

He nodded like an eager teenager. "Hell yeah."

With the flick of my fingers, my lopsided breasts welcomed their release. I tossed my bra to Luke and he caught it with one hand. He twirled it between his fingers before he hopped to the bed and sat down. Then he placed the bra over his thighs and rubbed his hands together like he was about to receive a serve of candy.

I pushed my thumbs into the elastic waist and eased my dress down over my hips until it fell to the floor and I kicked it aside. Now I stood before Luke wearing just a hot pink G-string and knee-high black boots. I wondered what the fashion designer thought of that. The question was on the tip of my tongue when I noticed the bulge in his boxer shorts growing. He did indeed like what he saw. I adjusted my shoulders, trying to work out which way made my boobs sit straight.

His eyes drilled into me and he leaned back on his hands, thrusting his hips forward. Luke ran his tongue over his lips, leaving moisture in its wake, and the way he did this showed that he was enjoying my show. His reaction was damn sexy and I was ready to give him more.

I reached up, cupped my breasts in my hands, and flicked my fingers over my nipples. They were already hard and tiny bumps had formed around my delicate buds, drawing out my arousal. Luke's cock grew to a dominant bulge lining his cotton shorts and edging toward his very sexy navel.

I put the toe of my boot up onto the chair and with my eyes on him, I rolled my tongue around my finger and then glided it into my lacy G-string. The air sucked through my teeth as I rolled my finger over my pulsing clit. I glided my finger around the most sensitive part of my body and then applied pressure until it just began to hurt, then I plunged my finger into my vagina.

Repeating the move again, I rolled around the bud, pressed down, then slid over my hot folds.

I closed my eyes, concentrating on my pleasure-seeking finger. With each thrust I teased my clit, drawing out the sensation with both the drive in and the pull out. The tingling pleasure building inside me grew fast, and I wasn't surprised. After all, it'd been thirteen days since my last orgasm.

A deep groan had me opening my eyes and what I saw had my insides clenching. Luke was naked now, his boxer short discarded at his feet. His cock was a rigid pole standing large and proud and his balls between his spread legs were full and round. He leaned back and propped up his elbows allowing him to see both his own arousal and mine.

I strode to him and straddled his hips, resting my long boots on either side of his thighs. Without a word, I dangled my breasts before his face and he obliged by taking my mounds in his hands and mouth. He caressed and sucked with equal intensity. I in turn ground my hips back and forward, gliding my G-string over his rock-hard cock.

Rubbing the lacy fabric over his solid muscle was glorious, providing the right amount of pressure and friction. I glided my finger into my G-string again and found my clit. As he sucked and caressed my breasts, I plunged into my hot hole with increasing intensity. My orgasm built with a vengeance, stacking up glorious layers of lust, begging for release. But it wasn't happening. The release was so close but the grinding, sucking, finger-fucking, wasn't quite enough.

I couldn't stand it anymore.

I snapped my breasts from his lips and stood above him. With one hand I tugged my G-string aside, and with my other I plunged my fingers into myself, bending my knees to delve even deeper. Luke reached up and I grabbed his hand.

"Yes," I cried out, as his finger drove into me, first one, then another. My knees threatened to buckle at the glorious pleasure of it.

Through my erotic haze I saw the concentration on his face match the intensity in his eyes. I rubbed my clit. Massaged my nipples. Bent my knees. I was there, oh-so close. The coil inside was wound so tight it was ready to snap. I sucked in. My insides tensed. I cried out and with one huge breath, release came. My juices spilled from my body, sprinkling onto Luke's inked torso.

It was long and sweet and exquisite, tearing at my insides with glorious rolling pulses.

My knees buckled and I fell to Luke's chest. His heart was a raging beat in my ear. My erratic breathing matched with his own.

He rolled us over so I was on my back and he at my side. Not a moment was wasted as he sucked my breast and his fingers once again found my throbbing hole. Before I knew it, my body reacted again and I raised my hips, begging for more. Another quick orgasm ripped through me, fast and explosive and completely unexpected.

My heart was a raging torrent and my head was a fuzzy erotic haze when he pushed up onto his knees. Seeing his glazed eyes, I knew he was ready. Thankfully, my brain kicked into gear. I held up my hand. "Hang on a second, big boy. We need a condom."

I rolled off the bed, discreetly whipped off my wet G-string and flicked it aside. My condoms were conveniently hidden in the side zip pocket of my bag. I grabbed one and passed it to him.

Luke rolled it in place and remained on his knees, his rock-hard cock extending from his body like a flagpole. I put my legs either side of Luke's knees, and reclined back. He put his hands beneath my legs and tugged me forward, then he raised my left leg at a ninety-degree angle, putting my boot on his shoulder and he leaned forward, opening me up wide.

Luke's glazed eyes looked at me, but he was lost in another world.

His penis nudged at my opening and I braced for the plunging that I expected to happen. However, it was the exact opposite. Ever so slowly, he entered me. His teeth were clenched. Air hissed between them, and his eyes flickered with the drawn-out glide of him entering my body. It was glorious to watch this man, this exquisitely fit yet flawed body, savor my deepest depths.

He filled me to the hilt, his balls flush against my ass, and it felt perfect. With his fingers digging into my thigh, he pulled out quickly and entered me slowly again. Luke repeated the move, each time getting just that little bit faster. He placed his thumb on my clit and I clutched at the sheets as he rubbed it with increasing intensity.

With my leg in the air and him plunging me full-tilt, his cock clawed at something inside me that begged for more. Each rock of his hips brought a new brick of pleasure, building an orgasm that was out of this world.

Luke stopped. I opened my eyes to witness his whole body tense. The tattoos over his pecks danced as they bulged. His eyes opened; he blinked. Then he released a primal growl, dug his fingers into my thighs again and thrust in and out, over and over and over.

My orgasm rocked through me, pulsing out a maddening beat in time to his movements. Over and over, with clenched jaw and glistening muscles he plunged, until his shoulders sagged and he gasped for air. Soon he slowed and I unfurled my clutches on the bed sheet.

Luke was covered in a fine lick of sweat that highlighted the contours of his sculpted torso. I took in every line of his magnificent body; the tattoos were intricate and perfectly matched his physique. This was an image I'd like to retain for the rest of my life.

Luke let out a huge sigh before he eased back and his cock popped out of me. He rolled around to sit on the bed and tugged the sheet to cover his damaged leg and his groin.

I gradually pulled myself up to sit beside him at the end of the bed.

"You have no idea how much I needed that," he said as I reached his side.

I huffed. "Me too."

"No," he said. "I'm serious. I haven't had sex in more than six years."

My jaw dropped. "What? A body like yours should be experienced by as many women as possible."

He blinked at me as if disbelieving. Then he shook his head. "Not since the accident."

I sensed that he wanted to say more, so I waited. For several heartbeats we sat side by side, looking out across the glorious bedazzled ocean, listening to the sound of the waves crashing below.

"I was drunk when I crashed the car."

I moaned and twisted my fingers together as I waited for the horrible story I knew was coming.

"Fortunately, I was the only one in the vehicle at the time. I lost my leg. But ultimately, I lost so much more. I was a crane driver, and I was good at it too. But of course I couldn't do that anymore. I grew angry at the world and it wasn't long before I lost my wife and friends, and with them went my self-confidence."

I had no idea what to say, so I waited out the silence.

"Three years ago, I decided it was time to change my life back around."

"I can see that you have."

He turned and smiled at me. Then he laughed, and it was so contagious I laughed along with him.

With that wonderful sound, I stood up and set about putting my dress on, and I shoved my G-string, belt and bra into my bag.

"What's your name?"

I swung my bag over my shoulder. "Memphis."

A little frown rippled his forehead as if he didn't believe me. "Well, Memphis, I think you're my lucky charm."

"Thank you." I smiled and turned, and with that lovely thought, I headed out his door and made my way to my room.

I showered and cooked myself eggs on toast for breakfast.

Then I grabbed my diary and sat out on the balcony to eat.

I turned to 21st May, and wrote *Mr. Luke Stone room 27*—and as I thought about the pristine suit that he'd worn on Friday night and the exquisite yet flawed body hidden beneath, I wrote *Surprise, Surprise.*

I thought I was going through a life-changing experience, but what he'd been through must've been horrific. Life was a rollercoaster, full of highs and lows. I'd had my share of lows. This year though, was showing me many, many highs.

As I breathed in the fresh ocean air and ate my eggs on toast, I detailed in my diary how wonderful sex had been with my hunky, tattooed, one-legged, fashion designer. When I wrote that down, he actually sounded too good to be true.

Another aspect of our encounter occurred to me too. For some inexplicable reason, men felt compelled to tell me things that they probably never told anyone else. I had become a therapist of sorts. Yet if anyone asked me, these men were my therapy. I was the one learning and growing from this journey.

I was also having the best sex in the world.

Leaning back, I propped my legs up on the table, and laughed long and loud at that incredible admission.

I was on the ride of my life, and it sure was exhilarating.

26TH MAY
SHAKEN AND STIRRED
Room 38 – Hot Horizon Hotel

From the second Mr. Dylan Ashley walked up to reception, I knew I'd found my next potential passion partner. He was tall and dark-haired, with lovely chocolate eyes framed by long, dark eyelashes. His smile lit up his whole face and he had a confidence about him that screamed sexy. He was James Bond and Bear Grylls rolled into one. I nearly giggled at that thought.

"So what brings you to the Gold Coast?" I asked as I completed the necessary paperwork.

He leaned sun-kissed arms onto the reception counter. "I'm a boat broker, here for the Gold Coast Marine Expo."

"Oh." The job suited his confident charisma perfectly. "Sounds interesting."

"It is. I love it." My heart did a little flutter as his eyes glistened, then I realized the discreet down lighting probably caused that.

As much as I'd like to chat to him all night, I finished the check-in process, programmed his room card and placed it on the counter between us. "Okay Mr. Ashley, you're in room thirty-eight on the seventh floor."

When he reached for the card, I noticed long tanned fingers, neatly trimmed nails and no wedding ring. Perfect.

"Thank you," he said. "Have a good night."

I watched his sexy butt as he walked to the elevator and moments later he disappeared behind the silver doors.

For the next seven hours I did nothing but imagine what was beneath Dylan's stylish outfit, to the point where I was actually buzzing from the inside out.

"Morning Jane."

I looked up and thanked the stars that Needledick was nearly on time for a change.

"Hi Mr. Karwatsky."

"I've told you a dozen times to call me John."

"Sorry. It's just habit."

"How was the night? All good?"

"No incidents." I felt like I should ask how his mother was, but I really just wanted to head up to room thirty-eight and get some action on. It was so unlike me to be this uncaring, yet it felt so right.

I did the usual morning handover to Needledick, and we said our goodbyes. I practically skipped to the elevator. It dinged open and after the doors closed I wanted to bang my head on the door as it made its incredibly slow crawl up to my floor.

Before I even reached my room, I'd tugged my hair out of the tight bun I'd had it in all night and I'd started to undo the buttons on my shirt. By the time I arrived at my room, I probably looked like I'd already been shagged.

I jumped into the shower, washed and hopped out again in record time. As sexy Dylan and I had spent some time chatting last night and I may or may not have drooled in front of him a bit, I needed to take meticulous care with my makeup.

I applied the fabulous electric blue eyeliner along both the top and the bottom of my eyelids in an attempt to detract from my green irises and I plastered on foundation, eradicating all traces of my freckles. My choice of wig today was the short blond bob and it took a while to wrestle my long dark hair into it. I finished with blush to accentuate my cheekbones and Pinky Promise lipstick. For something different, I dabbed on a touch of perfume today.

I flung open my wardrobe door and studied the collection. My knee-high boots that I'd worn with Luke Stone last Saturday caught my eye, and a cheeky little idea raced through my brain.

After a quick rummage through my sparse underwear drawer, I put on my last pair of French knickers. They were black lace, and as I'd worn them many times they weren't as tight as I'd like them to be. Sitting on my bed, I slipped my feet into my knee-high boots and pulled the zip up the back of my calf.

I stood to look in the mirror and grinned. Could I do this? *Hell yeah.*

Without a second thought I whipped my trench coat from the closet and put it on, did up the buttons, then wrapped the belt around my waist and tied it into a knot. Glancing down to make sure my boobs weren't visible, a delicious flutter rolled through me at what I was about to do.

I grabbed a black bag, transferred a few condoms to the side zip pocket and after one last glance in the mirror, I strode from my room.

I rode the painfully slow elevator up to the seventh floor and my eight-inch heels sunk into the carpet as I made my way to his room. My heart belted out a crazy, excited beat at the freedom of being practically naked beneath my black trenchie.

Normally I'd pause at the man's door and plump up my boobs. No need today. A cheeky smile curled at my lips and I knocked and held my breath as I waited.

One of the neighboring doors opened and a middle-aged woman in a dowdy floral dress poked her head out. She eyed me up and down, and her leering gaze made me feel cheap. I wanted to poke her eyeballs out.

Dylan's door opened and I swiveled around to him.

"Oh, you are here," I said with all the familiarity I could muster, and as I resisted glaring at the woman, I squeezed past Dylan and waltzed into his room before he could block my entrance.

"Can I help you?" he said as the door clicked shut.

I sighed an over-exaggerated sigh. "I hope so. I'm so horny I could just about burst."

His eyes bulged and his brows shot up his forehead.

"Do you think you can help me out with that?"

Dylan wore black slacks that were zipped up, but the undone button at the top splayed open below his navel. His very sexy navel. He was shirtless and a scattering of hair covered his chest, forming a line that ran down his torso and disappeared into his zipper.

He ran his hand through his dark hair and it instantly sprung back into place. "Mmmm." He tilted his head. "What's the catch?"

I plonked my bag down, and reached for my belt to untie it. "No catch." With the belt now hanging loose at my sides I began undoing the buttons, starting at the top. My nipples were already rock hard and I kept my eyes on him, drooling for his reaction to my nakedness.

He licked his lips and his eyes flitted from my face to what I was doing with my hands.

When my trench coat was completely undone I let it fall aside a fraction. Just enough that he could peak through but not so much that he could see my nipples.

"Do you want me to continue?"

His Adam's apple bobbed up and down and he nodded.

I hooked my fingers under my collar, glided the jacket off my shoulders, and let it fall to the floor. I stood there wearing just panties and knee-high boots.

Thrills of impending action coursed through me.

Dylan inhaled a shaky breath as he rolled his palm over his groin. I'd seen this move before; his penis was growing. I was incredibly horny knowing I could turn a man on by simply undressing.

It was time to capitalize on his interest. I was so ready—I'd been thinking of this for seven hours.

"Do you like to watch?"

He nodded again and swallowed so loud I heard it.

Stepping my boots apart, I glided my hand down my torso and began to rub my clit. My underwear lace provided the perfect friction and a quick little shudder rippled through me. I glided my hand into my knickers and with a bend in my knees, I rolled my finger over my clit and poked the tip of my finger into my hole. It didn't surprise me that I was already moist.

Dylan moaned, and I snapped my eyes open. I hadn't realized I'd shut them. His jaw was clenched, and he rubbed his hand over his pants with splayed fingers showing the amount of pressure he was using.

"Do you want me to set you free?"

He nodded quickly, as if I'd change my mind if he delayed his response. I strode to him and placed my hands on his waist, feeling the warmth emanate from his skin. His breathing was rapid, practically marathon-worthy. With our eyes locked, I felt for his zipper. The bulge of his cock pressed against the fabric. I repeated his earlier move and ran my hand over his groin. He did a cute little eye-roll thing and I did it again.

I glided the zipper down, peeled open his slacks and fed my hand into the opening. My breath hitched as I noticed Dylan was naked beneath.

"Well hello," I said, as I hooked my fingers around his cock and set him free. His pants fell to the floor and I stepped back to take in the spectacle. Mr. Dylan Ashley didn't disappoint. His erection stood large and proud. A slick of semen bubbled from the slit in his glorious swollen crown. It took all my might not to drop to my knees and taste him.

Anticipation was a glorious thing.

"Mmmm, yummy," I said, as I shifted my gaze from his cock to his eyes. Dylan had that wonderful lust-filled haze that I'd become accustomed too.

He didn't move; it was as if he were frozen. It surprised me how many men didn't know what to do when a woman took control.

Taking control was what I needed to do.

I stepped forward, and as I ran my tongue over his nipple I wrapped my hand around his shaft and glided my fingers up and down in a twisting motion. Dylan gripped my shoulders and hissed as if he were holding back a demon. His body was hard as steel, as was the muscle in my hand.

His fingers wove into my knickers and I spread my legs, allowing him entrance. A delightful shudder rolled through my body as he slipped inside me. I closed my eyes and allowed this glorious stranger to explore my depths with his fingers. He adjusted his stance to change his angle on my pussy, and a sharp ripping sound confirmed he'd torn my knickers. The sound had me bending my legs more, begging him to plunge deeper as I increased my pace on his cock.

"Stop. Stop." He stepped back and held his palms up.

I blinked at him.

"Sorry, but . . . you said I could watch." His chest heaved with rapid breaths and I realized he didn't actually want me to stop, it was just that he was close to release. Too close.

Understanding what he wanted, I spied the dining table and an idea formed. I slipped out of my knickers and tossed them at Dylan. He looked a little bewildered at first, as if he'd slipped into a mystical dream. Leaving him in his trance, I walked to the table, stepped up onto a chair, and hoisted my bottom onto the table. Placing the heels of my boots onto two separate chairs, I spread my knees apart, showing Dylan my most private parts.

His hand went straight to his cock and he wrapped his fingers around his bulging member and pulled it once, stopping at the top to squeeze. His reaction was glorious.

Ripples of want zipped through me and I was so ready to release the orgasm that'd been building inside me for hours. I licked my finger, then I glided it over my clit with enough pressure to have my insides clenching, before plunging it into my velvet folds. My insides were hot and wet and clamped around my finger like a fist.

I pulled it out, maintaining the friction over my clit on the way out and on the way in again. Moving my knees open and closed in a little game of peek-a-boo for Dylan, I drove my finger in and out in time to the motion. Soon my twitching insides had me plunging my finger in a frenzy. My erratic breathing matched my erratic heartbeat and I was close, oh-so close to incredible release.

I rubbed hard, punishing my clit like never before, drawing out the excruciating climax. Dylan groaned and I watching him punishing his cock, too.

"Wait," I yelled, and his eyes snapped to me.

"Wait," I repeated, and reached for my bag. Fumbling with the side zip, I opened it and pulled out a condom. "Here, do you want to have sex with me?"

His eyes were huge as he strode my way, his cock leading the charge. Dylan tore open the condom and rolled it on with expert speed.

He stood between my legs, every defined muscle slicked with sweat. His nipples were rock-hard pebbles. I put my legs in the air, pointing my sexy boots to the ceiling and Dylan closed the distance between us. His cock nudged my opening like a heat-seeking missile.

Dylan wrapped his hands around my leather-clad ankles and slammed his cock into me. I gasped at the speed of it. It was pleasure and pain, glorious and brutal, and I wanted it again. He spread my legs apart and with his eyes on my vagina he did it again, all the way in, fast and hard.

Dylan clenched his jaw as he alternated opening my legs and crossing them over with each plunge. The sensation was incredible—one second I was wide open, begging to be filled, the next second I was clamped up nice and tight, trapping him in my hot oasis. The intensity in his face matched the intensity of his focus as he didn't miss a beat. Open. Closed. In. Out. This new move was glorious, exquisite, and I quickly committed it to my ever-growing library of incredible sexual positions.

The orgasm that'd been building hit me, tearing at my insides with each hot plunge of his cock. I clutched at the table, trying to grab hold as Dylan took his thrusting to a whole new level. In and out he pounded, prolonging the moment until I thought I'd explode.

He crossed my legs and clenched his teeth, bulging out the muscles in his jaw. When his eyes snapped open but he wasn't actually looking, I knew it was the moment of no return. He let go of my ankles and pushed on my knees, bringing my ass off the table slightly.

Dylan growled, long, low and deep, and hammered all he had into me. His cock touched that wonderful thing inside me that was a cocktail of both pleasure and pain. I cried out, gasping for more.

It seemed like an eternity before Dylan's body relaxed from the erotic state that'd gripped him. His chest rose and fell with his rapid breathing. He opened his eyes and it was a moment before they focused on me.

A smile curled at my lips as a look of utter satisfaction crossed his features. He let out a huge sigh. "Wow." A dazzling smile lit up his face.

I nodded. "Wow."

He let go of my legs and as he stepped back, I lowered them to the table and sat on the edge.

He held up one finger. "Excuse me for a sec."

I admired his sexy butt as he walked to the bathroom and disappeared.

I used the isolation to climb off the table. One glance at my knickers was enough to know they were ruined. After wiping myself with them, I tossed them into my bag. As I was putting on my coat, Dylan returned with a towel wrapped low on his hips.

"Tell me that wasn't a dream?"

I chuckled. "No. It wasn't a dream."

"I've never had anything like that happen to me before."

"Really? You were amazing." Men seemed to need reassuring.

His smile lit up his face and it was that smile, the one that said the world was perfect. "What's your name?"

I tied my belt around my waist. "I'm Memphis."

Dylan ran his hand through his hair. "I feel like I've slipped into some kind of surreal world." He pushed the towel lower on his hips and took another step toward me.

Worried that he was about to kiss me, I grabbed my bag, blew him a kiss and headed for the door. With my fingers around the handle I glanced at him over my shoulder. "Have a great day."

"Are you kidding? Best . . . day . . . ever."

I smiled at that comment and left his room. As I tugged my coat around my nakedness, I headed to the elevator. Every muscle in my body pulsed in after-orgasm glory. The sharp ping announced its arrival and as I went to step in, I froze. Mr. Karwatsky was in there. His eyes bulged, and my heart stopped.

He ran his gaze over me and feeling completely naked right now, I stepped into the elevator and turned my back to him. My heart exploded in my chest as I realized I couldn't go to my room. I glanced at the button panel. We were going to ground. I had no choice—I was trapped.

I felt him leering at me and out the corner of my eye, I saw him lean forward to look at my face.

"I've seen you before." His accusatory voice was louder than it needed to be.

With all the courage I could muster I turned my eyes to him, forcing boldness into my response. "I beg your pardon?"

He squinted. "Yes, I've seen you before. What room are you in?"

I frowned and drilled disgust into my eyes. "That's none of your business."

"We don't accept people like you in this hotel. Now what room are you in?"

"Look, creep." Even I was shocked at how angry I sounded. "I'm not telling you my room number."

"I'm the hotel manager and I have a right to question--"

"Yeah, and I'm Daenerys Targaryen, mother of dragons." I waggled my head at him.

His jaw dropped, and I just about chuckled at my boldness. "I am the hotel manager."

The doors pinged open and I strode as fast as my six-inch boots could carry me across the marble lobby.

"I'll be watching out for you," he yelled after me.

My heart and head were ready to explode as I exited the building and raced down the front steps. Without any plan I continued walking up the path that ran parallel to the beach. Within a minute I was giggling. Within two minutes I was laughing so hard I could barely breathe.

As I strode up the path in the knee-high boots, wearing nothing but my trench coat, I passed women in bikinis and men in board shorts. Their accusatory glances were justified, and I felt completely out of place.

My brain was a crazy scramble as I tried to work out what I was going to do next. I couldn't believe I was stuck without a phone or money. I made a mental note never to do that again. Somehow, I had to get to Lolly—she was my only savior. With that decision made, I headed toward the tram station.

A heat wave of embarrassment coursed through me as I tried to ignore the glares from complete strangers and walked the half mile in the middle of the day in my trench coat and boots. I looked like a hooker and the elation I felt just ten minutes ago was replaced with ultimate humiliation.

Without any money, I'd have to take the tram and pray that no inspectors stopped me to ask for my ticket. *Maybe I could avoid a fine by flashing my boobs. Oh my god!* I'd never have considered that six months ago.

The tram arrived within two minutes and I slipped into a seat at the back. I wiped the sweat from my temple and with the inferno frying my brain, I wished I could take my wig off.

As the tram neared Main Beach Station, I stood and tried to ignore glares from random strangers as I waited for the doors to open. I did the fifteen-minute walk in ten, and my inner thighs were sweating by the time I stepped onto Lolly's driveway.

Please be home. Please be home. I chanted out the mantra as I strode to her door and knocked.

My embarrassment hit a whole new level when Calvin answered the door. I wanted to dive into the bushes and be buried beneath the compost.

"Hi." Calvin blinked at me, and I realized he had no idea who I was.

I was tempted to turn and leave, but my shoulders slumped as I realized I had no choice. I swallowed the enormous lump in my throat.

"Hi, is Lolita home?"

He shook his head. "No, she's—" He paused mid-sentence. His jaw dropped and his eyes bulged. "Jane!"

I wanted the earth to open up and swallow me whole.

"Holy fuck, it *is* you." He burst out laughing. "Come in, quick, before the neighbors see us."

He laughed all the way into the kitchen where I flopped down, rested my arms on the table and hid my face in my palms.

"Did you get caught again? Holy shit, you look hot. Lolly's going to be pissed she missed this." Calvin was an excited child as he laughed and spoke without waiting for my replies.

"Wait there, I'll call her."

I couldn't have moved even if I'd wanted to.

"Hey babe, you won't believe this." There was a pause. "Jane, or should I say Memphis, just showed up." I heard Lolita squeal. "Yes. Sure is. I know."

I could just imagine what Lolita was saying on the other end of the line.

"Okay, will do. Love you too."

I sensed him sitting at the table and I looked up at his enormous grin. "She's coming home."

"Where was she?"

"Halfway through grocery shopping."

I could just imagine her abandoning the shopping and sprinting to her car.

"Want a drink?"

"A water please."

He stood up and walked toward the kitchen. "I'd ask you what happened but you'll just have to repeat it when she gets here."

I groaned and plonked my head on the table.

Calvin touched my shoulder as he placed a glass of water down. "Just tell me you're okay. You didn't get hurt, did you?"

His concern nearly brought me to tears, and I shook my head. "No. No. Nothing like that."

"Oh good." He rubbed his hands together. "I can't wait to hear this."

I gulped back the water.

"No wonder you're getting these guys. You look amazing."

Coming from Calvin, that was like winning an Oscar. "Thanks."

"I mean it. Clayton told me how much he enjoyed your date."

Oh Jesus. I felt like a two-timing slut at the mention of Clayton. What would he think of me if he knew what I was doing? *Jesus.* I plonked my head on the table again and tried to force my racing heart to calm down as I waited out the silence.

A squeal of tires announced Lolly's arrival, and she bounced through the doorway about two seconds later.

"Holy fuck, babe, this's so exciting." She pushed her perky boobs into my shoulder as she hugged me.

"Calvin, get the champagne and glasses. Us girls have got some serious chatting to do." I didn't even bother pointing out that it was only nine thirty in the morning.

"And me," Calvin protested, and I groaned at the suggestion.

I looked up to see Lolita trying to shoo Calvin away quietly with her hand. His expression showed utter devastation.

The second he was out of earshot, Lolita clutched my hand in hers. "First, are you okay?"

"Yeah." I rolled my eyes to the ceiling. "And no."

"Okay, that's good. That's good. So start at the beginning and tell me everything."

"Can I at least have some clothes first?"

Her eyes lit up and I knew what was coming. She jumped up, ogled down my coat and burst out laughing. "You're naked. Hey honey, Jane's naked."

"What?" Calvin called from the kitchen.

I was tempted to stab my eyeball with the wrought-iron candelabra beautifully centered on the table.

"She's got nothing on under the trenchie."

Calvin grinned a deviant smile as he returned to the table with a bottle and three glasses. "Okay, I'm ready," he said.

"Really? Do I have to tell you?"

"Shit yeah. I'm here for you, you know that." Calvin's gorgeous profile was enhanced with his look of deep concern. I'd happily pass out right now if I didn't have to speak ever again.

I grumbled, but at the same time knew I had no way to get out of it. Calvin handed me a full glass of bubbles and I swigged a huge mouthful before I sat back, sighed, and accepted the inevitable.

I gulped the rest of my champagne and huffed. "Okay, so I met this guy."

"What'd he look like?" Lolly was insatiable, and I glared at her impatience.

"Sorry," she said. "Carry on."

"His name was Dylan, he's a boat broker, and I'd describe him as James Bond meets Bear Grylls."

Calvin frowned but Lolly snapped her fingers. "Oooh nice. So I'm picturing suave and sophisticated, yet hunky and brawn."

I nodded. "Yeah." She'd nailed him. "For some crazy reason I decided to wear just my boots and knickers, with my trenchie over the top."

"Holy fuck, that's hot. Right, babe?" Lolly turned to Calvin, and all I wanted to do was cover my ears and yell *la la la* at the top of my voice so I couldn't hear his answer.

I carried on, determined to get the humiliation over as quickly as possible. "Anyway, I went to his room." I squeezed my palms over my eyes so I couldn't see their reaction. "After we finished, I put my boots and coat on and headed to the elevator. Needledick was in there."

"Oh fuck. I bet you just died."

"Yep." I held my glass toward Calvin and he readily filled it. Gulping back liquid sanity, I carried on. "Needledick pointed his finger at me and said he'd seen me before, and then went on to say that they didn't accept people like me in the hotel."

"Like you? What did he mean?" Calvin frowned.

"A hooker." I bulged my eyes, angry that I had to state the obvious.

"What?" Lolly gasped. "He's an ass. You don't look like a hooker. You look shit hot. Right, Cal?

"Sure do."

"He's just jealous that some other lucky bastard in the hotel got laid. So what happened then?"

"He asked me what room I was staying in. So I called him a creep and told him it was none of his business."

"Then what?" Calvin leaned forward.

I giggled, barely able to believe what I'd done next.

"What? What?" Lolly pushed forward on her seat and gripped my arm.

"He said he was the hotel manager, and I said yeah, just like I was Daenerys Targaryen, mother of dragons, and then the elevator opened and I raced out of the building."

Calvin and Lolly roared with laughter and soon we were all in tears.

"That's fucking gold." She held her glass toward me and we chinked them together. "You, my girlfriend, are an absolute riot."

"Man, I'd love to have seen his face," Calvin said.

"Me too. Shit that would've been funny."

I shrugged. "So I did the walk of shame over here and once again I need to borrow some clothes."

Lolly frowned, all serious all of a sudden. "We need to give you a section of my wardrobe."

I huffed. "I don't plan on doing this a third time."

"Yeah, right. You're playing with fire, babe—who knows what's going to happen?"

I blinked at her. She was right. Playing with fire had consequences.

"What's wrong?" Lolita placed her hand on my arm.

I shook my head. "Nothing."

"Damn right it's nothing. Now come on, let's get you something to wear and you can tell me all about this guy's cock." She wiggled her head at Calvin and he just shrugged. He obviously knew when there was no point arguing.

Lolita hooked my arm into hers and led me to their bedroom. I sat on the bed as she went to her extensive wardrobe that not only eclipsed her side of the shelving but half of Calvin's too.

"How about this?" The dress she held up was a hot pink slinky mini that'd be more suited to a night out on the town than a tram ride back to my hotel.

"I'm just going home. Do you have anything black?"

"Black?" She wrinkled her nose at me. "Have you ever seen me in black?"

That was true. "Navy then?"

"Oh, here you go."

She held up at cute navy and floral V-neck romper. It looked tiny.

"Get your coat off. Come on."

Grumbling, but aware there was no point arguing, I stood up and undid the belt and buttons on my coat. I tossed the coat onto the bed.

"Jesus, babe, you are naked. Where're your pants?"

"It's a long story." I rolled my eyes.

"Oooh, do tell." She sat on the bed and as I stepped into the little shorts-suit she was lending me, I told her about my underwear dilemma.

She flopped back onto the bed and roared with laughter. "Oh my god, these guys are a hoot. What do you think they do with your panties?"

I shrugged; I hadn't really thought about it. To my surprise, the floral romper fitted me. I glanced in the mirror and instantly tugged the fabric at the V-neck together to cover my cleavage, but it was pointless. The elastic pulled it in at the waist and the shorts stopped high on my thigh. It would have to do. "I have no idea," I finally said.

"Babe, they're probably showing them off to any guy that'd listen."

"Ewww, that's gross."

She waved her hand at me. "Men are gross."

We both chuckled at that.

She reached for my arm. "Now don't let this little incident put you off your challenge. Oh, hey, you didn't tell me what his cock was like."

"Mmmm, well he wasn't huge and he wasn't small, but he did this scissor action with my legs that was incredible."

"Huh? What's that?"

I explained what Dylan had done and Lolita's eyes bulged. "Holy fuck, that sounds awesome. I'm getting Calvin onto that one."

I plugged my ears with my fingers. "La, la, la."

"Oh, stop it. Calvin and I fuck. All the time."

"I know. I just don't need to know about it."

"You're so mean." She pouted her lips but the twinkle in her eyes showed she didn't mean it.

I peeled my wig off and plucked at the pins to undo my hair. "Can I borrow some sandals too? I can't wear my boots with this."

"Sure."

By the time I left her bedroom, I was a new woman. I'd removed my makeup and fixed my hair and changed into something much more appropriate for the Gold Coast.

Calvin was fussing about in the kitchen when we returned downstairs. "I liked the trenchie better."

"Ha. Thanks."

"I'm serious." His grin perfectly matched his stunning looks.

"Thanks for your help. I need to go home and sleep."

"I bet you do." He wriggled his eyebrows and I just shook my head.

I said goodbye to Calvin and when Lolita offered to drive me home, I accepted.

"I meant what I said in the bedroom, babe," Lolita said as we pulled out of her driveway. "Don't go letting this little blip ruin your challenge."

"Okay."

"I mean it. Twenty-two men in twenty-two weeks. You're invested now. No deviating from the plan."

"Okay," I repeated.

Ten minutes later she pulled into the drop-off zone at the Hot Horizon Hotel and I climbed out of the car. My legs trembled as I walked up the steps to the lobby.

By the time I reached my room, I was exhausted. By the time I had a long, hot shower, I was completely shattered.

After shutting the blinds, I sat on my bed, reached for my diary and turned to 26th May. At the top, I wrote *Mr. Dylan Ashley, room 30* —and as I thought of my James Bond meets Bear Grylls analogy and then the disaster that happened after, I wrote *Shaken and Stirred.* I giggled at that and went on to describe today's lover who was mix of suave sophistication and hunky brawn. Dylan had shown me another sexual maneuver that would never have crossed my mind. But I'll certainly never forget it.

I put my pen and diary next to my alarm clock and curled onto my side on the bed. My mind bounced over everything that'd happened in the last four hours; it was a crazy concoction of elation and dread. But as the swirling emotions spun like a roulette wheel I realized that the thrill of nearly being caught was just as exciting as the thrill of pursuing my next random stranger.

I yawned loudly, and as crazy pictures of me running naked up the beach invaded my subconscious I closed my eyes, and sheer exhaustion dragged me to sleep.

1ST JUNE
MY RAUNCHY REVIVAL
Room 30 – Hot Horizon Hotel

Friday morning arrived and with it a brilliant spectacle of orange and yellow sky reflecting off an almost flat, black ocean. Giant cruise ships appeared as tiny shapes on the horizon, while close to shore, surfers bobbed like little black corks in the stillness, waiting for the next wave. The lack of breeze meant the only rustling in the Pandanus palms was caused by the rainbow lorikeets flitting from one branch to the next.

The morning was the epitome of peace and beauty. I inhaled the cool salty air in through my nose and out through my mouth in my own form of meditation. Even my green tea seemed a little sweeter today. I sat on the sun lounge out the front of the hotel swinging my legs back and forward as I watched the sun peek over the horizon. Today was the first day of winter and at this time of year, sunrise almost coincided with the end of my shift.

Aware that my boss might catch me if I stayed out too long, I reluctantly went back inside. Not ten minutes later, Needledick walked in through the sliding glass doors, looking as if he'd just crawled out of bed. His hair was a scrambled mess and he clearly hadn't shaved.

"Are you okay?" I didn't really want to ask, for fear of hearing too much about his private life, but felt I needed to.

He blinked down at me and nodded. Gradually his expression shifted to misery, and I dreaded what he was about to say. "We had a bit of a rough night. Had to call the ambulance out."

My hand snapped to my mouth as I gasped. "Oh no. Is your mom okay?"

"She's okay now, but it was a bit touch-and-go there for a while."

"How scary for you. Have you had any sleep?"

He shook his head. "Only what I had in the chair at the hospital."

I touched his shoulder. It was the first physical contact I'd had with my boss and it didn't repulse me as much as it should have. "Go home and get some sleep for a few hours. I'll cover for you."

He blinked at me as if seeing me for the first time. "Are you sure?"

"Of course. Just don't be too long or I'll pass out asleep on the counter." Although I was serious, I faked a chuckle.

"Oh Jane, thank you. I'll be back by ten, I promise."

In light of his usual tardiness, I took his promise with a huge dose of skepticism.

His step was just a little more lively as he walked out of the Hot Horizon Hotel.

Once he was gone I slumped into the office chair behind the counter and huffed. This wasn't how I'd planned my Friday morning. I'd wanted to run along the beach, and after a shower and a bite to eat, go pantie shopping. My underwear situation had become desperate. If Needledick came back at ten as promised, I'd still have time to shop but I wouldn't be able to fit my exercise in. I could just imagine Lolita's disapproval of my decision. She prioritized exercise above nearly everything.

I whiled away the hours cleaning out the drawers in the counter desk and dusting the shelves in the little office at the back of reception. Visitors came and went, and it was a nice change to meet guests who were not completely exhausted. The night shift didn't always bring out the best in people.

Ten o'clock ticked by. As did ten-thirty. I was on the verge of ringing Needledick and demanding he get his lazy ass into the hotel when he raced through the door.

"I'm sorry. I slept through my first alarm." He looked as if he'd showered because of his wet, slicked back hair, but he still hadn't bothered to shave.

"I'm glad you had a sleep."

"Thanks to you."

"Okay, I'll see you later." I practically raced away.

Rather than head to my room, I decided to go straight to the shops. As I strode out the doors and down the front steps a taxi arrived to offload guests, and in a snap decision, I took it to Pacific Fair Shopping Centre.

My stomach grumbled for the entire ten-minute trip, and as soon as I got out of the car I went in search of breakfast. I settled at Cafe Cherry Beans and chose a table that allowed me to people-watch as I ate a bacon and egg roll and sipped a cappuccino.

Crowd-watching had become one of my favorite pastimes and soon I was playing a little game of trying to guess the marital status and occupation of any man that didn't have a woman on his arm. It was a fun way to kill thirty minutes.

Then, with my tummy full, I headed toward Isabella's Passion, the lingerie store Lolita told me I just 'had to go to'. It was on the ground floor on the way toward Myer.

Crowds were not usually my thing. Maybe it was because I grew up in the country. Today though, I enjoyed being in amongst the throng of shoppers. People-watching was fun. Hunky-man spotting was even more so. And the Gold Coast offered an abundant selection of choices. Men in all states of fitness patronized the busy center, and I tried not to be too obvious as I checked them out.

It felt good to be out and about. I spend way too much time just lazing around my apartment. When I wasn't fooling around on one of my secret rendezvous, that was. I chuckled at that thought.

In amongst the thousands of people walking around Pacific Fair Shopping Centre, I was nobody. But put me in my sexy Memphis disguise and I could be whoever I wanted to be. It was a powerful concept that had me grinning as if I'd had a few tequila shots with my morning coffee.

I passed an optical store, and on impulse, I stopped, turned and walked in. Serendipity Optical was wall-to-wall with all manner of glasses frames. Maybe they had colored contact lenses too. I walked up to the counter and waited for the middle-aged woman with the short, uninteresting haircut to finish her phone call. She smiled at me, held up her index finger and mouthed *one minute*.

I tried on a few frames as I waited.

"Hello, can I help you?" she said as she put the phone down.

"I'm not sure. I'd like to buy colored contact lenses. Do you sell them?"

"Yes we do. I'll show you." She waddled toward one wall and pointed to a shelf of blue boxes.

"We have these Glamour contact lenses. They have an Aztec design that enhances the effect of your iris, giving you a glamorous look. For your green eyes you could wear aqua, blue, gray, honey or violet, which is a bit of fun."

I had no idea this would be so easy. "How much do they cost?"

She picked up one of the boxes. "They're $55 each. You get two lenses per box and they should last you about six months if you look after them properly."

The price shocked me—I thought they'd be so much more expensive. "Great, I'll take all of them."

"Oh." Her eyes bulged in surprise. "Have you used contacts before?"

"No. Are they hard to put in?"

"Most people find the first couple of times a bit fiddly, but after that you'll be an expert. Would you like me to show you?"

"Yes please."

By the time I walked out of the shop I'd managed to put contacts in and take them out of my eyes with success. I'd also bought five pairs of colored contact lenses, eye drops, a lens wash solution, a cute little travel box to store the contacts in, and a pair of sunglasses. She was an excellent saleswoman.

I checked my watch and couldn't believe it was already midday. With a skip in my step I made my way to Isabella's Passion. The second I walked in, a fresh-faced young girl offered to assist me. So, feeling lucky with my first purchase of the day swinging off my arm, I told her what I wanted.

I tried on many brands including Elle McPherson, Goddess and Playful Promises. I tried French knickers, G-strings, boy-leg, full briefs, crotch-less panties and a pair of gold hot pants that would serve as a great Kylie Minogue costume. Within no time I was sold on fifteen or so pairs. Then the lovely Catherina started to bring out the fun stuff. I tried on a Leather and Venice corset that was delightfully wicked and totally sexy at the same time. I added it to my "hell yes, I'm buying it" pile. She brought me tempting teddies and cheeky bustiers, everything from a collection called Sultry Seductress, full-body stockings, and other bits and pieces featuring barely any fabric at all.

I was both impressed and bewildered with the extensive selection. Before I lost an entire day in the lingerie store, I re-dressed and hefted my abundant selection to the counter. When I finally left the store I had four bags of goodies and $674 less in my bank account. As I hadn't bought lingerie since I left my hometown more than three and a half years ago, I wasn't worried. Besides, I was worth it.

Hunger pains dictated my next purchase, and back at the food court I ordered a lamb doner kebab with extra cheese, sour cream and barbeque sauce. As I ate, my head spun over my morning shopping success. Normally shopping was a torture. I could try on fifty things and walk out with nothing. My life really had become amazing.

It was one p.m. before I crawled my weary ass into bed and fell asleep.

* * *

It seemed like only twenty minutes when my alarm sounded at eight p.m. I'd slept like a log and the creases on my cheek were evident even after a long hot shower. Forty-five minutes after I woke up, I headed downstairs to start my night shift.

I hugged Marjorie's boney shoulders to my chest as we said hello. "How was your day?"

She rolled her eyes. "Not too bad, except for the weirdo in the bar."

"Who?" My eyes shot toward the Triple H Bar's entrance but I couldn't see past the doorway.

"This guy came down the elevator at about six o'clock, and asked me if I knew someone named Memphis. He's the second guy to ask that; I'm wondering if she's the hooker John was talking about."

My heart exploded in my chest and, before I oozed into the rubbish bin at my feet, I clutched at the counter top for support. "What hooker?"

"John said he's seen a woman here a couple of times who he thinks is a hooker."

I covered my mouth, feigning shock, and swallowed the enormous lump in my throat. "Why does he think she's a hooker?" I faked naivety.

"She was dressed in a trench coat and long black boots."

As I had thought, he was referring to me. "But it's winter; many women wear boots and a trench coat."

"Oh yeah, I know, but I saw her too. She just walked like one, you know?"

Ummm, no, I didn't. "How does a hooker walk?"

"You know, with the sexy confidence that says 'you can't touch me'. Besides she called him a creep and said her name was Daenerys Targaryen."

I faked a laugh, trying to sound as convincing as possible. "I wish I'd seen that."

Marjorie laughed now too. "It was funny. He was so pissed off."

She reached for her handbag and fished around in it until she removed her car keys.

"So who's the guy in the bar?"

"I don't know, but he's obviously staying here. John must've checked him in."

I wished I had supersonic eyesight right now.

She leaned in to whisper—not that she needed to. "Every twenty minutes or so he leaves the bar, walks around the lobby, goes out the front for a bit, and then heads back to the bar. He's a bit creepy."

My brain went crazy with the options. The mysterious man could be any one of the twenty-two men who'd been touched by Memphis. I had to see who it was.

"Anyway, I'm outta here. The kids are staying at Mom's, so I'm off to the movies with Helen."

As we hugged goodbye I wondered when I'd last been to the movies. The question was only fleeting because as soon as she left I turned my attention to my mysterious stalker.

I had to go see who it was.

Half way toward the bar, the damned phone rang and I raced back to reception. "Welcome to the Hot Horizon Hotel. This is Jane, how can I help you?"

As I went through the motions with the caller to make her booking, a tall man walked out of the bar. His significant height had me instantly recognize him as one of the guys I'd been with, yet somehow he looked different. I couldn't quite work it out. As I tried to talk coherently to the caller, I searched my brain for his name.

He did exactly what Marjorie had said he would. He scanned the lobby and then stepped through the glass sliding doors. He was outside when I finally finished the call. I plucked the check-in cards off the back counter and rummaged through them until I found a name I recognized. David Lawson was one of the first men I'd experienced this year. If my recollection was correct, he'd been incredibly timid and I'd had to practically force him to touch me. Well, not me exactly, but Memphis.

He re-entered through the glass sliding doors and I tried to work out what was different about him. And not just his looks—his demeanor, too. He smiled at me, a broad, welcoming smile and as he tucked his hands into his pockets and strolled toward me, my heart skipped a few beats.

"Good evening." His azure blue eyes were quite spectacular.

"Hello. Can I help you?"

"I hope so. Do you know a woman named Memphis?"

I'd already anticipated his question and was shaking my head before he finished. "No, I'm sorry I don't."

"I met her last time I was here." He sighed a huge sigh. "I was hoping to find her again so I could thank her."

"Thank her?" I blurted it out, unable to curb my curiosity.

"Yeah. It's a long story."

Oh, but I want to hear it.

"Sorry to bother you." He bobbed his head as if burdened with the weight of the world.

"It's no bother, really."

"I'll wait a bit longer. Maybe she'll turn up." He turned and I watched him walk all the way to the Triple H bar with my heart aching. David had been sad when I'd first met him all those weeks ago, but by the end of our bedroom romp he was delightfully happy. I wanted to see him smile again.

He didn't know it yet, but Mr. David Lawson had just declared himself my twenty-third sexy rendezvous.

My mind spun like a roulette wheel as I considered how this was going to play out.

Four times over the course of the next hour, David repeated his reconnaissance. With each appearance he looked more inebriated. *I hope he goes to bed before he completely passes out.*

At eleven-fifteen p.m. David did another round of the lobby. He was fairly unsteady on his feet when he walked past the reception desk.

"Maybe she'll come to you in the morning," I called out to him before he disappeared into the bar.

His eyes shifted to me. "Pardon?"

"I said, maybe this Memphis woman will come by in the morning." I deepened my voice in a lame attempt to disguise it.

He blinked at me, fluttering eyelashes that were as dark as his hair. "Maybe."

"How about you tell me your room number and if she comes in I'll ring you."

His eyes lit up. "Really? You'd do that for me?"

"Of course." Relieved that I could finally help him, I made a show of grabbing the notepad and pen and avoided looking directly at him so he wouldn't see my eyes. "What's your name and room number?"

He strolled up to the counter and I smelt both beer and musky cologne. "I'm David Lawson and I'm in room thirty."

I wrote it down and put the pad on the desk. "Okay then. If she turns up I'll ring you."

He nodded and looked like he was ready to fall asleep right there on the countertop. "Thank you."

After a brief unsteady wobble, he headed toward the elevator and within a minute he was gone.

As the night rolled into the early hours of the morning, I was consumed with the question of what David wanted to thank Memphis for. Our last rendezvous hadn't culminated in anything spectacular. Well, that wasn't exactly true—it was out-of-this-world-spectacular for me. I remembered standing above him, allowing him to watch as I did things to myself that I'd never done before. Just the thought of it had my insides curling. David, however, had remained fully clothed and for most of our encounter had looked completely petrified.

Maybe he wanted to show me another side to him. I was so ready for that.

The second Needledick arrived to take over my shift, I shot up to my room and into the shower. I pictured David in his white button-up shirt with the top button undone and wondered what delightful things he had beneath that clothing for me to explore.

I applied my makeup, and as I ran my favorite electric blue eyeliner along my eyelid, I realized I had a dilemma. David might remember Memphis had green eyes. And after talking to me several times last night, he could recognize my eyes too. The question was, should I wear my new contact lenses or not? On one hand, his encounter with Memphis was eighteen weeks ago, so there was a good chance he wouldn't remember her eye color. On the other hand, he'd had a bit to drink last night, so he possibly wouldn't recall my eyes.

Deciding not to, I applied elaborate shades of blue eye shadow and lashings of mascara to hopefully detract from my green irises as much as possible. Finishing my makeup, I tugged on the trusty black wig that came with the French maid costume. That was how David would remember Memphis.

I considered wearing the French maid costume for all of about six seconds before I decided on something a little less flamboyant. I chose my rose red halter-neck dress that I'd worn the day I'd lost my casual sex virginity to the gorgeous geek with the wonderful soft hands. I chuckled at the memory as I tipped out my entire assortment of new underwear onto the bed.

Normally I'd wash the new underwear before I wore them, but this was an emergency.

I chose a red G-string that just about matched the color of my dress. I couldn't wear a bra with this outfit, but that was okay—I was actually beginning to like the feel of boob-wobble when in Memphis mode.

I matched the dress with a pair of black and white patterned strappy heels that I'd never worn. Another positive about my raunchy escapades was that all my unworn pairs of shoes were finally getting a memory to go with them.

After a quick glance in the mirror, I applied a slick of Mac Chili Red lipstick. The black hair and red dress contrasted beautifully. I smiled, smiled some more, blew myself a kiss and then grabbed my bag and headed to my six-foot stranger waiting for me two floors up.

As I rode the painfully slow elevator alone, I jiggled on my toes, testing my boob wobble in the mirror. This simple little move that used to horrify me gave me a lovely thrill of freedom. My life had changed in so many ways this year and it was getting better and better.

I strode to David's room without any trepidation. After all, he was waiting for me.

At his door I rubbed my lips together, smoothing out my lippy one last time, then knocked twice.

I heard a crash of something and within two seconds the door opened.

David was practically gasping for breath in the open doorway. "Oh my god, Memphis, you came."

I looked up at him, once again surprised by his height. "Hi David. May I come in?"

"Yes. Yes." He stepped aside and I eased past him, strode to the table, flung my bag over the back of the chair, and turned his way.

As he ran his fingers through his thick dark hair, the door clicked closed. "I never thought I'd see you again."

I cupped my hands in front of me, acting coy. "You were wrong."

David wore a navy long-sleeved linen shirt with white buttons and a pair of khaki chinos. He looked so much more stylish than the last time I'd seen him.

"You look different," I said.

A giant grin lit up his face. "It's because of you. After we . . . were together, I felt like I could walk on water. I've lost weight. My sisters took me shopping for clothes and I shaved off my mustache."

The mustache. *That's right.* That's what was so different. His mustache would've given Tom Selleck a run for his money. "You look really good." I became caught up in his enthusiasm and grinned.

"Thank you."

I wriggled my eyebrows and stepped right up to him, placing my hands on his chest. "Mmmm, you have been working out."

"I've joined a gym and I go four times a week." His voice faltered as I undid a couple of buttons on his shirt.

"You changed me, Memphis, in ways you'll never know."

"Mmmm." He sure was chatty. If my memory served me right, he was practically speechless last time I was this close to him. I tugged his shirt open and was surprised to see a silver chain with a black crystal dangling between his superbly defined pectoral muscles.

"What have we here?"

His Adam's apple bobbed up and down. "My sister bought it for me. It's meant to bring good luck."

I ran my hands up his chest. "Is it working?"

He nodded and swallowed loudly.

I smelt both toothpaste and his musky deodorant as I leaned forward and ran my tongue over his nipple. David drew in a breath, and his entire body tensed as I dug my fingers into either side of his torso and flitted my tongue from his left nipple to his right.

"Mmmm, you taste yummy."

He gripped my shoulders. "Oh god, Memphis, stop."

I stepped back and blinked up at him.

"Sorry, but I'd like to ask a favor."

I frowned as twenty questions flitted through my brain in a nanosecond. "Okay."

He grabbed my hand and pulled me to the bed so we sat side by side. With his fingers driven between his knees, he clenched his jaw, and I began to fear what this favor may be.

I placed my hand on his knee and he flinched.

"Sorry. It's just . . . I get so nervous around women."

"I can see that. Just relax."

"That's just it. I've . . . I've . . . oh god." He closed his eyes, and as he rolled his head back to the ceiling his Adam's apple bobbed up and down again.

I squeezed his thigh. "It's okay; you can tell me anything. We're complete strangers and I won't judge you." All of a sudden I was a psychologist and it felt so right.

He huffed out a breath. "I had sex."

I just about burst out laughing, but resisted and patted his leg instead. "Fantastic."

"Twice," he blurted.

"Look at you go, you sexy devil. I bet it was good."

"Well you see that's the problem. I was . . . I was too quick and the poor ladies . . . I, I—"

"Do you want me to teach you some things you can do for them?"

"Yes." He turned to me. His eyes dazzled in the morning sun. "Would you?"

God, I love being Memphis. I stood up and eased my knees between his. With my hands on his cheeks, I drew his eyes to mine. "I'm going to show you a couple of moves that'll have women lining up."

He gasped for breath and I leaned down to kiss him. My world tilted into a blaze of lust as our lips met. This was the first man I'd wanted to kiss since my fiancé had cheated on me and I was so ready. His lips were supple and soft. As I tilted my head, I parted my lips, letting him know he could explore and his tongue entered my mouth. I tasted peppermint as our tongues moved in an exquisite tango. I drove my fingers through his thick hair and as our breathing became fervid I pushed my tongue into his mouth, wanting to taste more of him.

Remembering my role as teacher before I got too carried away, I eased back, cupped his hands again and watched as the erotic haze ebbed from his eyes. "You're an incredible kisser."

He blinked. "Really?"

"Start with that and you'll make a woman wild."

I turned my back to him and raised my hair above the knot of my halter-neck. "Undo my dress please." His fingers were delicate feathers on my neck and soon the dress fell over my breasts to stop at my waist.

Stepping forward, I kept my back to David. "Stand up and curl your arms around to cup my breasts."

The warmth of his chest caressed my back as his hands curled under my breasts. My nipples were already rising to his touch. I ran my finger up and down my neck. "You can kiss me all along here."

His breathing increased as his lips trailed little kisses from my ear to the base of my neck and back again. I cupped my hands over his, showing him how hard he could squeeze by boob. He was a quick learner and soon my knees were close to buckling with the sensation. A groan tumbled from his throat and I leaned my head back, offering him all of my neck.

"Squeeze my nipples."

David was an excellent pupil and followed my instructions without hesitation.

Fumbling for the zip at the side of my dress, I undid it and when the fabric fell to my feet, I kicked it aside.

Wearing nothing but my skimpy thong and sexy heels, I grabbed his right hand and trailed it over my body and into my G-string. A delicious shudder rolled through me at his very first touch. Guiding his finger beneath mine, I showed him how to apply pressure to my clitoris. Together we rolled our fingers around and then pressed down on my now very sensitive bud.

Our breathing became erratic, and David's hand delved lower of its own accord. His long arms afforded him excellent reach and as his lips continued to travel up and down my neck, one hand squeezed my nipple and manipulated my breast while his right index finger plunged deep into my pulsing hole. His ability to concentrate on all three areas was exceptional.

For me it was sensation overload and my insides begged for release. From this angle, each time he glided his fingers into my pussy they rubbed over my clitoris, drawing out every inch of my lust.

"Faster," I urged.

And as David plunged my throbbing depths, I bent my knees, giving him more. He moaned and his hot breath on my neck had me gasping as I tipped over the edge and let my orgasm overtake my body and mind. Waves of ecstasy shuddered through me as David continued his onslaught until I was completely exhausted.

I twisted out of his embrace and placed my hands on his chest. "Wow. Just wow."

His smile was glorious. "Really?"

"Yes, really." I glanced down at his groin to admire the bulge in his pants. "I see you're still with me."

He nodded, clearly pleased with himself. "Can you show me something else?"

I wiggled my eyebrows, delighted with the prospect. "I have an idea." I peeled off his shirt and tossed it aside, then I grabbed his hand and led him to the kitchen counter.

"Hang on a sec." My wet G-string felt very unsexy and I stepped out of it and tossed it aside. "Sorry about that."

"Don't be sorry. You're amazing."

I cupped his cheek. "Thank you. Now place your hands on my hips and help me onto the counter."

He did as he was asked and I spread my legs apart and indicated with my finger for him to step forward. Once he was close enough I wrapped my legs around him and locked my ankles, trapping him in my deviant lair. I nearly giggled at that thought, but the serious expression on his face stopped me.

"David."

"Yes."

"You're meant to be enjoying this, but you look like you're doing a math exam."

"Oh, sorry. I'm . . . I'm—"

"Would you like to taste me?" I diverted his attention with expert skill.

He nodded and his cock bounced in his belted pants.

I unlocked my ankles, placed my palms on the counter and eased back, thrusting my breasts out. Thankfully I didn't have to instruct him and he leaned forward. His lips latched onto my breast and drew the nipple into his mouth. "You can roll my nipple with your teeth, but be very gentle."

As I scraped my nails through his scalp, David pleasured my breasts. And what a pleasure it was. My nipples grew rock hard and as they begged for more of his attention, my clit pulsed out its own needy signal.

I braced on one hand and reached for his. With his hand in mine, I guided him to my pussy and as he plunged my hot abyss, I rubbed my clit. I grinded my finger over and over, each time pressing down harder. He plunged in and out, first with one finger, then two, thrusting out an urgent beat.

I flopped back onto the counter and lifted my ankles onto his shoulders so my stilettos framed his neck. His expression was a curious one. Maybe he was expecting an invitation.

I obliged by parting my knees, showing him all there was of me. His clenched jaw and quick inhale confirmed he liked what he saw. I nodded, giving him a silent go-ahead. David bent forward and ran his hot tongue up my pussy.

It was quick. Shocking. And fucking awesome.

His tongue was an inferno, slick and hard too, as it glided up and down my velvet folds and around my clit. Suddenly his finger was in me. Then there were two, prodding something deep inside that had my insides clenching every time he touched it. There was no pain, just mind-blowing pleasure.

He licked me up and down, and the heat of his tongue drove exquisite shudders through me. I raised my hips, giving him a new angle to play with, then reached down and used my own hands to rub myself.

My insides squeezed around his fingers, trying to trap them in my core.

He pulled his head back, and as his body shuddered, his eyes rolled and he licked his lips. Realizing that he'd tipped over the edge, something detonated deep inside me, ripping through me with a powerful tremor. I squeezed my knees shut, trapping his hand. Unable to move and gasping for breath, I rode out the glorious sensations thundering through my body.

It was a long while before whatever gripped me let go and my muscles eased. My breathing was still erratic, as was David's. I lowered my legs to the counter and sat up.

"That was amazing. You were amazing."

He leaned on the counter. Maybe for support. "Thank you. For everything."

"You're welcome. It was fun. Remember, David, sex *should* be fun. For both people."

He nodded, all serious again. "Excuse me for a minute."

While David disappeared into the bathroom, I jumped off the counter and re-dressed without bothering to put my wet G-string on. I was curling my bag over my shoulder when he returned.

"I'm so lucky to have found you," he said.

"Actually, I think it was I who found you." I reached up to kiss his cheek. "Now go and satisfy those women, David."

He laughed. "Okay."

I made my way to his door.

"Wait. How do I find you again?"

"Nothing in life is a certainty. If it's meant to be, it will happen." With that crazy comment echoing in my brain, I walked out his door. All of a sudden I was both a psychologist and a prophet. Life had become a complex riddle. Back in my room, I removed my makeup and wig and had a long, hot shower. Afterwards I sat on the bed, grabbed my diary and turned to the 1st of June. At the top I wrote *Mr. David Lawson, Room 30* and, as I thought about how much he'd changed since our last encounter, I wrote *My Raunchy Revival.*

I found it interesting to discover how many men were insecure about sex. All my life I'd assumed that men would just know what they were doing. I guessed to some degree they did, but really, many men only knew what pleased them. It was just as important that I showed them what I wanted. If I found the man of my dreams, he was going to be quickly educated on what pleased me. No, not if I found my man. When I found my man.

Closing the diary, I put it and my pen aside, pulled back the covers, curled onto my side, and pulled the sheet up to my neck. My body ebbed into relaxation as I inhaled deep, relaxing breaths.

As I remembered David's lovely soft lips threading up and down my neck, I drifted off to sleep.

8TH JUNE
A DATE WITH DOCTOR EXOTIC
Room 22 – Hot Horizon Hotel

A trickle of sweat rolled down my temple as I eased onto the mat for my standard core-strength routine. I counted my push-ups in my head, working my way to fifty.

"How many doctors are there?"

Lolita was the only person I knew who could talk through an entire workout, no matter how tough it was. "There are two hundred and twenty booked for the conference. And they're not just doctors, they're plastic surgeons."

She sucked in a breath and I'm pretty sure it wasn't from exertion, even though she slammed out push-ups at a frightening pace. "They're the best kind. How many men?"

"About one hundred and eighty."

"Jesus, it's a fucking smorgasbord. Literally." She burst out laughing as she rolled onto her back for fifty sit-ups.

"Most of them will probably be married."

"Yes, but all the single women in the world are counting on you to fish out those who are aren't."

I finished my push-ups and laughed as I followed Lolita's lead and rolled onto my back.

She crawled to me, and holding her hand as if it were a microphone, she spoke into it. "Do you, Jane Nichols, promise to fuck a random stranger tonight?"

"Lolly!" I gasped, and looked at the sweaty men positioned around the gym. Both Dean and Oliver, two of the Tuesday regulars, stopped their routines and grinned at us.

Lolita poked my ribs. "Is that a yes?"

"Yes. Yes," I spoke into her pretend microphone, giggling.

"Good." She laid on her back again and raised her straightened legs at a forty-five-degree angle. "Oh my God." She turned her head to me, and by the bulge in her eyes I feared what she was about to say.

"What?"

"You need to get a nurse uniform. Holy shit that'd be a hoot." She wiggled her head. "A little doctors-and-nurses action to spice up your challenge."

"Stop it, you crazy woman."

"I want pictures." She rolled to her side and started leg raises. "And I don't mean of you. I want to see him. Or them, if you decide to do more than one."

I rolled my eyes. "There won't be more than one."

"Yeah, yeah. Famous last words from a sexual deviant."

I pouted. "I'm not a—"

"Jane! I'm fucking with you. You know I'm just jealous."

"No, you're not. We've been through this."

Her eyes bulged again. "Oh shit. I have a great idea. Let's go to the costume shop together. We'll both get naughty nurse outfits." She jumped to her feet and reached for my hand. Obviously, the decision had been made. "Come on."

After I was hurled to a standing position she practically hustled me out of the gym.

My complaints were bound to be useless, but I decided to try nonetheless. "But I'm all sweaty."

"You look fine."

"I'm hungry, too; you know how much I love my coffee and cake after our workout."

We dodged the traffic to cross the road to her Jeep Cherokee. "This is an emergency, and emergencies call for sacrifice."

I hopped into her car and buckled up, fearful Lolly was about to catapult me through the bustling Gold Coast traffic. "Ummm, why is this an emergency?"

"Calvin's going on his two-day golfing trip." She screwed up her face at me like I should know the implications of her statement.

I frowned at her. "Annnnd?"

"I need to buy this sexy little nurse outfit and get back home to fuck his brains out before he leaves. God damn, I'm getting all horny just thinking about it."

I help up my hand. "Way too much information."

She gunned the car through a yellow light. "Ha, now you get a taste of what I go through every Tuesday."

I huffed. "I could stop telling you."

"Like hell you will. You're living my ultimate fantasy, babe, and I live for your sex stories."

I tried to ignore my growling stomach as we joined the throng of cars heading into Pacific Fair Shopping Centre. By some miracle of God, Lolita managed to snag a parking spot right out the front of the main entrance. I swear she did that nearly every time we went shopping together. The woman was a freak.

I felt utterly gross walking amongst the shoppers in my sweaty gym gear, but Lolita strutted along, with her perky boobs bobbing above her fluro-green Lycra top like she was the queen of the shopping center.

Costumes on the Coast was empty except for the lovely Asian woman behind the counter who'd served me a few times before. The quiet store was a complete contrast to the last time I was here. Then again, my prior visit coincided with the Supanova conference, so the craziness had been expected.

"Hi." Lolita didn't waste a second in approaching the staff member. "We're after a couple of sexy nurse uniforms. What've you got?"

The diminutive Asian woman clicked her fingers, rose from her chair and we followed her down one of the side aisles. "I have a few choices for you sexy ladies." She paused halfway along.

She handed me a white dress, which, based on the miniscule amount of fabric, was barely a dress at all. "This is perfect for you."

Lolita grinned at me as if the decision to buy it had already been made.

"And this"—the Asian woman handed a second dress to Lolita—"is for you. Now go, try on, you will see I'm right." She pointed to the back of the shop.

Lolita didn't hesitate. She turned and wiggled her non-existent ass all the way to the change room. I followed her and stepped into the cubicle beside hers.

"Oh, this is going to be so much fun." Lolly's high-pitched exclamation was that of a teenage girl on prom night.

Her enthusiasm was a living, breathing thing, and I was quickly swept up in it. I wrestled my gym top off but left my sweaty Lycra pants on. The nurse uniform had a zip that went from hem to cleavage, little cap sleeves, and a plunging neckline. It was white, but every edge was trimmed in red to match the red cross on the fake breast pocket.

I undid the zip, weaved my arm in, curled it around my back, put my other arm in and tugged the front together. It was going to be a tight fit. But, like all these costumes, it was designed for a variety of body sizes, so it stretched to fit. I hooked the zip together at the bottom and glided it up.

It sure was tight, but it did do up, and damn, if it wasn't as sexy as hell. The dress was extremely short, and I turned to check out my ass. I bent over and lucky for me, I was wearing my gym shorts, because as expected, my ass was in full view. The display picture that went with the costume showed a woman with white fishnet stockings and knee-length boots. The sexy combination looked amazing. So amazing, in fact, that I instantly decided I'd do a bit more shopping before the morning was done.

Lolita burst out laughing. "Holy guacamole, this is fucking fabbo."

"Show me." I stepped out of my cubicle, and she did the same from hers.

We burst out laughing at each other. "Shit babe, you look hot," she said.

"You do too." Lolita's dress was a perfect combination of cute and sexy. Her breasts bulged over the plunging cleavage. It pulled in at her tiny waist and then curved out to a skirt that was plumped up with layers of lace. "How cute is this?" she squealed. "Cal's going to blow his stack just looking at me."

She twirled around, fluffing up the skirt as she went. "Right." She stepped back into her cubicle. "I need to get home asap."

She was so excited I couldn't help but be happy for her. "I'm going to stay and see if I can find boots and fishnets to go with this costume."

"Oooh, good idea. Wish I could stay, babe, but—"

"It's okay, I get it. He's more important than me."

"Oh no, it's not like that."

"Lolly, I'm joking."

We stepped out, redressed in our gym gear again, and she put her arm around me. "You really are changing, and I like what I see," she said.

We paid for the costumes, and outside the store we said our goodbyes. After Lolita left, the first thing I did was head toward the smell of bacon that'd had my stomach growling from the second I'd entered the shopping center.

I stopped at the first coffee shop I encountered, ordered a cappuccino in a mug and a bacon and egg muffin, and then settled at one of the tables out the front. As I watched the people walk past, my thoughts drifted to Lolita and Calvin. Their love for each other was always present, even when they were apart.

I wanted a relationship like that.

I wanted to feel the simple thrill of holding a man's hand knowing that I'd go to bed in his arms that night. I wanted to be so in love that every time we separated I felt as if my heart would split in two. And I wanted to have the best sex in the world. The kind of sex that only two people who were so completely committed to each other could have. *Was that too much to ask for?* No. I decided it wasn't. I'd seen that kind of love in Lolly and Cal.

I wasn't being greedy. There was nothing wrong with creating a wish list.

My breakfast and coffee arrived, and as I ate and watched the anonymous people walk past, I considered what else I'd have on my wish list.

I'd want my man to be able to laugh freely. And enjoy the outdoors, and know how to cook and clean and choose the best wine. I'd like him to have a sound financial situation but be comfortable with me adding to our wealth creation. He'd need to want to travel, and eat interesting food, and take on the occasional heart-pounding rollercoaster.

He would also need to be able to show his affection freely. Ryan, the man I'd had the sneaky relationship with in my late teens, couldn't wait to get away from me after we'd had sex. And my cheating bastard ex-fiancé, Alexander, well, when I looked back now, it was like he was embarrassed to even hold my hand. I'd been a fool.

I wasn't a fool anymore. I was a woman who wouldn't take second best ever again.

It was only once I'd finished the last piece of crispy bacon that I realized my wish list didn't have any attributes that dictated what my man should look like. Clearly, his looks weren't as important as everything else. Which was interesting, because every one of my Memphis conquests had been chosen solely on their looks. "Hmmm," I mumbled under my breath. Maybe I should revisit my list later.

I finished my coffee and headed toward my favorite shoe store, Wittner. Shoe shopping was my kind of therapy.

"Hi Jane." One of the staff members greeted me with a huge smile. The staff always seemed so happy to see me.

It took me about five seconds to scan the latest trends, but despite their extensive collection of winter boots, they didn't have any white ones. They did, however, have a red pair. My spirits raised as I lifted the display shoe off the top shelf. It was divine soft leather and the heel was an acceptable six inches.

"Hi Jane." Stefanie, one of the junior staff members, sidled up beside me.

"Hi Stef. I have to have these; tell me you have them in my size."

"They've just come in, so we should." She disappeared through a back doorway.

I sat on the cushioned leather chair and undid the laces on my gym shoes. Rebecca returned holding a white box like it was the Holy Grail. The boots were expertly crafted leather masterpieces. I zipped them up and walked to the mirror. Everything about them was perfect. I didn't even bother looking at the price. I was worth it.

After the shoe purchase I raced up to Myer and scoured the department store for the intimate apparel section. The extensive range of hosiery was spectacular, and it took me a while to make a choice. In the end, I selected a pair of thigh-high white patterned stockings that stayed in place thanks to a broad, patterned elastic at the top. I bought a couple of other stockings too, but they were all black.

With my purchases hanging off my arm, I headed toward the taxi rank and within fifteen minutes I was back in my apartment. After I hung my nurse outfit on the hook outside my wardrobe, I took a long, hot shower.

It was already 11.15a.m. when I crawled into bed and set the alarm for six o'clock. Sleep didn't come easily though as my brain flicked around imaginary pictures of me in a nurse uniform with a hot naked guy kneeling before me, ready to perform whatever medical miracle I demanded. After rolling around for about for half an hour, I turned on the television, found a re-run of Friends and laughed along at the jokes that I'd probably heard three or four times before.

I woke to a siren, and it took me a while to work out it was the television. Annoyed at myself, I glanced at the clock, and was shocked that the alarm was just ten minutes off waking me anyway.

My neck was a bit sore from Lolita's punishing workout this morning, and I rolled my head from side to side as I crawled out of bed and walked to the bathroom. I showered, washed my hair, and did a face scrub, tone, and cleanse. My skin just wasn't used to all the makeup Memphis wore.

Loud voices drifting up from below caught my attention. I tugged on my bathrobe and glanced over the verandah to see a bunch of men come out of the hotel. The sun had set more than an hour ago, but the lights dotted along the walking path highlighted the way. They were dressed to go out in lounge suits and swanky shoes, and based on their boisterous laughter, they were in for a fun night.

As they disappeared into the distance, I wondered if one of them would need a nurse later. I giggled at that thought and then stood up and walked inside to make some dinner.

Fifteen minutes before my shift was due to start, I made my way downstairs to the lobby. Marjorie was almost hidden behind the reception counter as she tapped away on the computer.

"Hey Marj, how's your day?"

"Oh Jane." She sighed. "I'm bloody exhausted."

I frowned at her. "Are you okay?"

"Yeah. Sammy had me up all night, vomiting. Fortunately, Mom looked after her today while she was home from school."

I tutted. "Aww, that's not good."

"I feel like I could sleep for a week. Hopefully she's better by now."

"Well off you go then. Hopefully you'll have a better night."

"Thanks." She grabbed her bag and disappeared through the glass sliding door, leaving me to the peace of the large marble expanse.

It was a Tuesday night, and as expected, it was quiet. By eleven o'clock, I'd finished all my usual duties; by one a.m. I was bored out of my brain. I grabbed the check-in cards and for a bit of fun, I laid them out on the counter. First, I shuffled out all the women. Then, with the driver's licenses my main focus, I tried to work out which of the men were married. The license photos were terrible, not only were they grainy and weathered, but there wasn't one smile amongst them, which was to be expected I guess, given that you're not supposed to smile for a license photo. In the end, my experiment was pointless.

The glass doors glided open, and the rowdy mob tumbling into the foyer were the same men who'd left the hotel before I'd even started my shift. They were as happy as they were loud, hanging off each other's shoulders and tripping over each other's feet. I found myself smiling at their frivolity.

"Well hello." One of the guys with stylish blond hair and a neatly trimmed beard headed toward me. He sprawled his hands across the marble counter. "What's your name?" He had lovely long fingers and no ring. My stomach did a little flutter at how supple his hands were, and his nails were perfectly trimmed. Hands were quickly becoming important to me.

The blue of his eyes caught my attention, like a moth to a flame. "I'm Jane." I barely managed to speak.

"Hi Jane. I'm Mike, pleased to meet you." More like Magic Mike. He held his hand forward and when I reached for it, he grasped my fingers in his and kissed the back of my knuckles. I wanted to fan myself like an old-fashioned movie heroine.

"Hey Mike, you're not annoying the lady, are you?" A second man joined Mike, and I just about passed out with his beauty. He had to be a model. *Tell me he's a model.* His eyes were the color of the outgoing tide and his olive skin screamed mixed exotic cultures. And his teeth—oh my God, dazzling perfection. I swallowed, hardly able to believe my eyes as two of the sexiest men to ever talk to me actually talked to me.

"I'm not annoying you, am I?" Mike's smile was an equal match to his friend's.

I shook my head. "No."

"He's always annoying."

"No I'm not."

The second man placed his hands on the counter. He did have a ring, however the chunky gold square with the black stone in the middle was on his right hand.

I'd officially fallen into heaven. A heatwave coursed through me and as a tidal wave of opportunities flooded my horny brain, I was certain I'd be bright red in a flash. I needed to focus on them, not my quivering insides.

The rest of the men disappeared in the elevator, leaving me alone with the two hotties. I cleared my throat. "Are you here for the conference?"

"Yes."

"Yep."

Their smiles were sex magnets. *Holy smokes.* "Are you both doctors?"

"Yep."

"Yes."

Oh God. Tie me up and spank me now.

Doctor Exotic put his hands on Mike's shoulders. "Come on, buddy, we've got an early start tomorrow."

I bit my tongue, fearful I'd say something stupid, like "I'm not wearing any panties".

Mike screwed up his face. "Oh yeah, I forgot about that." He peeled his hands off the counter. "Bye Jane."

"Bye." *For now.*

They turned, and with their arms over each other's shoulders, they headed toward the elevator. "Whose idea was it to go for a run before breakfast anyway?" Mike grumbled.

"Dominic, of course. You know what he's like."

"Yeah, fucking showoff."

They burst out laughing as the elevator arrived. Once they disappeared, I picked my chin up off the counter and collapsed into the office chair.

"Holy shit." I wiped my lip for fear I may have dribbled.

My eyes fell on the check-in cards still laid out across the counter, and like a crazy woman, I fished through them, searching for my two doctors.

My brain had vacated the building and my libido was in charge. I found Mike first. Mike Sexton. Ton of sex appeal more like it. The driver's license of the second man didn't do him any justice. His skin was so much more heavenly than the insipid photo. Doctor Exotic was in fact Maxwell Bradford. "Well hello, Doctor Bradford."

I shuffled all the other cards back into alphabetical order and sat with my two lovely suitors on the counter. After my shift tomorrow, one of these men was going to be my twenty-fourth conquest. But how to choose? Both were suitable for about a thousand reasons. I glanced at the clock. It was two a.m. and way too late to ring Lolita. I giggled at the conversation we'd have.

Maybe I could flip a coin? I reached for my purse and plucked out a fifty-cent piece. Head for Maxwell. I giggled at that. Tails for Mike. Mike and Maxwell—they sounded like some kind of male review duo. I tossed the coin in the air. Tails landed facing upward. Mike was the victor. He had a lovely trimmed beard. I'd never been with a guy with a beard before. But then I thought of Maxwell's gorgeous olive hands and pictured them on my breasts, and I tossed the coin again. Heads landed this time. Head for Maxwell. My insides squirmed as I pictured me in my sexy little nurse uniform and his gorgeous hands all over me.

As I twirled their check-in cards around, I revisited our conversation, trying to work out which one of them appealed to me more than the other. There were so many boxes being ticked that my head began swimming, and my insides started curling. I sat up in my seat as I recalled the last thing they'd said before they'd disappeared. They had to get up early for a run.

"Oh shit." That could be before I even finished my shift. "Shit," I repeated. The lobby was quiet. Before those guys arrived, I hadn't seen anyone since eleven p.m. and since then I hadn't seen anyone. Most nights I didn't. Adrenalin coursed through me, and my heart galloped as I committed to doing the irrational. But I couldn't help it. Could I really leave reception again? The idea gripped me as if it were a muscle-bound soldier.

The last time I'd vacated my post, I was caught. But this was once-in-a-lifetime stuff. I may never have this opportunity again. Was it worth the risk? "Hell yes."

With my heart in marathon mode, I put the "back in five minutes" sign on the counter, practically ran to the elevator and jabbed the button several times. As I waited for it to open, I scanned the lobby. Then I remembered the last time I'd got caught and how Needledick's name and phone number were on the emergency contact notice out the front.

I raced to the sliding doors, tore the sign off the glass and ripped it in half. Problem solved. But I had to leave my number. With my fingers trembling from lust-loaded adrenalin, I pounded the keyboard, opening a Microsoft Word document, and in giant letters I wrote: *In case of emergency call Jane Nichols* and listed my cell phone number.

As I waited for it to print, the elevator I'd ordered before arrived and the door dinged open and closed again before I finally had my printout. I grabbed it and the sticky tape and literally ran to the front door. The damn tape rolled around my finger twice before I managed to stick the new sign to the glass.

With that done, I raced back to the elevator. The doors opened immediately this time and I jumped in and jabbed the button to my floor a million times before the doors closed and the elevator rose. As I waited out the eternity for the doors to open, my brain swirled over which doctor I'd go to. Would it be Magic Mike or Doctor Exotic? Nicely trimmed beard or eyes the color of the outgoing tide?

As I debated the pros and pros of each doctor I tugged my hair out of its bun, wrestled my shirt from my skirt, and undid a couple of buttons. If anyone saw me now, they may think I'd already had a horny romp.

With time at a premium, I forfeited the shower, stripped off, and went straight to the mirror to ply on my makeup. Then, with eyeliner in place and mascara on, a sudden horrible thought gripped me. As Mike and Maxwell had only just spoken to me, there was every chance they'd recognize my eyes.

I had no choice but to use my new colored contact lenses. With trembling fingers, I tore open the pack for the blue contacts.

As the lady in the shop had instructed, I balanced the disk on the tip of my finger, pulled down my lower eyelid, and as I held my breath, guided it in. The second it touched my eyeball, I winced and blinked. When I opened my eye, I found the folded up disk dangling from my mascara-clad lashes.

"Shit." I plucked it off and placed it back into the small pod of solution it came with.

I gripped the counter and glared at my reflection. "Calm down, you horny bitch."

After a couple of deep breaths, I tried again. My breath caught in my throat as the lens neared my eyeball again, and then suddenly it was on. I blinked at my reflection.

"Holy shit. I did it."

I was surprised at how comfortable it was. The left eye contact went in without a hitch and I stared at myself in the mirror. The transformation was so stunning, I grinned.

I tugged on the red wig, deciding it was the obvious choice with my flashy new red boots. As I picked through my vast new collection of lingerie, the cheeky little thought I'd had downstairs when the two men were in front of me flashed through my mind. My heart was set to explode as I made the outrageous decision not to wear any underwear.

Giggling like a schoolgirl, I pulled on the patterned stockings, securing them at the tops of my thighs, then slipped into the nurse uniform and zipped up the front. I turned my backside to the mirror, bent over a fraction, and gasped. My cheeks were in full view. There was no need to bend over any further; I could already imagine what else would be on show. I covered my mouth with my hands and peeked at my reflection through my fingers. Gradually, I straightened up and removed my hands as I realized this was just perfect.

"Memphis, you've outdone yourself."

After I zipped up my new red boots, I grabbed a big red bag that I'd bought at the sales last Christmas and shoved my phone into the side pocket, along with a condom, and a twenty-dollar bill. With my survival kit in place, I put on my trench coat, swung my bag over my arm and went in search of one of my doctors.

As I waited for the elevator, I utilized my time to decide which man I'd go to. By the time the elevator opened, I'd made my decision.

When I arrived at his door, I removed my trench coat, draped it over my arm and fiddled with my boobs to make sure they were in place. With one last deep breath, I knocked. The hall was silent as I waited for my sexy doctor. I was just about to knock again when the door opened. It took all my might not to let my jaw hit the floor. Maxwell had been smoking hot in his clothes, but in the white, hotel-supplied bath robe, he'd hit the top of the Sexiest Man Alive list.

A smile curled on his mouth, and he wriggled his eyebrows. "Hello."

"Hi." I made a show of running my eyes over his glorious body. "I heard there was a doctor in the house."

He chuckled. "Yes, me and about two hundred others."

"Well, Doctor, I have an emergency."

He swallowed loud enough for me to hear. "You'd better come in then."

He stepped aside, and it took all my might not to drive my hands into his robe and feel his sculpted torso. The heels of my boots sunk into the carpet as I crossed the room and tossed my bag and jacket over the chair. When the door shut, I turned to him and paused with my fingers on the zip at my bust. I ran my tongue over my lips as I ogled the most handsome man I'd ever seen.

"So . . . what's this emergency?"

"I have a problem."

"Mmmm."

My clitoris actually pulsed when that rumbling sound hummed in his throat. "I'm horny, and I hate to be alone when I'm horny." Those words had become my best friends. And right now, with just one zipper between me being naked with Doctor Exotic, I was so glad I'd discovered them.

"Well, you're not alone anymore."

"Thank God." I glided my zipper down, gradually exposing my nakedness underneath. I paused just below my bust. "Oh no. I think the zipper's stuck."

Maxwell rubbed his hands together and stepped toward me. "Let me see."

He ran his tongue over his lips as he closed the distance between us. His wonderfully soft hands cupped my neck and cheeks, and his eyes revealed ravishing desire as he guided me in for a kiss. Our lips met, and I melted into a wonderful world of pleasure. When I parted my lips, our breaths entwined and our tongues performed a delightful dance, tasting, probing with equal intensity.

I reached for his torso, seeking out all the exquisite muscles beneath the robe. His nipples were hard pebbles that I pinched between my fingers. Our kiss deepened as he found the zipper at my cleavage and rolled it down my body. As the dress eased apart, the tingles already coursing through me hit electric mode as I waited for the moment when he realized I was naked beneath.

He pulled back and when his eyes lowered, I witnessed that delightful reaction. His eyes bulged, his pupils widened, and his lips parted. Movement between the split in the bathrobe was unmissable, and I reached for the bulge that rapidly grew. He moaned at my touch, a deep, guttural moan that rumbled from his chest and off his lips.

Suddenly, he pulled my zip all the way down, and once I eased it back over my shoulders the dress fell from my body. I stood before Doctor Exotic wearing nothing but knee high red boots and stockings. The blue in his eyes darkened as they devoured me. He took in every aspect of my flesh like he was about to eat me. I'd let him, too. The way my nerve endings tingled like crazy, I'd let him do whatever he wanted.

He leaned forward and sucked my nipple into his mouth. As he worked his magic, licking, sucking, gently nipping, I clawed my nails up his back and through his thick hair. He eased me backward toward the table and lifted me up like I were merely a feather.

I leaned back, offering him my breasts, and he wasted no time in ravishing them. His hands—soft exquisite, professional hands—glided from my breast to along my thigh. I spread my legs, letting him know I wanted more. As he continued his undivided attention on my breasts, he trailed his fingers up and down my inner thigh, from my knees to my pussy. Up and down, up and down, drawing out goose bumps until they were ready to burst.

I could hardly believe my eyes as I watched one of the hottest men in the world suck my breast. His skin was flawless, a delicate blend of honey and chocolate, and his long lashes that flickered as he savored my nipple would make any woman jealous.

He eased back and opened his eyes, and our gazes met. The fire I saw in those aqua irises set my insides to inferno mode. In one swift movement, Maxwell gathered me in his arms, and as I wrapped my hands around his neck he carried me to the bed. That one romantic move had my already racing heart thundering out an exotic beat.

He laid me down, and as he eased away to stand at the edge of the bed, he retained hold of my hand. Our palms came together and a delicious heat passed between them as he examined my body like I was a living masterpiece.

"You're magnificent."

It took all my might to stop my chin hitting my chest. Between the two of us, Doctor Exotic was the magnificent one.

He sat beside me, and as he trailed his finger around my nipple then down to circle my belly button, the blue in his eyes dazzled. He ran his tongue over his supple pink lips, and with each breath his chest rose and fell.

I reached up, opened his robe to touch his hairless chest, and flitted my fingers from one hard nipple to the other. His hand continued its exploration up and down my torso, exploring every inch of my skin, each time drawing closer and closer to my pussy. My insides throbbed with aching desire, and all I wanted to do was tear the soft waffle-weave fabric from his body. The anticipation was both agony and ecstasy.

He turned slightly, and hoping I read the move correctly, I parted my legs, letting him know I was so ready for whatever he wanted to do to me. I was correct, as this time his fingers glided from my belly button, down between my thighs. Doctor Exotic didn't miss a beat, and I raised my hips as his finger slipped into me.

The angle of his position meant that each time he drove into me, he ground over my clitoris, driving me wild. I bucked under the glorious onslaught and in a flash, an orgasm ripped through me. I gasped for breath, tore the sheets from the bedding, and let my body do what it did best. It was fast, explosive, incredible.

When I opened my eyes, Doctor Exotic and I stared at each other like only two random strangers could do after a moment like that. It seemed completely improbable that someone who didn't even know me could take me to that kind of limit. Hell, he didn't even know my name. Yet I wanted to shove all those untimely thoughts aside and do it all again.

It was time for me to take him to the stars.

I sat up, reaching for his robe to shove it off his shoulders. It fell away, to reveal more exotic skin. Maxwell was a flawless example of what man's body should look like. His large, solid cock was perfect and the pink head at the top begged for me to touch it. As I wrapped my hand around that glorious muscle, a groan tumbled from his throat and his knees bent. For a second, I feared he'd crumble to the ground. But he didn't. Instead he closed his eyes, clenched his jaw, and turned his face to the ceiling. If it weren't for his erratic breathing and rock-solid shaft, I'd have no idea if he was enjoying it.

As I carried on rubbing my hand up and down his groin, his position remained the same, and I had a feeling he could do this all night. It was time for the attention to be returned to me. I let go of him, glided off the bed, and strode to my bag. In a flash, I'd plucked out a condom and walked back to him. "Can you put this on please?"

He tore the packet open with his teeth and the second he'd glided the condom on, I reached for his shoulders, turned him, and made him sit on the bed. I was just about to straddle him when he grabbed my hips, turned me around, and nudged his feet between my legs. I now stood with my back to his chest and each of my long red boots on either side of his calves. With his hands still on my hips, I hovered with the head of his penis nudging at my already throbbing opening. Anticipation was a glorious thing. When he reached for my breasts and pinched my nipple, that was the signal I needed. Ever so slowly, I bent my knees and lowered onto him, drawing that fabulous pole into me. When I sat on his lap, every last inch of him was inside me, stretching me and filling me completely.

His fingers dug into my flesh, and I rose back up again. I paused for only a second at the head of his penis before I plunged him into me again. I did it again. Each time, I increased my pace just a fraction. To have this ultimate control was magnificent.

With his vice-like grip on my hips guiding me, I rode up and down, feeling the glorious orgasm build to mammoth proportions inside me. Suddenly, Maxwell lifted me off and spun me around so my hands were on the bed, and he thrust into me from behind.

His jackhammer pummeled me; his balls slapped against my ass as he grunted a primal sound with each movement. His cock touched that place inside me that loved and hated it at the same time. The pounding hit fever-pitch, and I clutched at the bed and gasped as an orgasm shuddered through me.

Maxwell froze and sucked the air through his teeth, and I knew this was the point of no return. I planted my feet, squeezed the sheets in my fists, and prepared for the pounding I was about to receive. He cried out and thrust in and out, over and over and over until finally he flopped forward onto my back.

His gasps for breath showed that his workout was as intense as mine had been, and it seemed like an eternity before he finally slipped off me and flopped back onto the bed at my side.

He blew out a breath of air. "Wow. I wasn't expecting that at this conference!"

A fine layer of sweat made his already glorious skin positively shimmer, and I drilled every aspect of his physique into my memory bank.

"There's nothing like a sexy surprise." Embarrassed at yet another one of my lame comments, I walked away from him, gathered my dress off the floor, and shoved it into my bag.

I suddenly remembered that I'd snuck away from reception and hit panic mode. *How long have I been away?* At breakneck speed I put my coat on, grabbed my bag, and strode to his door.

"Wait, wait, what's your name?"

I paused with one hand on the handle. "Memphis."

"Bye Memphis." My name was whispered off his lips, and with that lovely sound echoing in my ears, I raced to the elevator while tying up the belt on my trench coat.

Back in my room, I was horrified that I'd been gone fifty minutes. I tore off my coat, boots, and stockings, and removed my wig in a flash. I nearly plucked out my eyeballs in the rush to remove my contacts, and I scrubbed off my makeup. I jumped in the shower, had a quick scrub, and jumped out again.

I redressed, and not willing to risk another minute away from my desk, I grabbed my diary, shoved it in my bag, and headed downstairs. As I braced for the elevator to open at the lobby, I checked my reflection in the mirror. It was frightful. My skin was red and blotchy and my hair scrambled in all directions.

As I attempted to fix my hair, the doors pinged open. The lobby was as silent as a church, and I let out a huge sigh at the relief of it. I flopped into the office chair and after ten or so minutes, I opened my diary. I turned to 8th June and wrote *Doctor Maxwell Bradford room 22*. And as I thought about just how horny I'd been before I even reached his doorway, I wrote: *A Date with Doctor Exotic*. After I'd detailed his exquisite skin and wonderful contours, I then wrote about how much I'd enjoyed the thrill of anticipation.

The next couple of hours went so slowly that I was certain several minutes actually scrolled backwards. When the sun finally lightened the horizon, I made a cup of green tea and headed out to the sun lounge.

As I imagined Doctor Exotic sleeping naked upstairs, I inhaled the fresh sea breeze and welcomed in another glorious day.

Kitty Kendall

17th JUNE
DANGEROUS GAMES
Room 15 – Hot Horizon Hotel

The sun began its slow crawl across the horizon, signifying the end of my shift. I loved winter for its spectacular sunrises and would rather sit at my favorite seat out the front of the hotel until the golden glow in the distance finished its show, but any minute now, Needledick was due to arrive to take over from me.

I wandered back inside, washed up my tea cup, and tried not to constantly check the clock as my knock-off time came and went. He was now fifteen minutes late, and although I knew he was often delayed because his mother was very sick, my patience was starting to grow thin.

I reached under the counter to grab my bag, ready to leave the moment he walked through the door.

"Hello." I looked up, and my heart just about launched out of my throat. Billy. Cowboy Billy. Holy hotness in a cowboy hat leaned his muscular arms over the counter.

My bag tumbled from my fingers, spilling the contents in a noisy clatter onto the floor.

"Are you okay?" His southern accent was unmistakable.

I couldn't breathe, and I was certain my bulging eyes would make me look like some kind of crack addict. Searching for a distraction so I could get my thoughts in order, I fell to my knees to gather my bits and pieces from the floor. "I'm fine," I mumbled, as I reached for two tampons that'd rolled over to the base of the bin.

"Did I scare you?"

"Yes." Yes, that's the reason I'm a mumbling idiot. "It's okay."

He came around the counter and knelt at my side. "Here, let me help." As he reached for my brush and handed it to me, I inhaled his leather and spice perfume. I could enjoy his scent all day long.

When all the contents from my bag were back in their rightful places, Billy stood and offered his hand to help me up. Our palms touched and with his calloused fingers wrapped around mine, he launched me upright. We were barely inches apart, and I swallowed the lump in my throat and stepped back to look up at him. He grinned at me, drilling two perfect dimples into each cheek. Then his eyes changed, darkening with what looked like curiosity.

A hot flush boiled my blood as fear gripped me. *Oh god, he knows my secret.*

He touched my arm. "Are you sure you're okay?" His deep baritone was a song to my ears.

I nodded and lowered my eyes. A shiny object on the floor caught my attention, and I just about died. A foil condom packet was right next to his foot. *Faarrrkkkk.* I was about to self-combust.

"Thank you for your help." I stepped toward him, expecting him to step back and return to the customer side of the counter. But instead, he cocked his head and frowned. His molasses eyes darkened further as he studied me, really, truly examining me, like I was the Mona Lisa. *This is it; my ruse is up. I, Plain Jane, am about to be exposed for the lying fraud I am.*

I had to get him out of there. "Sir, you have to go around the other side of the counter."

"Oh, sorry, it's just . . . you look familiar."

I put my hands on his narrow hips, and trying to ignore the feel of those sexy muscles that I knew threaded down to his groin, I guided him backwards. At the same time, I kicked the condom under the counter. A solution to his confusion suddenly hit me, and I just about did an Irish jig when I thought of it. "We've met before. You helped me take my groceries up to my apartment a few weeks ago."

He clicked his fingers. "So I did. It's Jane, isn't it?"

"Correct." I turned my name badge upwards so he could see it properly.

He nodded, yet the confused look remained. "I know I asked you this last time, but do you know a woman named Memphis?"

I shook my head, my confidence gaining traction. "No, never heard of her."

"Mmmm, you said that last time, too." It may have been the discreet lobby lighting, but I was certain I saw a twinkle in his eye.

"Morning Jane."

"Mr. Karwatsky. You're here." Damn, his timing was impeccable.

Billy tapped the counter with his hand twice. "If you see Memphis, can you tell her I'm in room fifteen?"

I nodded and as Billy turned to walk away, all I wanted to do was watch that sexy swagger, but I turned to my boss instead.

"Who's Memphis?"

I blinked at him. "Sorry?"

"That man. He asked about Memphis."

I swallowed the lump in my throat. "I think it's his girlfriend."

He screwed up his face. "Weird."

"What's weird?"

"He's the second man to ask for Memphis."

My jaw actually dropped, and I turned around to hide my shock. "Really? That is weird." Two men asking for Memphis? My brain spun as I tried to picture who the second man could be.

"I'm wondering if she's that hooker I've seen lurking about."

I moved closer to the rubbish bin, certain I was about throw up the yogurt I'd had about three hours ago. And that was when I noticed the condom packet on the floor again. *Holy shit, can this morning get any worse?*

"Have you seen her?" Needledick opened the drawer to toss his car keys in it, and I used the moment to pick up the offending packet and conceal it in my hand.

"I don't think so. No." I reached for my handbag, desperate to get out of there.

"You'll know what I mean when you see her. She has this rude, untouchable attitude."

"I'll keep an eye out. Anyway, I'm off now."

"Okay, sorry I was late again."

Yeah, yeah. I turned and walked to the elevator. As I stepped in, adrenaline pumped through my veins, making my head spin and my knees weak. The elevator was so slow, I wondered if it had stopped. Finally, it pinged open on my floor, and I made it to my room. My legs were a quivering mess by the time I flopped onto my bed.

"Bloody hell!"

As I lay there listening to the waves crash into the shore below, I debated whether or not Cowboy Billy knew who I really was. The way he'd looked at me was as if he was trying to work out a piece of a puzzle. Maybe my voice gave me away. I should've disguised it somehow. I wanted to kick myself for not thinking of that earlier.

I reached for my phone and dialed Lolita. For the first time ever, it rang out, and I left a message after her perky little voicemail response. Three seconds later, my phone beeped. It was Lolita with a text message. 'Sorry, I'm in parent/teacher interviews. Are you okay?'

I texted her back. 'Yes I'm fine, I'll tell you later. Have fun.'

'Fun?' she replied in a flash. 'I'd rather pull my pubes out one by one.'

'Ha ha. You love it. Bye.'

'No I don't.' She ended the conversation with a smiley face.

I sat up and finger-combed my hair. The last thing Billy had said indicated that he didn't actually think I was Memphis. Then again, maybe he had put two and two together, yet he was still telling me to go to room fifteen. Could that be it? Even though he knew Jane and Memphis were both me, did he really still want me to visit?

My heart did little summersaults at that thought.

I had to find out. My brain skipped over the possibilities as I showered and applied my Memphis makeup. As I layered my mascara, I realized I had a problem. Billy had really, truly looked into my eyes this morning. But as he'd been with Memphis twice, he may have remembered my green eyes. So although I had the colored contact lenses, I couldn't wear them.

No matter which way I looked at it, I was playing with fire. And yet, I had this crazy, uncontrollable desire to still go to him. The times with him had been amazing. I wanted that again, and according to the last words he'd said to me downstairs, he wanted Memphis too.

With that decision made, I put on my black wig again and went to my closet. After my last wardrobe disaster with him, I needed a dress that was easy to remove. As I tugged the dresses aside, struggling with indecision, a shirt caught my eye. It was the one and only man's shirt in my closet. Billy's shirt, the one he'd lent me last time. I removed it from the closet, and the decision to wear it was an obvious one. Although I'd washed it, I wished I hadn't as his wonderful scent had lingered when he'd given it to me.

After a quick rummage through my now overflowing lingerie drawer, I decided to wear my new little white teddy. The sheer fabric alternated with stripes of white satin and see-through lace that lined my torso. It slipped on without any zips, clips, or buttons, which was perfect for easy removal. My dark nipples were easily visible through the lace, and although this would have once horrified me, it now had my nipples practically rising to the occasion.

A quick scan of my extensive shoe collection had me choose my new red boots. Boots for the cowboy seemed totally appropriate.

I glanced in the mirror and felt sexy just looking at my outfit. The shirt sleeves were too long, and I rolled the cuffs over a few times to my wrist. I did up the buttons at the front of the shirt but left the two top ones undone so that my white teddy was just visible. Although everything was suitably covered, I should wear my trench coat over the top, but with a cheeky giggle, I decided I'd run the gauntlet to his room. Besides, based on my shopping expedition at Pacific Fair the other day, this outfit was on trend and I was totally smokin' it.

After a brief check in my handbag to ensure I had my essentials, including money for an emergency, I dabbed on my Ciate Liquid Velvet Matte lipstick. Once it dried, it was supposed to stay on for at least eight hours.

I checked my reflection again and loved what I saw, except for one thing—the frown on my face.

My stomach did as many flips as my brain as I debated whether or not I should go to Billy's room, just two doors down. My challenge this year was meant to be fun, and I wanted to slap myself for making it so serious. So what if Billy recognized me? What could be the worst that happened?

Prime-time television as my dirty little secret was exposed to the world.

That horrid thought flashed into my mind at frightening speed, and I decided that would definitely be the worst. But after a brief panic attack that had my pulse raging and a heatwave cooking my skin, I decided the chances of that actually happening were negligible. After a couple of deep breaths, I shoved the doubts to the back of my brain, pushed my shoulders back, smiled at my reflection, grabbed my bag, and walked out my room.

Billy was just two doors down, and with every step my heartbeat raised a notch. I closed my eyes, sucked in a huge breath, and let it out very slowly. I reminded myself to disguise my voice and tried to ignore the pounding in my ears as I knocked twice.

A few seconds later, the door opened and all my worries vanished in a second. Cowboy Billy was stunning in faded jeans, a short-sleeved shirt that he'd left unbuttoned, and a smile that could light up New York City.

"Hello Memphis. I see you've brought my shirt back."

"Hello Billy." My high-pitched voice sounded silly, but I cast the thought aside as I inhaled his delightful scent. I entered his room and forced myself not to touch him as I squeezed past. At the table, I placed my bag down and turned to him. Billy was the epitome of guy-next-door hunky. He had a strong jawline that accentuated his muscular physique, yet his dimples gave him a softness that made me want to fall into his arms.

"You're a hard woman to find."

I tilted my head, unsure what he was talking about. "Oh?"

"I was beginning to think you'd forgotten about me."

I cocked my head. "Why?"

"I stayed here a couple of weeks ago, but you didn't come to me."

My eyes bulged. "Really?"

He ran his hand through his brandy-colored curls and nodded. "Uh huh."

Well that might solve the mystery of who's been asking for me. "I'm sorry I missed you."

"You're forgiven. Especially when you look so damn sexy in my shirt."

My heart skipped a beat at the way he gazed at me. "It'd look even better on the floor." That sounded cute in my head, but when he didn't move I began to wonder if it was just another one of my lame comments.

A couple of heartbeats later, he stepped toward me, and my breath quickened as I acknowledged that smoking-hot Billy actually wanted me. As his hands touched my hips I reached for the gap in his shirt and glided my fingers up and down his glorious well-developed muscles. Billy's incredible body was the result of a lifetime of work. A sculptor would be blessed to have him as a model.

As he undid the buttons at my breast, I in turn undid his belt buckle. The silent communication between us was electric. Desire sizzled as an inferno between our bodies, and my urgent fingers couldn't get his clothes off quick enough.

I pulled his belt from his jeans and let the thick leather fall to the floor. Then I tugged at his shirt, and he helped by whipping it off in a flash. If it were possible, I thought he looked even more toned than he had the last time I'd seen him. His arms were perfectly developed, not too bulky to put him out of proportion, but just the right amount of muscle to have me believe he'd save me, no matter what the situation was. Billy the Cowboy had the ultimate dream body.

He undid my last button, glided the fabric off my shoulders so his shirt fell at my feet, and stepped back. "You're beautiful."

The way he said it, like a breathless whisper, was as if he were in a wonderful dream. My heart skipped a beat as his molasses eyes travelled up my body. I did the same with him, savoring every inch of his sculpted torso, and stopping at the now unmistakable bulge in his jeans that strained against the denim.

He reached for the spaghetti strap on my shoulder, and as he glided it off, he stepped in and kissed me from my ear right down my neck. The combination of his hot breath and soft lips had my pulse racing. I closed my eyes and rolled my head to the side, offering him all of my neck. Tingles prickled my skin, drawing my nipples out to meet him.

I reached for him and explored the contours of his body. His nipples were as hard as pebbles, and when I pinched them he groaned. The rumble off his lips thrummed over the nape of my neck. My fingers found the button on his jeans and I undid it, then unzipped him and that sound turned me on like I wouldn't have believed.

Maybe it turned him on too, because he curled my other strap off my shoulder, lowered my teddy to below my breasts, and leaned over to take my nipple in his mouth. My insides clenched, and my pussy pulsed with want for him. As one of his hands manipulated my breast and his tongue and lips explored the other, I clawed my nails up his back and into his wavy hair.

My teddy fell to my feet. I hadn't even realized he'd pulled it the rest of the way down, and I kicked the flimsy fabric aside. Billy's hand slipped between my legs and I stepped my boots apart, letting him know that I was oh-so ready for him to touch me.

Billy obliged, gliding his finger over my clit and into me with delicious repetition. He sucked my nipple, drawing it out until it snapped from his lips, and then he latched on again. As he repeated the teasing motions with my nipple, he played my pussy like it was a lover's song, drawing out exquisite sensations that started deep within me and shivered across my every inch of my body.

I bent my knees, and Billy pushed two fingers into me, driving them in and out with repeated thrusts that had me at his mercy. As I clutched the corded muscles of his shoulders, an orgasm of immense proportions ripped through me. My juices spilled onto his hands as he continued to draw out every ounce of lust from me.

In one swift movement, Billy launched me into his arms and carried me to his bed. He lay me down, and I rolled onto my side to watch him strip out of his jeans and white jockey underpants. For a brief second he stood before me, allowing me to witness the male miracle. His cock was aimed right at me, the pink head swollen, and a droplet of semen glistened at the slit in the top.

I wanted to taste him. To suck him. I rolled onto my stomach, crawled toward him, and beckoned him forward with my finger. Billy stepped closer, so his knees butted up against the edge of the bed. I raised onto my elbows and was at the perfect height to suck his glorious muscle into my mouth.

I wrapped my lips around his crown, rolling my tongue over the smooth skin and tasting the saltiness of his juice. His knees buckled slightly, and as he drew away from me I chased him, gliding my lips over his solid shaft and sucking him into my throat. From this position I was also able to hold his balls in my right hand. He parted his legs, and I took the full weight of his scrotum into my palm.

With each glide of my lips down his shaft, his balls sucked upwards. Billy may have been a man made of muscle, but in my hands and mouth he was as malleable as putty. It was ultimate power to have this control.

I rolled my lips down, taking him into my mouth as far as I could, then I glided back up, stopping at the very tip. When he moaned, I moaned with him; his enjoyment was equally enjoyable for me. Feeling confident, I thrust his cock in and out of my mouth with increasing speed. Billy clutched my shoulders and in the next second, he shot his load into my throat.

I gagged and pulled back in time to watch him ejaculate again, shooting a long white stream onto the bed sheets. Certain I was pulling a very unsexy scowl, I plonked my head down and tried to swallow back the last of it without hurling. *Holy shit, that was dreadful. Ewww.*

When Billy stepped away and headed toward the bathroom, I quickly wiped my hand across my lips and rolled my tongue around my mouth. I'd give anything for a gallon of water and a toothbrush right now.

Billy returned moments later with a towel around his hips, and when he offered me his hand, I rolled to sit up. He grinned at me, that glorious model-worthy smile with the deep dimples on either side that said everything was perfect.

Judging by the look on his face, I didn't think he'd noticed what had happened, which was good. The last thing I wanted was for him to think I didn't like it. Because I did. Except for the last bit, that was.

I felt a little weird sitting there with nothing but my red boots on and was about to stand up when he sat beside me. He placed his hand on my knee, and when he sighed, I felt like I was about to need my therapist hat again. "I know who you are."

My heart skipped a beat, and my shoulders slumped as the urge to throw up gripped me. I wanted to believe he was wrong, but somehow I knew he wouldn't be. "What do you mean?" I twirled a lock of my wig around my finger in one final futile attempt to retain my secret identity.

He reached for my hand and entwined his fingers within mine. "Your eyes give you away. They're beautiful, Jane."

I was completely torn. On one hand, happy butterflies danced in my stomach at his comment; on the other, I was completely embarrassed by my sneaky indiscretions. I covered my eyes with my free hand. "I'm so sorry."

He slipped off the bed, knelt at my feet, and pulled my hand away from my face. "I'm not."

I blinked at his extraordinary molasses eyes with a thousand unanswered questions swirling around my brain.

He squeezed my hands. "I feel like the luckiest man alive to have met you."

I frowned. "Really?" A strange music started up, and it took me a moment to realize it was my phone.

He glanced over his shoulder at my bag and then turned to me. "Do you want to get that?"

I rolled my eyes. The timing couldn't have been worse. "No." It was probably Lolita.

He cupped my hands in his. "I don't know why you pretend to be Memphis, and I'm not complaining because she's amazing, but I'd love to know Jane a little better too."

My jaw dropped. The hottest cowboy in the world wanted to know more about Plain Jane. This, whatever *this* was, just didn't happen to me.

My damn phone rang again and I clenched my jaw, willing it to go away.

He stood up, reached for my hand, and lifted me to my feet. "You better get it; it must be important."

My feet moved like lead weights and with my swirling thoughts, I felt like I was walking in a pool of clear jelly. The ringing stopped, but I still reached for my phone to check the missed calls. As I'd thought, both were from Lolita. Suddenly, it rang again and I frowned briefly at the strange number on the screen before I pressed the green button. "Hello?"

"Hi Jane. It's me, Clayton."

My head exploded, as did my galloping heart. "Oh, hi." I was surprised any words came out.

"I just wanted to confirm you were still okay for lunch today."

I'd been so caught up in Billy that I'd completely forgotten about my lunch date with Clayton.

I blinked, trying to force my brain to stop spinning. With Cowboy Billy sitting practically naked on the bed and looking at me as I stood wearing only a pair of red cowboy boots, I told another man that I was indeed ready to see him in a few hours.

I'd totally hit mental-asylum mode.

Maybe I was bi-polar. Or just plain crazy. Either way, I shouldn't be allowed to roam the streets.

A scathing flush burned my cheeks as I said goodbye to Clayton and ended the call. Guilt had me feeling very naked, and not just because I wasn't wearing anything. I picked Billy's shirt up off the floor. "May I borrow this again?"

"I told you, you can keep it."

Completely dazed, I didn't bother with my teddy. Instead, I redressed in his shirt and buttoned it up. "I've got to go." I shoved my teddy into my bag and hooked the leather strap over my shoulder.

"Are you okay?"

I nodded, barely able to speak. "Yes, I'm sorry, but I really do have to go." As much as I wanted to stay and talk over about a thousand things, I couldn't do it now that Clayton had reminded me of our lunch date. It just didn't seem right.

He reached out and stroked my forearm. "Don't worry, Jane; your secret is safe with me."

The tenderness of his touch nearly brought me to tears. "Thank you." A thick fog gripped my brain.

"I'll be back for you."

I just nodded and headed for the door.

Somehow I made it to my room, undressed, removed my wig and makeup, and stepped into the shower. As the hot needles of water pummeled my body, I rehashed everything that'd happened during the last hour. My thoughts bounced from exquisite sensations rolling through my body to mind-numbing terror. It was a wonder my heart was still beating.

I dried myself, and flopped onto the bed. On a whim, I grabbed my phone and dialed Lolita.

"Hey babe, I was so worried about you. I called you twice. Are you okay?" Lolita spoke at a million miles an hour.

"No." Tears pooled in my eyes as I told her everything from my choice of lingerie to Billy's confession.

"Oh, babe. Don't cry. It's not that bad."

"I just feel terrible."

"Okay, sit down for me."

I sat on the edge of my bed. "I am."

"Let's go through this logically."

I wiped a tear from my cheek. "Okay."

"Right, first up, are you dating, engaged, married, or have you pledged your love to either Billy or Clayton?"

"Lolly, this is serious."

"I am being serious. So what's your answer?"

I rolled my eyes. "No, I haven't pledged my love to either of them."

"Have you had sex with either of them?"

Although this was my third time with Billy, I knew for a fact that I still hadn't had sex with him. "No."

"Was your morning with Billy fucking hot?"

I chuckled. "Yes."

"And he knew it was Jane he was with the whole time?"

"I think so."

"So what are you worried about? You're not cheating on anyone, and I'd say Billy likes Jane just as much Memphis. So your secret is safe."

I sat cross-legged on the bed and scowled at my disastrous peeling toenail polish. "Are you sure?"

"I'm not just sure. I'm one hundred percent positive."

I flopped back on the quilt as relief washed over me. "Okay."

"Do you feel better now?"

I sighed. "Yes. Much better, thank you."

"Babe, you really aren't doing anything wrong. You're a single woman playing the field a bit and loving every minute of it. Sex is a good thing, and just because you're not dating a guy doesn't mean you shouldn't get it. Besides, what will we talk about next year when your challenge is over?"

She laughed, and as I laughed with her the final shred of my doubt evaporated. "You'll just have to give me a whole new challenge."

"I like the sound of that. Now get some sleep and wake up all ready for a hot lunch date with Clayton."

I smiled as I thought of him; he seemed like a really sweet guy, too. "Okay, I will."

"Love ya, babe."

"Love you too, Lolly."

I hung up the phone, placed it on my bedside table, set my alarm, and then crawled under the covers. The second my head hit the pillow, my eyes felt like lead weights. Sleep dragged me into another world.

* * *

When the alarm sounded, I was still in the same position I'd collapsed into when I'd first hopped into bed, and based on my tingling fingers, I'd say I hadn't moved for the whole four hours.

I groaned like an old woman as I rolled off the mattress and headed for another shower. As the hot, cascading water woke me up, I reflected on what I used to do all day, every day, before this year's madness. Sleep was about all I could think of.

My life had been boring. Not now though.

After my shower I toweled off, and during the annoying twenty minutes it took to blow-dry my hair, I considered cutting it short. I'd never had short hair; actually, I'd barely changed my hairstyle since I was a little girl. But the cute little bob-cut wig I'd been wearing showed me a style that I never would've dreamed of trying. Not only was it easy to manage, but I was surprised at how much it suited me. Maybe a change of hairstyle was on the cards soon.

I decided to wear my hair down today, and it fell heavily over my shoulders and down my back. Winter was the only time I usually didn't pull my hair up. As was I applying a touch of makeup, I realized that I hadn't written in my diary.

With a towel around me, I walked to my bed, sat on the edge, and reached for the diary. I turned to 17th June and at the top I scribbled *Cowboy Billy, room 15*. I wrote how wonderful it was pleasuring him, but how disastrous it'd been when I'd gagged. I didn't hold back describing my surprise at how awful semen had tasted. I vowed never to fall for that little mistake again. It was all about the timing, and I needed more practice.

I giggled at that thought. Obviously, I was keen to try it at least one more time.

Then I wrote about how Billy knew who I was and although it had been a shock to hear his admission, deep down I hadn't been surprised. Even this morning, when he'd studied me at the counter, I'd had an inkling that he knew my secret. I'd still wanted to go to him. I'd been willing to risk it. With that thought, below his name I wrote *Dangerous Games*.

I closed my diary, and as I turned my attention to my lunch date with Clayton, I walked to my wardrobe. It was a bit cooler today, so I chose to wear denim jeans. I matched them with a simple white cotton button-up shirt and a red blazer.

For a bit of spice, I chose to wear my D'orsay leopard-print stilettos with eight-inch silver-spiked heels and a strap that went around my ankle. They were so damn sexy, yet I'd never worn them. Fortunately, I'd bought the matching purse when I'd purchased the shoes, and I dug that out from the back of my wardrobe too. It was wonderful wearing all these accessories that'd only seen the back of my closet since the day I'd brought them home. I checked my reflection in my full-length mirror and blinked.

I liked what I saw.

It was an unusual admittance. Normally, the only time I liked my reflection was when I was dressed up as Memphis. Maybe my alter-ego was rubbing off on me after all.

With my purse clutched beneath my elbow, I made my way downstairs.

Like last time, Clayton was waiting for me beside his Audi. Today he'd matched classy jeans with a linen navy shirt and tanned leather shoes. My heart skipped a beat as he walked toward me.

He leaned in to kiss my cheek, and I inhaled his cologne that somehow smelt of pine forest and oriental spices at the same time. "You look fabulous," he said as he touched his hand to my lower back and guided me toward his car.

"So do you."

"Did you get any sleep after your shift?"

"Slept like a log."

"Oh good." He opened the car door, and I slipped into the passenger seat. He climbed into the driver's side and put his seat belt on.

"Now before we head off," I said, "I just want to remind you that I'm paying for lunch."

His eyes lit up. "Oh, I know, that's why I booked the eight-course degustation menu at Allure restaurant."

It took all my might not to bulge my eyes. I'd heard of that restaurant; it'd been voted the best in Australia, and was probably the most expensive in the country too.

He turned to me, grinning. "Gotcha."

I slapped his arm. "Geez, you had dollar signs whizzing through my brain."

"I wouldn't do that to you." He started the car. "Not on our second date anyway."

As the car left the curb, I stewed over his comment of this being our second date. Were a dinner and a lunch considered dates? I guess they are. Guilt crept into my brain like a stream of poisonous mercury. The devil and angel in my mind belted out a furious debate as I turned my attention to outside the window and watched the Gold Coast whiz by in a kaleidoscope of color and movement.

"Aren't you curious about where we're going?" Clayton said as we stopped at a red light.

"Oh, umm, okay, where are we going?"

"It's a surprise."

"Really?" I cocked my head at him.

"You'll see soon enough. It's one of my favorite restaurants; hopefully you'll love it too."

"If they have food, I'll love it."

"Well you're easy to please."

"Yep. My mom always said I had a hollow stomach."

He laughed. "My daughter has one of them too." His face lit up at the mention of Telitha.

"Where is Telitha?"

"She's at school."

"Oh right, of course."

"You must get your days mixed up all the time with that shift of yours."

"I guess so. The only two days I look forward to are Tuesday and Wednesday."

"I understand Wednesday because it's your day off, but why Tuesday?"

"It's the day before my day off," I said, deadpan.

He turned to me with a curious look, maybe unsure if I was joking, and I giggled. "You're a funny woman."

"Thanks. Tuesday's the day Lolita and I get together to exercise and have coffee. Actually, I have coffee and cake; she just has green tea."

"That sounds like Lolita. So you like to exercise?"

"I do. I try to do something every day. How about you?"

He sighed. "I haven't done any decent exercise in months, maybe longer. It's hard with work and getting Telitha to school and meals and stuff."

"Oh." I didn't know what to say. I had nothing to compare that with, and his comments were exactly the reason why I was unsure if I wanted to settle down with a man who already had a child. There was a whole world out there I wanted to explore.

"Here we are." He turned the car into a parking lot that overlooked the ocean and walked around to open my door. I reached for his offered hand, and he helped me out of the Audi.

We walked side by side toward the whitewashed restaurant situated right on the beach. "I asked for an outside table. I hope you don't mind?"

"Sounds great." With the lovely blue sky and slight breeze, the idea of sitting outside was perfect.

One of the waiters greeted Clayton by name and promptly led us to a table on the outside deck. The view was spectacular, taking in golden sand, crashing waves, and the busy Burleigh Heads skyline.

We sat opposite each other, and the waiter filled our water glasses.

I sighed a contented sigh and reached for my water. "This's fabulous."

"I thought you'd like it."

"So you come here often?"

"Not as often as I'd like. One of the head chefs bought an engagement ring from me about a decade ago. Anyway, we struck up a friendship that's lasted through his divorce and mine." He chuckled, so I did too.

The menus were handed to us, and after I spent a while scouring the extensive selection and salivating at nearly everything on the menu, Clayton cleared his throat.

"Would you like me to suggest a few meals?"

I flipped the menu shut. "Yes please, or else I'll order everything."

He grinned at me. Clayton was very handsome. His clean-cut skin indicated he'd shaved before he came out. His hair was very dark, almost black, but in this sunshine hints of copper caught in the light. As he ran through his suggestions, I couldn't help but stare at his long, dark lashes that framed his equally dark eyes.

"What?" He paused during his description of the meals.

"What?" I bulged my eyes at him.

"You're staring at me again. Did I leave toothpaste on my mouth or something?" He ran his tongue over his lips.

"Oh. Sorry, I didn't realize I was staring."

"Well, you were. Have you even heard a thing I've said?"

"Of course," I lied.

He cocked his head at me. "Okay then, what was the last dish I mentioned?"

"Ahhh, it was eye fillet." I rolled my eyes, fully aware that I'd been caught out.

"Wrong. I said pig's eyeballs in tomato garlic sauce."

I screwed up my face. "Gross."

"Clearly you weren't listening. So do I have toothpaste on my lip?"

I giggled. "No, you're fine."

Our bottle of wine arrived, and once we each had a glass and the waiter left, Clayton held his glass toward me for a toast.

I raised my glass, curious as to what he'd say.

"To new beginnings."

I smiled at his splendid proposal. "To new beginnings."

The afternoon rolled on as if it was perfectly choreographed for our lunch date. I inhaled the fresh ocean breeze, relaxed in the gorgeous winter sunshine, ate exquisite seafood, and laughed freely with yet another new stunning man in my life.

25TH JUNE
SEDUCING THE SPORTSMAN
Room 19 – Hot Horizon Hotel

Tonight was up there as one of the most hectic Friday nights I'd worked since I started the night shift at the Hot Horizon Hotel. The culprits of the madness were the Irish Warriors football team that were here for two nights. On Sunday they were playing against our Gold Coast Suns in what they called a "friendly match." In the meantime, though, they seemed hell bent on reveling as much as they could.

My brother, Tyler, played professional football and as a consequence, I'd spent most of my youth being dragged to every one of his games and practice sessions. Some weekends we spent hours in the car just to watch him play. I grew to hate football because of it.

Much to my parents' delight, Tyler had been drafted to the West Coast Eagles. This meant Tyler and I were literally on opposite coasts of Australia. My brother and I talked on the phone occasionally, and the main conversation was around his stellar career. I was proud of him; he deserved everything he got. He certainly worked damn hard for it.

One of the things that always surprised me, though, was how forthright he was about sharing what he got up to in his so-called downtime. According to him, women hung around the team like hungry lionesses, just waiting to pick up any man who was keen. I, of course, being the naïve country girl I was, had never believed him. But after tonight and the number of women I'd seen coming and going, I now had faith in every word he'd said.

What amazed me the most, was just how stunning the women were. Every one of them could win a bikini model competition. They certainly weren't afraid to flash their flesh either.

As if on cue, two women strode into the lobby. Their stilettos were high enough to cause serious back damage and their skirts short enough that they could almost be called belts. The ladies had their arms hooked together, and neither of them glanced in my direction as they made a beeline for the thumping music coming from the Triple H bar. A shout erupted when they entered; clearly, they'd been expected.

The Gold Coast was renowned for its gorgeous girls, and I think every one of them had visited the Hot Horizon Hotel tonight.

I glanced at the clock and sighed. We had extended the closing time of the bar to three a.m. to cater to the footballers' party-time request. They still had one hour to go. But even then, if I managed to get them out and the bar closed by four it would be a miracle. Maybe I could call last drinks at two thirty and see if anyone noticed.

A couple emerged from the bar, arm in arm. The guy, with dark curly, almost afro-looking hair was tall, at least eight inches taller than the woman. His thick arm was draped over her shoulder as they headed toward the elevator. His attire looked a little shabby. She, on the other hand, was stunning. Her flaming red hair with copper highlights fell in a luscious waterfall over her shoulders. Her skin was china-doll perfect, and had obviously never been kissed by our harsh tropical sun. She wore a green velvet dress with thin straps that crossed over at the back. It was backless and plunged away to just above her bottom. It sounded terrible, but on this woman it was classy and slutty at the same time, if that was even possible.

This was the second time I'd seen her go upstairs with a man; the last guy had been blond.

My initial reaction at thoughts of what she was doing hadn't been pleasant. But then I compared her to what I did when I slipped into my sexy Memphis disguise. Obviously I'd never had two guys in one night, nor did I think I ever would. But both of us were women who went after men purely to satisfy our sexual desires. *Was that bad?*

Why were women considered sluts when they needed their sexual thirst quenched, while men could have a different woman every day and suffer no derogatory labels? Of course, women and men who cheated were both considered to be sluts by me. Having lived through the wrong side of that experience, I abhorred anyone who did it.

My mental debate was interrupted by a tall redheaded man who stumbled as he came out of the bar. At the last second, he managed to save himself from face planting on the marble tiles. Laughter erupted from the bar and the stranger's already red face flushed even brighter as he scurried away from their sight and headed toward the elevator.

As he waited for the elevator to arrive, he glanced over at me and for some inexplicable reason, I waved. He stared at me, and for a moment I wondered if he were seeing double or something.

I smiled, making sure he knew I'd been waving at him. This was not something I normally did. It was just a bit of fun, but when a small smile curled at his lips I was glad I'd done it. Then the elevator arrived and he disappeared.

Four more young women entered the foyer. Again, they were all dressed in scanty clothing and again, they headed straight for the Triple H bar. Maybe there was someone on a microphone outside announcing the hot guys gyrating in and around the hotel. Despite their sky-high heels, the women strode across the marble as if they were in runners.

It was now well past two a.m. and yet the party wasn't slowing down. The last thing I wanted to do was go in there and break it up. But that was part of my job. That was the reason I was paid the big bucks . . . apparently. In the three years I'd worked here, I hadn't had to do it yet.

Each time a man and/or woman left the bar, I did a silent little happy dance. Soon three a.m. rolled around, and although I hadn't actually done a head count, I was fairly certain there were at least fifty people still in there. The music died as the DJ promptly stopped at his designated finishing time, and barely five minutes later, he left the bar with a cursory wave in my direction before he vanished out the sliding glass doors. He was gone less than two minutes before the bar's in-house music picked up where he'd left off.

At 3:25, the noise seemed to get even louder, and I used that as motivation to do the inevitable. I tightened my ponytail, put my shoulders back, strode across the lobby, and weaved my way through the muscly giants. The combination of the throbbing music and exquisite bodies from both the men and the women was an attack to my senses. Odors of perfume, cologne, alcohol, and sweaty men abounded. The energy of the room had its own presence. There was so much to take in; I didn't know where to look.

It seemed like forever before I reached the bar. Peter, the bar manager, and Tania, the barmaid, looked as if they'd been breakdancing all night. Their cheeks were flushed and they both had sweaty hair clinging to their foreheads. That alone was justification to call an end to this party.

"Hey guys, it's time to stop serving."

Pete looked at me and his eyes lit up. "Thank God."

A tall muscular guy, with the biggest biceps I'd seen all day, leaned on the bar top. I waited to see what Tania did and readied myself to take over should the need arise.

"I'm sorry, sir, but the bar is now closed." Her confident assertiveness proved she'd done this before. I admired her fortitude.

The footballer grumbled. "Ahhh, what the hell? I didn't hear no 'last drinks' call."

He had a point; they should've called last drinks thirty minutes ago. Too bad. It was after three a.m. and well past everyone's bedtime. Except for mine, of course. I still had three more hours until the end of my shift.

The guy with the massive biceps turned to a group of men. "Bar's closed."

The collective moan was loud, yet it wasn't as bad as I'd predicted. It was almost as if they'd expected as much. I strolled to the stereo and turned it off. The adjustment in noise volume was confronting and several people turned around with confused looks on their faces, as if trying to work out what had happened.

"Let's go to Cavill Avenue," someone called out, and there were just as many cheers as there were groans.

Within ten minutes, half of the patrons had vacated. Within thirty minutes, the only people left with me were Peter and Tania. I'd like to let them go home, but until all the glasses and beer bottles were collected and the bar cleared, they had no choice but to stay.

It was nearly five before I returned to my post behind reception. My body was exhausted, but my mind buzzed. Images of those incredibly fit men dancing and smiling whizzed through my brain. Before long, I knew without a doubt that one of them would be my twenty-sixth sexual adventure, but how on earth would I pick which one?

I jumped on the computer and typed in Irish AFL team, and within seconds I was comparing faces on the screen with the men I'd seen in the bar. It was a game of celebrity snap and a little bit of fun to while away the final hours of my night.

The remaining ninety minutes of my shift whizzed by and just after quitting time, Needledick arrived to take over. I didn't bother telling him about the night I'd had; all I wanted to do was get out of there. We did our usual handover and I made my way to my room.

I had a long, hot shower and with one towel around my body and another around my wet hair, I cooked myself eggs on toast for breakfast. Once it was ready, I took my plate and an extra-strong coffee and headed out to my balcony.

It was only seven thirty in the morning, and yet the beach was dotted with dozens of people enjoying the early-morning sunshine. The ocean had never really appealed to me. Not from a swimming point of view at least. However, I could sit and watch it all day long. There was something mesmerizing about endless waves crashing into the shore.

I finished my breakfast and put my feet up on the other chair as I cupped my mug and sipped my coffee.

My scenery suddenly improved as about thirty men poured out of my hotel and headed straight for the beach. I couldn't believe my eyes as I realized they were the football team that I'd kicked out of my bar just four hours ago.

Standing up to improve my view, I watched as they stripped down to tight little shorts and headed straight for the water. Maybe this was their idea of a wakeup call or a hangover cure, but the fact that they were even upright was unbelievable.

As most of them dove under and over the waves, a couple of guys remained on the beach and began pacing out a playing field with colorful cones and flags that flapped in the morning breeze. Having been brought up in a football-loving family, I recognized that they were about to do a few drills.

An idea suddenly hit me. This was my chance to choose my man.

I plonked my coffee mug on the table and stripped out of my towel as I re-entered my room. In a flash, I was dressed in my exercise gear and with my wet hair tugged up in a ponytail, my sunglasses and room key in hand, I headed out my door.

I was a woman on a mission.

The sunshine was the right mix of light and heat as I crossed the small nature strip and strolled onto the sand. Thirty or so of the hottest and fittest men in the world were frolicking before me. I had my own Magic Mike show. I giggled at that as I remembered Mike and Maxwell, the two sexy doctors from the other week.

Now that I was here, I didn't know what to do. I was a deer in headlights, stunned beyond moving. Which was okay, considering my surroundings, but it made me look like some kind of weirdo pervert. I really had become quite the voyeur.

And I loved every minute of it.

As the men came out of the ocean, water glistened off the defined muscles lining their torsos. The setting was exquisite. Everything from the weather to the crashing waves to the smoking-hot bodies before me. Realizing I'd paused halfway between the nature strip and the ocean, I snapped my jaw shut, took a large breath, and jogged away from the men.

It really was nice to fill my lungs with the fresh ocean breeze. The sun penetrated my flesh with just the right amount of heat, and I made a conscious effort to acknowledge just how alive I felt.

After about fifteen minutes, I stopped and turned back the way I'd come. I was confident the men would still be on the beach. If my brother's AFL training regime was anything to go by, they'd be there for at least another couple of hours.

To my delight, not only were they there but so was a crowd of people. Young women, old women, kids, men—all sat alongside the witches-hat marked field to watch the Irish Warriors complete their training.

Now, I could fit right in.

I kept my pace up, right until I reached close enough that I could smell the combination of suntan lotion and sweaty bodies. As I slowed, I spied a couple of girls in gold hot pants and bikini tops. The Gold Coast Meter Maids were quite a tourist attraction. And why wouldn't they be? Sexy women in tiny gold bikinis who paid for street parking was a brilliant idea.

Now though, they were nowhere near any parking meters. Instead they were enjoying the footballers' rigorous training routine, along with another thirty or so people.

I made my way toward the crowd and eased myself between a chubby man with a young child upon his shoulders and a bunch of giggling young women. The meter maids made sure they had front-row seats to the action.

The footballers set up with half of them lined up on each side of the field. As they commenced a series of drills that they'd obviously practiced many times before, I set about investigating which one of the men interested me the most.

With thirty-plus options to choose from, it was quite a challenge. I decided to treat it like a project. The goal of my fifty-two-week challenge was to experiment. So my first step in the elimination process was to take out the physical attributes I'd had before. That excluded the dark-skinned guys, the Asian-looking one, and the guy who could give Arnold Schwarzenegger a decent arm wrestle.

Giggling discreetly as I crossed off the men like a wicked queen with a magic wand, I eliminated one after the other for all sorts of random reasons. By the end of my fussy decision process, I had eight men to choose from. Each one was a muscle-bound god most women would dream of. Me included.

The men set up again for another drill, then spaced around the four perimeters of the designated field. At the sound of a whistle, they raced for a ball positioned in the middle of them. An almighty roar erupted from the men as they dived into the sand. A sweaty wrestle of man muscle ensued with bulging biceps, laughter, and grunts. Their commitment was impressive. The man at the top of the pile was dark-haired and had skin that was made for our glorious sunshine, and when he grinned, his entire face lit up.

I kept my eyes on him, watching his every move like an eagle watched its prey, but then he did something that completely put me off . . . he turned to make sure the young women to my side were watching him. One look at the gaggle of ladies was enough to know they were. That simple little move scratched him from my imaginary list.

It wasn't long before I realized several of the other footballers enjoyed the attention, too. That put me off them altogether. It was getting close to total annihilation when the redhead who'd caught my eye last night captured my interest again. He wasn't on the field, though; he was on the sideline.

His shirt was off, showing muscle upon muscle and a thick mop of red hair covered his head and chest, and travelled in a line down into his shorts.

I licked my lips as I studied him. He commanded attention in so many ways, and yet unlike the other men, didn't ask for it. Mr. Redhead may not have been a footballer, but somehow he was part of the team. A couple of minutes later, a blond-headed footballer hobbled toward the redhead. The footballer lay on his back on a towel and my redhead reached for the footballer's ankle and manipulated it from side to side.

My jaw dropped as I watched the redhead's arms bulge as he applied pressure to the footballer's ankle. I moved around the crowd to get a closer look, and when he sprayed something onto his patient's skin, I smelt hints of eucalyptus and mint. As his thumbs threaded up and down the footballer's calf, his biceps moved and flexed. Up and down. Bulge and flex. It was the best show on earth, and I remained mesmerized until the footballer returned to his feet and Mr. Redhead sat back in a chair to watch for his next patient.

The muscle-bound sports physician had just declared himself my twenty-sixth sexual adventure. My insides quivered at the thought of his hands running up and down my thighs.

I just had to figure out which room he was staying in.

Despite receiving much more sun than I'd usually allow, I stayed right until the very end of the training session and so did the young girls. The meter maids had long gone, as had all the young families. I felt as if I'd joined the realms of my young counterparts as I drooled over Mr. Redhead while he left the field.

Somehow I needed to get myself into the elevator with him, see what floor he was on, and then in stealth mode, I had to watch which room he went to.

In the end, the first part of my plan was easy. As every other footballer jostled for a place in the elevator, he held back, patiently waiting his turn. Eventually there were just four of us remaining, and after watching how different he was to the other men, I liked him even more. Redhead was an introvert compared to the other gregarious footballers. My mind went crazy as I wondered what he was like in the bedroom.

When the doors pinged open, he turned to me. "After you."

"Thanks." I stepped to the back of the elevator.

The remaining three men, including Mr. Redhead, stepped in after me and pressed a floor button each.

He turned to me, and before he even said anything my stomach flipped as I realized my error.

"What floor would you like?" His Irish lilt caught me off guard, though it shouldn't have. After all, he was travelling with the Irish Warriors football team.

"Oh." *Oh crap.* "The ninth floor, please."
His blue eyes were the color of Artic ice—crisp, clear, and breathtaking.
"The penthouses. Nice?"
I nodded and inwardly cringed at my lack of foresight.
The Redhead stepped out of the elevator on the third floor. My floor. But
because of the other men with me, I couldn't wait to see which room he
walked to. So, as I rode the painfully slow elevator up to the penthouse
floor without a single word from the remaining two men, I stewed over
how I'd work out which room the redhead was staying in.
After the remaining men vacated the elevator, I pressed the button for the
third floor again. By the time the doors re-opened, I had a plan to find my
man that was so simple it bordered on ridiculous.
I went to my room and set about transforming myself into Memphis. As I
pictured my hunky redhead and his fascinating blue eyes, I used that as my
inspiration. My red wig was nothing compared to the locks of the flaming
redhead I'd seen last night in the green velvet dress, but it was still very
good. And for a bit of fun, I wrestled my new blue contact lenses into
position.
When I glanced in the mirror, the transformation was confronting. With
these changes in place, I could walk right up to my mother and she
wouldn't recognize me.
A scenario played out in my head. I decided that for today's outfit, I'd wear
my bikini. It was maroon with a white floral pattern and maroon string
straps that tied at my hips and over my neck. I slipped a sheer white cover-
up with a plunging V-neckline over my bikini and added a set of chunky
wooden necklaces and earrings to give it a funky, hippy feel. The
accessories weren't exactly practical for swimming, but they were perfect
for jazzing up my style.
With a pair of flat sandals on my feet, I grabbed my bag, confirmed I had
my basic essentials of condoms, my phone, and some cash, and headed out
the door.
With a plan to simply knock on all the doors on my floor until I found my
man, I walked to the opposite end of the corridor and started knocking. It
was a bold plan, and I guessed I could use my master key, but the thought
of walking in on the wrong person was enough to put me off it. I loved a
simple plan.
The first four doors I knocked on went unanswered, and I began to wonder
if I'd taken too long to get ready and had somehow missed him.
The fifth door was opened by a young fair-skinned woman with bloodshot
eyes and hair that scrambled in all directions.
"Oh God, sorry," I said, as I realized I'd probably woken her up. "Wrong
room."

She just rolled her eyes and closed the door in silence. After she shut the door, I leaned back against the wall and covered my face with my hands. Knocking on random doors proved I truly had gone nuts. My insatiable libido was making me do things that I wouldn't have even dreamed of before. I should just walk to my room and crawl into bed for the rest of the day.

But then I thought of my redhead and his stunning blue eyes, his rippling abs, his gorgeous smile. And I decided to knock on the next door.

There he was. Mr. Redhead, dressed in a tiny pair of black shorts, was one of the most naturally beautiful yet uniquely different men I'd ever had the pleasure of being this close to. Words trapped in my throat as he looked down at me.

"Hello."

I stepped back, making a show of looking him up and down. Actually, it wasn't really a show; the vista was excellent. "Wow," I said.

He blinked and raised his eyebrows up to meet his red bangs.

"You're incredible."

His lips parted and he blinked some more.

"May I come in?" I curled some of my wig over my shoulder, and as I studied his remarkable eyes, I waited out his decision.

He scratched the hair on his chest and stepped aside. "Sure."

As I eased past him, I trailed my fingers across his chest, feeling the coarse hair beneath my touch. That was the first time I'd done that and despite my brazenness, it felt so right.

I tossed my bag on the back of a chair and turned to him. He'd paused halfway between the now shut door and me, and stood with his feet slightly apart and ran his hand through his hair.

Clutching at my wig, I twirled it around my hand. "I saw you down on the beach."

"Oh."

"Couldn't take my eyes off you."

"Oh." It appeared that Mr. Redhead was a man of few words.

I stepped forward, placed my hands on his chest, and felt both the warmth and the taut muscle beneath. He just stood there, a statue in the making. I twirled my fingers through his ginger chest hair and followed the line of it down his torso, then paused at his navel. His reluctance to move caught me off guard, and I stepped back. "Are you married?"

He looked down at me, his brilliant eyes piercing my soul. "No."

"Engaged, girlfriend, partner?"

"No."

"Good." With that settled, I needed to figure out what got Redhead's heart beating. Maybe he'd had so many women fall at his feet that he considered my advances blasé.

I'll show him blasé.

I kicked off my shoes, clutched at the hem of my cover-up, drew it over my head—careful not to take my wig with it—and tossed it aside. He still didn't move, but he did run his tongue over his pink lips. That was good enough for me. His chest rose and fell as I reached up behind my neck and tugged at the string of my bikini. I released the knot and let the fabric fall off my beasts. As I watched his eyes, I reached behind my back and undid the strap there too and let the flimsy fabric fall to the floor.

With my naked breasts now in full view, his eyes widened, and he shuffled his feet a fraction. I stood there, topless, my heart thumping out a crazy beat as I waited for his reaction.

And suddenly, react he did.

He crossed the distance between us in a flash, grabbing my breasts in his hands with a greedy ferocity. They were soft and supple, yet strong. I tilted my head back and he took my lead graciously. His lips latched onto the flesh on my neck, sucking a slice of my skin into his mouth. A groan tumbled from my throat as I pinched his nipple, squeezing the hardened flesh between my fingertips. With his hand around the back of my neck, I heard a click and my wooden necklace tumbled away and fell at my feet.

His hand skimmed down my body and fed into my bikini. I spread my legs, letting him know I wanted him to explore. His finger slipped inside me, and I gasped at the swiftness. The restrained man I'd met just moments ago was gone and as I bent my knees, allowing him to plunge my depths, I experienced the new man he'd become.

Redhead was on a mission to make me orgasm, so I closed my eyes and allowed my body to take over. He bent down, and as his lips moved to my breasts, I eased back, placing my hands on the back of a chair, giving him more. He sucked my nipple into my mouth, first one, then the other. His hot breath combined with his slick tongue danced across my nipples, and his probing fingers had my insides pulsing.

I reached down and tugged at the straps at my hips, setting my bikini bottoms free.

My sudden nudity had him stepping back, and as his stunning eyes travelled up my body, devouring me in a blue haze, tingles of want coursed through me. The bulge in his shorts was unmistakable, and I wanted to see what was there. I reached for him, wove my fingers into the elastic at his hips, and wrapped them around solid muscle. The head of his penis nudged over the top of the elastic, teasing me with its appearance.

I fell to my knees, and with his rock-hard cock in line with my eyes, I eased his shorts down. His penis fell forward, pointing right at me, and without a moment's hesitation, I sucked that luscious part of his body into my mouth. Redhead gripped my shoulders as I glided my lips up and down his shaft, savoring the silky smooth skin. I reached around and clutched his firm butt cheeks for support as I gave him the best damn blow job I'd ever given. In my humble opinion, anyway. Based on his groans and his bending knees, he was loving it too.

As I glided my lips along his shaft, drawing them up to the very tip, I looked up at him. Muscles bulged along his jawline and his eyes drilled into me.

Next second, he had one arm beneath my knees and one arm around my back and I was swept off my feet. As I wrapped my hands around his neck and stared into his dazzling blue irises, he carried me to the bed. The intensity I saw in those eyes had my clit purring.

He lowered me onto the mattress and by the look on his face, I knew this was going to be a frenzy. I was so ready. But he wasn't. Yet.

"Do you have a condom?"

He blinked at me, suddenly dragged from the lust-filled haze that'd trapped him. He shook his head, fear marring his beautiful features.

"I do. Grab my bag."

Quick as a flash, he brought my bag to me and I pulled a condom from my side zipper. I handed it to him, and he tore open the wrapper and glided the condom on.

I spread my legs, showing Redhead everything I had. His chest rose and fell with deep breaths as he devoured me with his gaze. This stunning man, rippling with muscles and gentle in demeanor, wanted me. And that made me feel invincible.

As I explored his body with my eyes, he did the same to me. My insides clenched with the intensity of it, and I squirmed on the sheets. He placed one knee on the bed and raised my right leg so my foot sat on his shoulder, and as his eyes pierced mine, he pushed a finger inside me. As he bent forward, opening me up even more, he probed in and out of my pussy. First one, then two fingers, and I couldn't keep my eyes open a moment more. As he alternated between bending forward and easing back, he plunged my throbbing depths.

The orgasm building inside me rolled from deep within, drawing out tingling sensations that ripped through me with greedy intensity. I snapped my arms out, clawing at the sheets, ready, oh so ready to explode.

And suddenly, he stopped.

I opened my eyes, blinking at the unexpected halt to his magic, and what I saw just about had me orgasm right there and then.

Redhead's glorious smile lit up his whole face, and his eyes dazzled like brilliant blue diamonds. I wanted to slap him. I wanted to grab his fingers and stick them right back into me. I wanted to scream.

"Are you ready?" His voice quivered with masculine control.

"Yes." I was so ready I thought I'd implode.

Easing me backwards, he then spread my legs apart and knelt on the bed between them. With his hands hooked under my knees, he raised my bottom off the mattress and then my back, so only my shoulders touched the sheet. He wiggled forward so his knees were flush against my lower back for my support. He leaned forward, bending me so my knees rested on his shoulders and my feet protruded above our heads.

Redhead literally had me doubled over in two. It was a little awkward, a little uncomfortable, yet I couldn't wait for whatever new move he was about to show me. His hand moved down by my backside, and for a God-awful moment I thought he was about to do something that I hadn't signed up for. I prepared to karate chop his Adam's apple.

But then the magic happened.

The head of his penis nudged at my pussy, and ever so slowly he glided into me. I felt as tight as I'd ever felt as he entered, filling me until his balls slapped against my ass. His eyes rolled, his jaw clenched, and his breath hissed through clamped teeth. He froze in that position and for one exquisite moment, he opened his eyes and we looked deep into each other's souls. I was about to discover something so uniquely special.

He was about to rock my world, and I was oh so ready.

Redhead pulled out slowly and then entered me with exquisite precision again. He repeated the move, in and out, slowly, slowly savoring me as much as I savored him.

He pulled out again, but this time he rammed full-tilt into me. I clawed at the sheets, gasping at the shock of it. Something deep inside me screamed at the pain, and yet I silently begged him to do it again. And he did. Slowly out and fast and hard all the way in. I gripped his shoulders and dug my fingers into the rock-hard flesh.

He repeated the move a couple more times, then he opened his eyes. His pupils were huge, almost swallowing his blue irises. He plunged into me. In and out. Fast and hard. I clawed at the sheets. I squeezed his shoulders. My libido feasted on both the pleasure and the pain. I wanted to beg for more, but I couldn't stand it either. It was exquisite confusion.

Just as suddenly as he'd started, my redhead stopped. His arms trembled as he held us in position. Sweat glistened on his forehead. His ragged breathing matched the rise and fall of his chest, and he clamped his jaw so tight I thought he'd break his teeth.

This was the moment. Both of us were about to make magic, and I clutched his shoulders and clenched my insides around his cock, letting him know I was ready.

Redhead plunged into me with jackhammer blows. He cried out, and I did too as he pounded me over and over. My orgasm rolled through me, shattering me into a thousand pieces until I crumbled into a quivering mess.

My sexy redhead gasped for breath, and it was a long moment before he finally lowered me to the bed and pulled out of me for the last time.

He rolled to sit at the edge of the bed, and I lay staring at the ceiling until I could breathe again.

"You said you saw me on the beach?" He spoke with his back to me.

I propped up on one elbow. "That's correct."

"Then you know I'm not a football player?"

"I do."

He turned to look over his shoulder at me, and a frown marred his beautiful face. "Why did you pick me then?"

I blinked at him. The poor man was obviously burdened by the competition of being surrounded by a bunch of macho footballers. I knew what it was like to be surrounded by beautiful people. I knew what it was like to feel inadequate and unworthy next to my friends. I smiled at him, sat up, and cupped his cheek. "Because you were by far the most handsome man on that field. I couldn't take my eyes off you."

He swallowed, and his eyes softened. For a moment I thought he'd lean over and kiss me. I would've let him too.

I shuffled forward so my legs dangled over the side like his. We sat side by side, and I felt completely comfortable with the familiarity of it. I put my hand on his leg and tried to form the right words in my head before I spoke. "Sometimes men who have everything going for them become too cocky. They try to be something they're not. Your stunning looks are what caught my eye. Your casual understatement is what made me chose you."

His eyes glazed and for a moment I feared he may cry, but instead a huge smile lit up his face. It was that smile . . . the one that told me I'd made him the happiest man in the world.

With that glorious vision permanently etched into my brain, I stood up and collected my bikini bottoms off the floor. As I stepped into them, Redhead disappeared into the bathroom. By the time he returned, I had my bikini on, my cover-up over the top, and my wooden necklace back around my neck.

"I don't even know your name," he said.

I stepped into one sandal and hooked the strap over my heel. "I'm Memphis."

"Hi Memphis. I'm Adam."

I put on my other shoe. "It was lovely to meet you, Adam."

With my bag on my shoulder and the image of that glorious man smiling at me, I returned to my room. I turned the taps on the bath to full and while I waited for it to fill, I removed my wig, makeup, and colored contact lenses. And then I saw it. On my neck—a purple oval blemish. I leaned in and tugged at my skin. My eyes bulged, and my heart jumped to my throat as I realized what it was. A love bite.

"Shit."

What am I? Seventeen?

I didn't know whether to laugh or cry as I tried to rub it away. "Jesus."

After a while, I laughed. It'd only taken me twenty-eight years to experience my first ever love bite. Lolita would have a fit over this one.

As I wondered how long it would stay there, I poured a good slosh of scented bubble bath into the water and once the foam began its own little party, I headed to my bedside table, grabbed my diary, and placed it on the edge of the tub.

As I slipped into the bath, the water hugged me in a wonderful embrace. I lowered my shoulders below the waterline and sighed deeply at the simple pleasure of a beautifully scented bath. Much like the simple pleasure of a beautiful, muscular man's penis deep inside me. After I relived each moment of us exploring each other's bodies, I sat up and reached for the diary.

I turned to 25th June and wrote *Mr. Redhead Room 19*, and as I was the one who'd chased him, I wrote, *Seducing the Sportsman*. It didn't matter that he wasn't actually a sportsman. He was a winner in my mind.

In great detail I described the new position he'd introduced me to, and how he'd alternated from slow and seductive to rocking my world.

As I closed the diary and slipped below the water again, I thought about his insecurities. How was it that a man as uniquely beautiful as Adam could feel so insecure? With that in mind, what hope was there for a woman like me? There was nothing about me that was unique or interesting. Even my wonky boobs were probably a common occurrence.

Except . . . I was certain I'd be the only woman in the world to ever take on a crazy year-long sexual challenge. That was what would make me unique. But would it ever make me an attractive partner? I thought about this long and hard before I decided that yes, yes it would.

I, Plain Jane, would be a fucking diva in the bedroom. Literally.

I laughed aloud as I pictured smoking-hot men lining up to experience my magical abilities.

Keep turning the pages for a sneak peek at the next book in this series...

ABOUT THE AUTHOR

Kitty Kendall is a bucket list achieving, junk jewelry collecting, hopeless romantic who loves great wine and a good adrenaline rush from time to time. She also collect classy shoes and expensive perfume. But her greatest thrill in life is writing romance and the steamier the better.

Bring It On!

She's travelled extensively, some 37 countries and counting and she's addicted to experiences that make her scream… white water rafting, scuba diving with sharks and hang gliding are just a few. Her stories reflect her sense of adventure and her love affair with her very own hero.

Kitty also writes romantic suspense under the pen name of Kendall Talbot. She's won numerous awards, including Romantic Book of the Year, and several of her books are Amazon bestsellers. Check out www.kendalltalbot.com to find out more.

Read more at www.kittykendall.com

Keep turning the pages for a sneak peek of the next book in this series...

ACKNOWLEDGMENTS

I couldn't have written the Rise of Memphis series without my husband. His willingness to help out with the necessary choreography was commendable. But seriously, I wouldn't be an author without his unwavering support. He entered my heart more than thirty years ago, and I'm crazy lucky to have a man like him at my side.

Writing a book is never a solo effort, and I wouldn't have survived this series without my wonderful editor Lauren at McStellar Editing. Lauren's tough love helped me polish the rough drafts until they were shimmering diamonds.

Along this journey I started a secret Facebook group - Cheeky Memphis, and although I've never met any of the women who joined me there, I want to thank them for making this journey so special. Without their very intimate details and stunning pictures of totally hot men, this Memphis project would've been a very lonely one.

So in no particular order, special thanks goes to:
Brandi Warhank, Dawn Viertlbeck, Revva, Janet Ross, Sarah Frost, Raven Johnson, Vikki Clay, Michelle Harris, Jay Epiha, Ronda Thayer, Sunny Lane, Kathy Allred, Jennifer Kennessey, Tina Whitley, Sam Young, Evelyn Lazenby, Romana Purkiss, Maria S, Nicole Holt Sexton, Nicole Betalon, Vickie, Amanda Petersen, Gayla File, Angela Davisson, Babel of Literaria, Michelle R, Christina Conrad, Barbara Laarhoven, Lala Poara, Debbie Schrum, Emily Maynard and Marita Lightbody. I hope I didn't miss anybody, but if I did I apologise from the bottom of my heart.

I'd also love to acknowledge my writing buddies who are all incredible authors too. For more than a year they've had to hear me bang on about Memphis, and this journey has been made much more enjoyable knowing that they've been there with me. Special thanks to: Tania Joyce, Noelle Clark, Isabella Hargreaves, Anthea Jones, Matt JX and Claire Austin.

And finally and most importantly I want to thank you—my readers. I wouldn't be living my dream of being an author if you didn't support me along the way. I hope my stories take you on an emotional journey that fills you with joy, makes you laugh, and helps you to believe in true love.

You can write to me any time at kitty@universe.com.au.

Rise of Memphis Tease Me

This three book box set contains:

Rise of Memphis July Chronicles
Rise of Memphis August Chronicles
Rise of Memphis September Chronicles

KITTY KENDALL

Kitty Kendall

1ST JULY
SEX FOR BREAKFAST
Room 4 – Hot Horizon Hotel

Today was not only Friday, it was the first day of July, which meant I was officially halfway through my challenge. It was difficult to comprehend what I'd done so far this year, and my heart fluttered as I contemplated what wonderful surprises were yet to come.

I didn't have to wait long. The first surprise was Needledick actually walking through the front doors prior to his shift. It was the first time he'd been early in more than a year.

The second surprise walked in right alongside my boss. Mr. Hunter McCall, my perfect stranger from a couple of months ago, who made exquisite chocolates. He wore a tiny pair of shorts and jogging shoes, and based on the fine sheen of sweat covering his body, he'd been outside doing an exercise regime, probably similar to the punishing one I'd witnessed him doing the last time he was here.

Needledick and Hunter laughed together, sharing a private joke as they walked toward me, and I quickly tugged my hair out of my bun and tousled it around my face in some lame attempt to avoid Hunter recognizing me. In the back of my brain I knew my panic attack was foolish because Hunter only knew me as Memphis, yet I couldn't help it.

As the men neared the reception counter, I swallowed the lump in my throat and tried to ignore my thundering heartbeat as I studied them. They were complete opposites in every way. While Hunter could be the lead actor on some kind of outdoor reality show, Needledick had sickly white skin, a physique that showed his lack of attention to his body, and a smile that verged on a grimace.

Hunter said goodbye, tossed me a cursory wave, and then headed toward the elevator. I was torn between watching his sexy butt and turning my attention to my boss. *How could Hunter have stayed here and yet I'd missed it altogether?*

"Morning," Needledick said, as he opened the top drawer to toss his keys in.

"Morning." I had to find out which room Hunter was staying in without my boss watching me. All I needed was two seconds on the computer. Normally, as soon as Needledick arrived, I escaped as quickly as I could.

"Has it been busy?" He put his hands together above his head and stretched as if he'd just woken up.

"Just a typical Thursday night. Nothing special." *Except for one of my previous sexual partners popping in unannounced.*

Needledick went into the staff room with his lunch, presumably to put it in the fridge, and I jumped straight onto the check-in screen on the computer and typed in Hunter McCall. The fact that I even remembered Hunter's surname was not only a miracle given that there'd been about a dozen men since him, but it also showed how much it suited him. Hunter McCall had it all going on, and his name was just the beginning.

"What're you doing?" Needledick's accusatory tone was like nails up my back, and I jumped.

"I was just finishing off some stuff." The name Hunter McCall was like a blazing hazard symbol in the search button on the screen.

"Want me to do it?"

I just about fell off my chair. This was a first. He never offered to do anything for me. "No. No. It's okay." I pressed the enter button and after a millisecond the screen changed to Mr. McCall's details, and I quickly scanned the computer. He was in room four.

"What are you looking for?" Needledick was right behind me.

"Oh, ummm." I cleared my throat. "Mr. McCall wanted a wakeup call for tomorrow and I hadn't had time to do it yet." I cringed at my terrible lie.

Needledick mumbled something under his breath, and as he watched over my shoulder I recorded a wakeup call on Mr. McCall's room for six a.m. tomorrow. *How had I become so evil?*

I clicked off the screen, said goodbye to Needledick, and then headed up to my room.

The usual niggling doubt that plagued my mind when I prepared my Memphis disguise had taken a backseat this morning. In its place was sizzling anticipation as I transformed myself into a sexy minx for my perfect stranger. The idea of going up to him kick started a lovely purring through my insides. It was like he was already calling to me, telling me to hurry up.

I tried to picture what I wore with him last time, in particular, which wig I chose? In my mind I went back to that night with him. We'd gone to the bar, and later in his room we'd played a guessing game with his delectable chocolates. I closed my eyes and had perfect recollection of him undressing me and placing his lovely hands on my hips. By the time I reopened my eyes, I knew I'd worn my red dress and my cute blond wig. It was amazing how much recall I had. Maybe I had a photographic memory.

That'd be nice. For the rest of my life I'd have a perfect recollection of all the wonderful men I'd met this year.

I chuckled at that thought as I checked my reflection. Despite being halfway into my transformation, I liked what I saw. Plain Jane wasn't so plain anymore.

My diary would help me remember too. Although I had no idea what I'd do with it once the year was over. The things I'd written were sacred. For my eyes only.

God help me if anyone got their hands on it.

Turning my head, I checked my love bite again. Although it'd been six days since my sexy red-headed sports physician had left his mark, it was still noticeable. Thanks to my Nars Luminous Foundation, it was now sufficiently concealed. I tucked my hair up into my blond wig and examined the finished result thoroughly to ensure my dark hair didn't peek out anywhere.

The last time I'd gone to Hunter was at night, and the dress I'd chosen was perfect for an evening on the town, but now, this early in the morning, I was torn over what to wear. On the Gold Coast, most people wore barely anything at all. Last week I'd worn my bikini and it'd felt just right.

A cheeky little idea popped into my head. I could wear one of my fancy-dress costumes. The French Maid, Poison Ivy, or the nurse outfit. I giggled as I tugged each of them out and tossed them onto the bed. Black, green, or white. Hunter had seen Memphis as a normal, supposedly sane woman. Little did he know just how far that was from the truth.

It felt so weird thinking of Memphis as another woman, and yet it had become so natural. How would I cope next year? I huffed and quickly moved on from that thought. I didn't even want to go there. Not while there was a hot guy waiting for me just two floors away. As I picked up each costume and held it against my body to look in the mirror, I tried to picture the look on Hunter's face when he opened the door.

An idea formed in my mind, and although the French Maid costume had already received more than enough outings it was perfect for my plan.

I put on red French knickers and a matching red bra, and tugged the costume over the top. The edge of my bra peeked above the white lace at my bust. Once upon a time this would've bothered me. Not anymore; I liked it. I matched my sexy lingerie with a pair of killer red stilettos with an eight-inch silver-spiked heel.

Continuing the red theme, I selected my cherry red Gucci handbag. Then I opened the zipper on my black bag to transfer my emergency supplies to my new one and was shocked to discover I had just one condom left. Lucky last.

Mental note to self: Buy more condoms. And soon.

With a bunch of butterflies dancing about my stomach, I put my coat on to conceal my dress, then walked out my door and headed to the elevator. By the time I reached Hunter's room I was jittery with excitement. The idea of spending the morning with the hunky fitness fanatic who made exquisite chocolates was the best way to kill a few hours.

Standing outside his door, I removed my coat, plumped up my boobs to ensure there was a sufficient amount of red lace showing, and then knocked. "Housekeeping," I called out.

I heard him groan, and I giggled as I waited for the door to open. A couple of heartbeats later the door swung wide, and the scowl on his face vanished in a flash. His eyes lit up, and his cute smile dominated his face. My perfect stranger was at the top of the sexy-hunk food chain.

"Just Memphis!"

"Housekeeping at your service, sir?" I tugged at the layers of lace in my skirt and did a little curtsy.

He chuckled and stepped aside. "Quick, come in before someone sees you."

I laughed as I wriggled past him, strolled to his table, and tossed my bag and coat aside.

"Oh, wow. You look incredible."

"Thank you." I swung my hips from side to side, swishing my skirt around my thighs.

"How did you find me?"

I didn't have an answer for that, so I shrugged, acting all coy. "I have my little spies."

He walked from the now closed door toward me. "Well, I'll be forever grateful to them." Hunter had taken off his shoes and socks, but he was still wearing the shorts he'd been in when I saw him downstairs.

"I waited up all night, hoping to continue our chocolate guessing game."

I put on my best sad face. "I'm sorry I missed it. But I'm here now."

He scrunched up his nose and ran his hands down his sides. "If I'd known you were coming, I would've had a shower."

"Mmmm." The idea of watching him shower had my insides curling. "You can still have a shower. As long as I can watch."

* * *

Thank you for reading.

Hopefully your sneak peek has left you wanting more. This good news is there is... a whole lot more.

MORE BOOKS IN THIS SERIES

Rise of Memphis Box Sets:

Rise of Memphis Touch Me (January, February, March)
Rise of Memphis Tempt Me (April, May, June)
Rise of Memphis Tease Me (July, August, September)
Rise of Memphis Tame Me (October, November, December)

Rise of Memphis Monthly Chronicles

Rise of Memphis January Chronicles
Rise of Memphis February Chronicles
Rise of Memphis March Chronicles
Rise of Memphis April Chronicles
Rise of Memphis May Chronicles
Rise of Memphis June Chronicles
Rise of Memphis July Chronicles
Rise of Memphis August Chronicles
Rise of Memphis September Chronicles
Rise of Memphis October Chronicles
Rise of Memphis November Chronicles
Rise of Memphis December Chronicles

Printed in Australia
AUOC02n0708270417
285145AU00002B/3/P